THE INDEPENDENT

BY

JUSTIN LOWE

THE
INDEPENDENT

JUSTIN LOWE

INSPIREBYTES OMNI MEDIA

This publication is co-published and distributed worldwide in the English language in the following formats:

ISBN Paperback: 978-1-953445-47-6
ISBN E-Book: 978-1-953445-48-3

This book was responsibly printed using print-on-demand technology in order to minimize its impact on the planet and the environment. Learn more at: www.inspirebytes.com/why-we-publish-differently/

Library of Congress Control Number: 2023941725

INSPIREBYTES OMNI MEDIA

Inspirebytes Omni Media LLC
PO Box 988
Wilmette, IL 60091

25 & Y Publishing
1250 S. Buckley Road, #143
Aurora, CO 80017

For more information, please visit www.inspirebytes.com
For more information, please visit www.25andy.com

DEDICATION

For My Heavenly Father,
For whom the first portion is called
to be reserved and set aside.

In Memory of My Earthly Father,
Ernst L. Lowe
1924–2021
Whose Loyalty, Kindness, and Excellence
were examples to all who knew him.
I miss you every day.

PROLOGUE

August

By the sound of his voice, it was clear he'd woken the man on the other end of the call. "The Crockett story broke this morning. Networks picked it up just in time for coffee on the East Coast."

"Good," was all the voice could muster through the fog of his broken slumber.

Conversation at the Republican National Committee Headquarters was getting heated. Miranda had never seen a man's face go from sickly yellowish-white to deep pinkish-purple as rapidly or often. If Wade didn't calm down, she might need to call an ambulance.

"Look Wade, Crockett was heading for a runoff so long as Stowe remained in the race. If this news came out during the runoff, we'd have far fewer options. It's too late to get another name on the ballot. Back Stowe!"

Wade wiped sweat from his brow. "I guess denying the Democrats the seat is better than losing it to them. I hope you're right about Stowe, Miranda. I'll make the call, but if this goes south, you go down with me."

CHAPTER 1

This was no ordinary year, and it seemed that nature knew it too. By this time last year, most of the leaves would have fallen and the few remaining would be brown and dry. Despite being well into autumn, a bright array of colors continued to cover nature's palate. It was the first Wednesday in November.

Parker Stowe placed his phone on his desk as he drew a long, deep breath, utterly depleted. The call he just finished was the last he intended to entertain before taking a shower and getting some sleep. He swiveled in his chair to gaze out the window and across the sunlit field to the tree line that marked his property's edge.

As his eyes wandered to the clock on the bookshelf next to the window, Parker sighed. It was five minutes to ten. He had been up for the better part of seventy-two hours, and he finally had a few minutes alone while his wife and children still slept. It had been an exhausting night. He and his family had only arrived home five hours earlier.

They'd considered staying at the hotel, intended to really, but there would have been no rest from the press. Parker Stowe was their hot political story of this election cycle: the senator-elect from the great state of North Carolina was an independent, making him, for the moment, the most powerful man in American politics.

Being an independent candidate in and of itself was not special. In an ordinary election, it would have made some news that an independent candidate beat out a better-funded, more organized campaign backed by a major party. It may have even drawn some curiosity, and the win might get a page two or three headline before the popular news culture would quickly move on to a sexier topic.

Not this time.

This time, the outcome of this election was unique, given the current makeup of the Senate. As a result, it put Parker in a position he had not anticipated. Now there were difficult choices to make. No matter what he decided to do, he would make powerful enemies. Enemies who would be determined to take him down.

His phone rang and vibrated, interrupting his thoughts. Parker pushed a button, silencing it, and then put it on Do Not Disturb. Humility did not come naturally to him. He had worked hard over the years to be less prideful and more gracious. Part of him was tempted to get drawn into the frenzy and let all the attention feed his ego. After all, it was no easy feat to be elected to the Senate of the United States, let alone as an independent candidate. So many people wanted to speak with him.

Powerful people.

Important people.

He yawned. Parker closed his eyes and thanked God for all His blessings. Feeling the weight of the decision before him, he asked God to grant him the wisdom to make the right choice.

He stood and yawned again. They were coming faster now, and he had to lay down. Going up the stairs felt like climbing Everest. He unbuttoned his shirt as he looked in on the kids, then proceeded down the hall to his bedroom. Veronica lay under the comforter with just her forehead and a thick wave of brown hair poking out the top.

Another yawn came.

Skipping the shower, he smiled as he undressed and slipped under the covers. Parker was tempted to reach over and kiss her but thought better of it. She needed her rest, and it would not be good if he woke her, plus the bed felt good. He was asleep before his head hit the pillow.

CHAPTER 2

"Have you reached out to him yet, Mr. President?" Mike Thach, the current Senate majority leader, was asking. Before the president could respond, Rachael interjected with a reply.

"Rodger Hall's the only one who's spoken with him. That was to concede the election and offer his congratulations." Her voice was hoarse, and she took a sip of hot tea.

She placed the china cup back on its saucer, adjusting it so that the presidential seal faced her directly. She'd been to the White House many times but never took the opulence of the People's House for granted.

Rachael Rosen-Zimmermann, listed in Forbes's *Top 40 under 40,* was the head of the Democratic National Committee and a congresswoman from Manhattan. Well educated and extremely well connected, her father was the founding partner of Rosen, Otto, Stewart, and Eckhart, a Manhattan-based litigation firm specializing in class action lawsuits. They had massive divisions that focused on environmental, product liability, securities, and discrimination law. She had intended on immediately joining the firm after doing her undergraduate work at Columbia University and receiving her J.D. from UC Berkeley. She postponed those plans when she met Stanly Zimmermann, the son of a wealthy Hollywood producer, while she was still a second-year law student.

After graduation, the two wed in the summer of 1996, and Rachael gave birth to their only child, a daughter named Gabriel, in February of 1998. By this time, they were back in New York, and Rachael was ready to take the Bar exam. Having utilized her time being pregnant to diligently study, she passed at her first sitting, and by early 1999 was beginning work at her father's firm.

Being new at the firm and the daughter of Arthur Rosen created a dichotomy of roles. She was not treated like the other first-year associates. Ninety-hour weeks are not compatible with being a mother, no matter how much domestic help one can afford. Her schedule was much more like that of a full partner than of an associate. She was resented for this as her peers were desperately vying for every chance to distinguish themselves. If they could hang on for five or seven years, they might get a shot at becoming a junior partner.

The junior partners did not much care for her either. She hadn't earned the kind of access she had to the inner circle. She attended gatherings that some of them, even as partners, had never been invited to attend. She knew more about the firm than people who worked through holidays and evenings away from their families. She had hours of attendance with Arthur Rosen, who rarely took a meeting if he could not bill it back to a client at the sum of fifteen hundred dollars per hour. They were jealous, envious, and angry.

During the presidential election cycle of 2000, the law firm of Rosen, Otto, Stewart, and Eckhart worked hard to support then Vice President Albert Gore's bid for the presidency. Gore's fervent belief in environmental causes would certainly have opened new opportunities to sue major industrial producers. The new tech boom would eventually produce opportunities for securities litigation. A liberal-leaning administration would most certainly provide a multitude of deep pockets to sue. So when the chance came to liaise with the campaign, Rachael was not only a good fit for the role, but eagerly looked forward to time away from the haters at the office.

Rachael was a hit with the Gore campaign. She was smart, attractive, wealthy, and connected. A young, energetic mother and wife, she was the woman the other women wished they could be if only someone or something wasn't holding them back. She perfected the art of networking and found she had a love for it.

When election night came, she was devastated. She volunteered her time and talents to help Gore and the DNC in their failed attempt to contest the election that put George W. Bush in the White House. She helped organize resources from the firm and the media to correct the mistake that would allow a popularly elected candidate to lose. She was outraged by the whole affair. When it was finally decided and Gore conceded, she felt cheated. She decided right then and there that she was going to Washington to protect America. After all, if George Bush tried to bring tort reform to Washington as he brought it to Texas, who would be willing to take up the case for the little guy, punish evil corporations with obscene judgments, and collect a fortune in fees for being the hero?

She proved to be an exceptional fundraiser and was easily able to win her bid for Congress in 2002. In fact, she was so good at shaking the trees on the West Coast utilizing her father-in-law's connections, as well as on the East Coast using her own family's influence, that the DNC started to tap her to help with national fundraising efforts. Her access to wealthy donors was so exceptional that state committees across the country consistently courted her. It was just inside a decade before she was able to trade her fundraising prowess to become head of the DNC. She was just shy of her fortieth birthday.

Maybe someday she could be sitting behind the president's desk. The desk that was currently in front of her.

"We wouldn't contest it anyway," said the president. "Stowe won by eight points. Contesting his victory will just tick him off and push him to the other side. Making an enemy of him before he declares is a bad idea."

Thach was six-foot-two with a wide chest, and unlike many at his age, he showed little sign of atrophy in his muscles. His thick, silver-white hair and goatee gave him a distinguished look. Combined with the powerful appearance of his ample frame, his look portrayed him as someone to be sought out for wisdom and friendship. He made sure the president was done before continuing. "We're contesting the results in Alaska, Arkansas, and Virginia. All we need is one to break our way and the Senate stays ours, even if Stowe caucuses with the Republicans. We could still pull this off without him."

Thach was technically right, but it was unlikely. In a mid-term election, even when a president's popularity is high, outcomes in swing states tend to go for the other party. While Congress had an approval rating of just forty percent, the president's was even worse at thirty-four. The Republicans had already picked up two Senate seats from them, one in Georgia and another in Louisiana. They had managed to hold all their existing seats. Four more losses to them and the Senate would turn red.

"Not going to happen, Mike," Rachael said. "We're going through the motions, but even our people are saying it's done. Dowd and Henry would have already conceded their races if we hadn't asked them to hold off. Tapp in Arkansas is the only one who thinks he can still pull out a win, but his numbers look worse than Dowd's in Virginia. The uncertainty buys us time, but not much. The only real question is, what are we going to offer Stowe to caucus with us?"

CHAPTER 3

President Marcus Jenkins was watching it slip away. His influence was eroding, and if his party lost the Senate, his legacy would follow quickly. Jenkins didn't care what anyone thought about him today. He knew history would be kind to him. The results of his presidency were transformational and justified how they were achieved. Rules and traditions had to be bent, broken, or ignored sometimes to get things done. He was a man of action. But a Congress controlled entirely by the other side would now pose a serious hurdle to finishing his agenda.

Born in 1954 to Dwight and Pearl Jenkins, Marcus grew up better than most black boys of his generation. They lived in Baltimore, Maryland. Dwight migrated with his parents and six older siblings in 1916 from the tobacco fields of Southern Virginia to the booming industrial cities farther north. Marcus was proud of his father and grandfather, and he often cited their struggles as a basis for his actions.

Dwight saw his father sweat out a living to support his family, shoveling coal into the hot furnaces to make steel. The steel he made built the ships that carried men and equipment first to destroy, and then to rebuild, Europe during and after the Great War. But his father's career was limited as he was uneducated and unskilled. He shoveled coal and scrubbed the furnaces for almost fifteen years until his body could take no more of the coal dust, soot, and heat. He died of black lung at the age of forty-seven in 1930, two weeks after Dwight's fifteenth birthday.

Dwight's mother was educated and acted as both librarian and secretary at the local, segregated school, taking great pride in making sure her children could read and write. Between his mother's insisting on an education and his father instilling a work ethic in him, Dwight got himself a good-paying job as a skilled welder. He built ships and mended machinery at the same shipyard where his father's steel had been made into great ships, later, putting his skills to work at the same steel mill his father worked at Sparrows Point. In 1938, he married Pearl, the daughter of the local doctor. The couple had four children together, Marcus being the youngest.

Having been born in 1954, Marcus grew up during the height of the civil rights movement in America—the same year as the landmark Supreme Court decision in Brown versus Board of Education. By the time he was six, the Baltimore schools were desegregated, and most Jim Crow laws had been repealed. In the 1960s, Marcus was old enough to watch television recording the crowds of peaceful demonstrators being beaten and broken down by the authorities. In the newspaper, he read accounts of lynchings and cross burnings. He heard stories of Klansmen in white hoods doing unspeakable things to people that were the same color as him.

His parents were not activists, but at the age of nine, Marcus went with them to Washington on a hot August day to hear Dr. King deliver a dream. He was mesmerized. He wanted to live in Dr. King's America. He believed it was possible, too.

On the way back to Baltimore, Marcus asked his parents if they thought he could be president when he grew up. His father told him, "Son, you can do anything you set your mind to as long as you are prepared."

"What does it mean to be prepared?" asked Marcus with all the legitimate interest of an impressionable nine-year-old mind.

"It means you need to know a lot of things about a lot of things. It means you have to do well in school and go to college," Dwight responded.

"Like Doc Pops and Ben?" Marcus asked. "Doc Pops went to college and knows a lot of stuff, and he helps people. Ben is going to be a general in the Army."

Pearl said, "Yes, like Doc Pops."

Pearl's dad had hoped one of his children would become a doctor and take over for him. Pearl trained as a nurse and worked with him in his practice. That was as close as Doc would get with one of his own. Doc was now hoping for one of his grandchildren to follow in his footsteps.

It was at this time that Marcus' older brother Ben was entering his third year at West Point. Dwight and Pearl were so proud of Ben. He was top ten in his class, and he hoped to go to medical school to become a surgeon. Doc Pops might get his wish after all. Dwight and Pearl just hoped he didn't end up in Vietnam.

"What do you think it will take?" President Jenkins asked no one in particular. Thach's heart rate increased, and he noticeably winced. The president and the party were playing with his chips.

Rachael was cool and direct. "It'll need to be significant from the start. The Republicans will come out strong. We're playing defense. Nothing less than a standing committee chairmanship will do."

From Agriculture to Veterans Affairs, there are sixteen standing Senate committees, five select or special committees, and dozens of sub-committees. They exist to streamline the process of writing and passing legislation, and to oversee the other branches of government, especially the Executive. They also perform oversight by holding hearings and calling witnesses as the committee chairman sees fit with few exceptions.

Chairmen can, and regularly do, kill bills in the legislative cradle of their committees, effectively blocking the proposed law from ever being debated. In other words, they wield a lot of power. Of course, some committees are deemed more significant than others, and committees are classed in order of importance, from A to C. Rachel knew that Parker Stowe would be getting the chairmanship of at least one of those Class A committees as tribute from one party or the other.

The president started to think about what he wanted to complete before the end of his term. "Give me more background on Stowe. He's conservative but not traditional. I think we can work with him. Let's find out what makes him tick and do what we did with Lackey. Offer him a committee chairmanship. Something that interests him, but not one where he can do damage to our agenda."

Bob Lackey was the only other independent in the Senate. Though officially an independent, Lackey consistently voted with Democrats when he was a member of the House of Representatives. In his 2006 run for the Senate, he received endorsements from powerful Democratic senators, all but assuring him no serious opposition to his candidacy from the left. This was a practical move by the Democrats, as putting up a candidate would have likely divided the liberal vote and handed the victory to the Republicans. It was a low-risk move as he had consistently voted with Democrats when he was a member of the House of Representatives from New Hampshire. To consummate the marriage and ensure that Bob would caucus with the Democrats in the Senate, he was promised the chairmanship of Small Business and Entrepreneurship, a Class B standing committee.

Here we go, thought Thach. Whatever they decided, one of his own would have to step aside. He would have to sell it. Shuffling the deck would mean calling in favors or handing out promises. It would be easier to fill a vacancy and deny a ranking member their next step up than ask a seated chairman to give up their position, particularly in favor of a newly elected independent who hadn't earned his stripes. The only thing he liked less than spending his political capital this way was the idea of the president and the chairwoman spending it for him.

"Let's start with what's open and see if we can make a fit," Thach said, hoping to guide the process. But Rachael cut him off before he could finish.

"We get one shot, and it will have to be our best offer. If we blow this, we lose both chambers of Congress. The next two years will be one standoff with the president after another. It could set us back years on immigration and gun control. It could set the stage in the next cycle for the Republicans to control the presidency and Congress. We've set some precedents that could spell disaster for what we've already accomplished if that happens."

"Best offer," the president repeated. "But what is best for us, and what is best from his perspective? Judiciary? Foreign relations? Appropriations? I'll say it again, we need to know what makes Stowe tick!" Marcus was annoyed and losing patience with the conversation. "He's the only one I have not called and congratulated yet. We're running out of time, and I have a country to run. We give him whatever he wants because anything less means we get nothing. It would be best if we had a clue what he might want before we make an offer.

"I'm going to call him, congratulate him, and invite him up here for dinner tomorrow. That gives us about thirty-four hours to prepare. I want to know everything. Circle back here at nine-thirty tonight."

And with that, Rachael Zimmermann and Mike Thach understood it was time to go.

CHAPTER 4

Parker Stowe was also the topic of conversation across town, in the executive conference room at the Republican National Committee Headquarters. The mood was, however, less tense and more optimistic. The prospect of gaining control of the Senate created an air of palpable enthusiasm.

"Of course, he'll caucus with us," Wade Wilson stated with the utmost confidence. "He's more conservative than some of our colleagues, and he knows he owes us for his win. If we had put another candidate in the race after the Crockett affair, it would have split the conservative vote. Rodger Hall would still be the senator from North Carolina."

Steve Crockett, the Republican candidate, had to pull out of the race with only eleven weeks remaining before Election Day. Much to the surprise of everyone, especially his wife, it was revealed that he was having an affair with his campaign manager. The problem for the party was that he was now labeled a cheater and a liar. Realizing that there was little time remaining to campaign, the Republicans decided their best opportunity to defeat Hall was Stowe.

Crockett was at forty-one percent and Hall was leading with forty-three. Parker had only been polling at about twelve percent before Crockett's campaign imploded, and the Republicans had been looking for a way to get Stowe to drop out of the race.

Then, overnight Stowe was up to twenty-eight percent. He began to get a lot of attention from the North Carolina conservatives who could no longer support the Republican candidate. As soon as Crockett announced that he was pulling out of the race, the Republicans threw their support behind Stowe. Parker leaped ahead of Hall in the polls with a fifty-two to forty-four percent lead. In the remaining weeks of the campaign, they split the undecided, and Parker Stowe won with fifty-four percent of the vote to Rodger Hall's forty-six.

"We just need Dowd, Henry, and Tapp to concede and this election is all wrapped up." The normally serious and stoic Wade was beyond happy. "Giddy" might be the word that best described the head of the Republican National Committee. So much so that someone who didn't know he never took a sip of alcohol might think he'd had a few already this morning.

"Don't start counting chickens, Wade," Miranda Cortez cautioned. Miranda was head of election strategy at the National Republican Senatorial Committee and largely responsible for their mid-term landslide victory. Wilson looked directly at her; his smile was gone.

"You convinced us that supporting Stowe was our best move, Miranda. Everyone got on board because of you. Now you're telling us that he might not support us?"

"I told you that the only way to beat Hall was to support Stowe. It looks like I was right. I never said that endorsing him would get us his support. Did you ask about his intentions when you spoke to him this morning? Did he hint at what he might want?"

"No and no." Gone was any hint of cheerful Wade. He focused again, resuming his reserved and controlled manner. "I just congratulated him. Told him to get some well-earned rest and that we'd be in touch soon to talk about next steps."

"Okay. I'll get on the phone with Jason and arrange to get him up here ASAP. We need to get to him before the Dems do. To be sure, Jenkins will get him to the White House before week's end. Control of the Senate is at stake, and the sky's the limit."

Wilson grimaced. "What do you think it will take? We can offer him anything they offer, and with us, he gets to be with like-minded people. Why would he even think about caucusing with them?"

"I agree. He will likely caucus with us. We need to let him pick the committee he chairs because the other side will give him whatever he wants. They need him on their side to keep the Senate. It's what I'd do if I were in their position."

Wade was thinking, *No way is Stowe going to call the shots.* "It'd be political suicide for him to align with the Democrats. He was elected by conservatives in North Carolina. He'd never get reelected, and they might even find a way to get him thrown out before his term is up."

"We'll offer him a chairmanship. Give him a choice of a few of our pickings. See if he comes back with something different. We'll give him whatever he wants, but I'm not opening the field if I don't have to. Let's see if we can lock him down before the White House gets to him. We'll get him up here tomorrow. Better yet, let's go to him. Make the call to Jason and set it up."

To say that Miranda Cortez was an attractive woman would be like saying that an Aston Martin is a car. However true the statements are, they grossly misrepresent the exquisiteness in every detail of finely crafted components. Blessed with perfect proportions and thick, dark hair, she possessed a youthfulness that hid her years by more than a decade. Her soft brown eyes and tan skin tones all spoke to the blend of her Latin and Asian heritages, granting her a mystique that Hollywood could only mimic, but only nature can create.

That men seldom noticed her intellect first was an advantage she used often, especially effective with male politicians tripping on their sense of self-importance and hunger for power. At any given time, she would be one of, if not the smartest person in the room.

Born to Hector and Mi-Hi Cortez of Houston, Miranda was the only daughter of a successful upper-middle-class family of four. Her older brother Heriberto ran the separate but affiliated service businesses that her family had built over the past seventy-five years. When Miranda was not orchestrating one election campaign or another, she went back to her humble roots in Texas and reacquainted herself with her three nephews and two nieces.

Her father, Hector, was a first-generation American. His parents legally emigrated from Mexico in 1929, just in time for the Great Depression. Hector's father, Paulo, worked at whatever he could find. His mother, Maria, was able to secure a good job as a housekeeper with the Ross family seven months after Hector was born.

The Ross family developed a fondness for Maria right away. She had a kindness and warmth about her that most agreed Miranda had inherited from her. Mrs. Ross was so impressed with the way Maria looked after the house and family that she convinced her husband to hire Paulo. He kept the grounds of their Houston estate, and the Ross property became the envy of Houston society. Social events held at the Ross Mansion were always described in magnificent detail in the society pages, which never failed to mention some fantastic aspects of the grounds.

At first, his employer thought that Paulo was looking for a raise when he came to him. Paulo assured him that was not the case. Over the years, Paulo had developed a reputation of excellence, and he only sought Mr. Ross's permission to do a few side jobs. He assured Mr. Ross that they would not interfere with his work at his estate.

Grant Ross made his money in oil. Besides viewing himself as a successful businessman, Grant fancied himself as a pillar of the community and a philanthropist. He knew Paulo had just the right mix of humility, talent, and work ethic to be successful at running his own business. He suggested that Paulo start a landscape enterprise with some seed money that he would supply. Paulo should view the money as a no-interest loan and could pay him back as the business grew. Before a year had passed, Cortez Estate Services employed ten men and was servicing over a dozen of Houston's most affluent families.

By the time Hector was nine, he was helping his father after school and on the weekends. He would clean up the shavings from trimmed hedges or grass clippings from walks. His father insisted that all aspects of the landscape should be perfect and harmonious when his men left a client's property. Paulo instructed Hector that in addition to collecting the normal debris from the grounds, he should also skim any wayward items from pools. This desire to always leave a property in its best condition led to an expansion of the family business into pool care and maintenance.

Because of his age, Hector was fortunate to have missed the Second World War, but not Korea. Shortly after he graduated high school, he was drafted and sent overseas to fight the Communists. Paulo and Maria were both proud and frightened for their only child, and they dutifully prayed for his safe return to them. When he finally came home, he not only returned to them safely but brought with him his Korean wife, Mi-Hi.

CHAPTER 5

Roni kissed Parker softly on his neck as she snuggled up next to him. "Senator Stowe? Are you awake yet?"

He smiled and said, "Senator-Elect Stowe. It's not official until I've been sworn in." Parker grunted as he began to wake in earnest. Her hair smelled fantastically floral, and the bed felt so good. He had no desire to get up. He opened his eyes and saw that it was two twenty-two in the afternoon. Five hours of sleep wasn't too bad, but he could certainly use more.

"Well, what does the senator-elect plan to do with the rest of today?"

He loved her southern accent. It was cute and seductive all at the same time, and even more so endearing when she batted those long eyelashes at him. He enjoyed locking eyes with her—she would always turn away first. It was as if she were embarrassed by what his look was revealing about his thoughts. It only made him desire her more.

"I need to talk with Jason. I'm sure the media and others have been blowing up the phones. Getting elected as an independent has real implications in this cycle. It's not just a novelty." He slid his fingers into his hair, rested the palm of his hand on his forehead, and massaged his scalp.

"What do you mean?" She feigned interest. Veronica loved her husband and was proud of him, but she had never aspired to be a politician's wife. She was one of a half-dozen or so vice presidents at a small information technology consulting firm. She was about processes and systems, not appearance and perception. With Roni, it was always what was right, not what was popular, that made sense.

"Well, if I choose to caucus with the Republicans, they get control of the Senate. If I caucus with the Democrats, they get to keep control. Essentially what I decide to do will determine if one party controls or both parties share control of one-third of the government." Parker ran his hand over his face and scratched the stubble of his beard. "I never really thought I'd win, let alone have such power."

She turned on her side, bent her arm, and cradled her head in her raised hand. Her chestnut brown locks fell like a curtain, enveloping and highlighting the olive tone of the limb. "Don't you owe your win to the Republicans? They did back you, after all. Besides, you're not exactly liberal. Seems like there really isn't a question here of what you'll do."

"I know, but right now I can't help but feel there is an opportunity here. It just hasn't revealed itself yet. They'll both offer me whatever I want to caucus with them. I can have the chairmanship of any committee."

"That's a good thing, right? More visibility, an opportunity to lead…"

"I'm not so sure. There is a pecking order to these things. I will make an enemy of the ranking member that has to give up his place for me, even if technically we're on the same side. I'll have the title, but I will be less effective because I will now have powerful enemies on both sides of the aisle. They'll work against me, and I'll have all the fingers pointing at me as the problem. I'll have no cover or support, except for maybe the American people. But even then, the press tends to heavily influence public opinion."

"The press seems to like you, honey."

He stood up and turned around to face her. "The press likes the story, which is why they are nice to me now. But our views differ on most things and will make it hard for them to support me if I get embroiled in a battle. I need to think about all this. I'm going to take a shower and get woken up." He headed for the bathroom.

"Want some company in the shower, Mr. Senator?"

"It's still Senator-Elect. And a little distraction is exactly what I need. Would you care to join me in the Capitol, Mrs. Senator-Elect?"

He could hear the smile in her voice. "There's nothing wrong with your decision-making abilities," she said as she climbed out of bed and headed into the bathroom behind him. "You'll figure it out."

"Hello, Jason? It's Miranda Cortez at the RNC. Congratulations on getting your man elected last night."

"Well, thanks, Miranda. It's always a pleasure to hear from you. What's up?" Jason was not immune to the charms of Miranda Cortez. His wife had died after a long battle with breast cancer about five years earlier. His two children were grown and out of the house. His eldest, a daughter, was at law school in Georgia and his son was an undergrad at UNC. He didn't date much, but Miranda certainly was on his radar.

"So, I was meeting with Wade earlier today, and we wanted to get a meeting with Parker on the calendar for tomorrow. I know it's short notice. We're willing to come to you, or we'll fly you to Washington if you prefer. Do you think that's possible?"

"I'll have to check with Parker. He was hoping to take a few days with his family. I'll get back with you tonight after I speak with him."

There was no discussion about the reason for the meeting. It was understood.

"Thanks, Jay. Appreciate you. By the way, while I have you on the phone, when are you going to take me out for that drink you promised me?" She thought the hint might encourage him to get Stowe to take a meeting sooner rather than later.

Miranda liked Jason. Quiet, observant, and always pleasant, Jason Tuttle was distinguished both in his looks and his accomplishments. She had been the one who offered Stowe the NRSC's backing and non-financial support. When Parker agreed, she and Jason had worked out the details. He had been firm about not committing to caucusing with the Republicans. When she relented, Jason had tested the water by mentioning that he owed her a drink.

Jason was pleased that she remembered his offer and smiled at the prospect of getting to know her better. "Maybe we can do something after the meeting with Parker since we'll already be in the same city."

"Okay, sounds good. I look forward to hearing from you. Bye." Miranda was also satisfied with herself. She had him on the line and just needed to be patient about reeling him in.

Jason arrived at the Stowe residence promptly at 4:30 p.m. Parker had sent him a text earlier in the afternoon and asked if he could come out to the house. Jay had had a long military career, so promptness was in his DNA. He was surprised at the number of media vans parked at the edge of the property and was glad to see a State Police car preventing the exceedingly zealous reporters from overtly harassing Parker or his family.

The property was an old tobacco plantation about forty miles southwest of Winston-Salem that Parker and Veronica had bought some ten years earlier at a steep discount because of the softening demand for the controversial crop. They sublet most of the fields to other farmers, retaining only enough of the acreage around the grand old house to ensure their privacy. The property was a compromise of sorts between Parker, who grew up on the North Carolina coast in Wilmington, and Roni, who grew up in Kingsport, Tennessee just south of the Kentucky border. Parker did not want to be too far from the ocean, and Roni was a mountain girl through and through. They met at Wake Forest University as lab partners in a Physics 101 class.

Parker was on the porch, swinging with his daughter, when Jason pulled the black Lincoln up in front of the house. Samantha jumped up, waved at him before he shut the engine off, and ran in to announce to the rest of the household that Uncle Jay had arrived.

Parker came to the top of the stairs and said, "Long time no see, my friend," and then he laughed.

Jason snickered too. "Could 'a sworn I just left you a few hours ago, but you look much better now than you did then."

"You, too. It's amazing what a few hours of sleep in your own bed and a shower will do for one's looks." The two men shook hands and hugged. "Let's go inside, it's getting chilly out here."

In the foyer, Roni hugged Jason and took his coat. "Would you boys like a drink before dinner? You are staying for dinner, Jason, aren't you?"

"Nothing to drink right now, thank you, but yes, I'm staying for dinner. What are we having? The house smells fantastic."

She smiled at the compliment. "Just a pot roast and mashed potatoes." The rich aroma of the roast filled the house and made it feel warm and cozy despite its rather large size. "How 'bout you, Parker? Want anything?"

"No thanks, sweets. I'll probably have a glass of wine with dinner."

Jason waved at the kids, who had now gathered on the landing at the top of the stairs. "Hi, guys," he said and smiled one of his biggest smiles.

"Hi, Uncle Jay." They spoke almost in unison and waved back. The boys were seven and nine. Samantha would be fourteen in a few months. And then, as if on cue, they all disappeared back down the hall, presumably to their rooms.

Jason followed Parker into his study, which was at the front of the house to the right of the foyer. It had a set of heavy, wooden pocket doors that reflected the age and elegance of the home. Directly across from them on the other side of the foyer was another set that opened to the dining room.

"It's still hard to believe we did it, Jay. If you had told me eight weeks ago we would be in this position, I'd've said you were nuts."

"I know. It's been a wild ride. Any regrets?"

"Not yet." Both men laughed and smiled.

"Have you talked to anyone?" Jason probed.

"Who do you mean? Like the press? No."

"Good. Have the Dems reached out yet? You should have heard from the White House by now. It's protocol for the president to reach out and congratulate the newly elected. Given your position, I'm surprised you haven't gotten the call."

"I went to bed at about ten-thirty this morning and slept until about two-thirty this afternoon. I bet he calls in the middle of dinner. That'll make Roni oh so happy. Who's been blowing up your phone over the last few hours?"

"All the Sunday shows want to book you. Every reporter from Boone to Kitty Hawk wants an interview. You should see the line of TV trucks at the edge of your property. Miranda Cortez called too. She and Wade are hot to trot and want to meet tomorrow. Didn't care where. They'll come to us, or we can go there."

"We'll go there, but not tomorrow. Tell Miranda it'll be Saturday morning, and we'll get back to her about the time and place. Make sure the minority and majority leaders will be available and present. Let's get a suite and a conference room at the Willard and set up a press conference for Saturday evening. Contact *60 Minutes* and tell them I'll do an interview Saturday night at the hotel. Book all the shows on Sunday morning starting with Fox, then ABC, CBS, and NBC last."

"What are you going to say? You don't even know what's on the table yet. Don't you think it's premature to do all this, Parker? We haven't even discussed all our options."

"No. I want everyone to expect an announcement Saturday night. If it's one thing I've learned, it's that Washington works best on a deadline."

"You're about to take me on another wild ride, aren't you?" Jason sighed, looked down at his feet, and laughed. "I think I'm ready for that drink."

"Don't be so glum, pal. This is about to get real fun. Remember my favorite verse from the Bible?"

"Matthew 12:48: *To those who are given much, much will be required.*" Jason looked directly at Parker. "I hope you know what you're doing."

"Why should that stop me now?" Parker's attempt to ease his friend's mind wasn't working. The phone on his desk began to ring.

"Hello."

"Parker Stowe?" the female voice on the other end asked.

"Yes, this is him. How can I help you?"

"Please hold for the President of the United States."

There was a brief pause while he was placed on hold. Parker pushed the speaker button and hung up the handset.

"It's the president," he told Jason, who nodded his understanding.

"Hello, Parker? This is Marcus Jenkins. I'm calling to congratulate you on your win yesterday and welcome you to the family of government service."

"Thank you, Mr. President." Parker fervently disagreed with most of the policy decisions the president made but personally found the man to be quite pleasant. He had a lot of respect for the office, if not the man himself. It was not his way to let a disagreement about beliefs scuttle a relationship with the man or the office.

"I hope you got some rest today. I hear you're the most sought-after interview in town." It was clear he was making small talk, as it was new territory for both of them.

"I got some, Mr. President. Thank you for asking."

"Listen, Parker, I was hoping to have you up to the White House tomorrow night for dinner, just you and Veronica with me and the first lady. Then maybe after dinner you and I can chat privately for a while. In fact, why don't you plan to spend the night in the Lincoln Bedroom?"

"That's very generous of you, Mr. President. I appreciate the invitation, but I'm afraid that will not work for us. I promised my wife a few family days after the election was over. I don't want to start my new career as a politician by alienating my most important constituent. I would be setting a bad precedent by breaking a campaign promise before I even take my oath of office."

The president did not hint that he was offended at the refusal. Despite his annoyance, he had to admit to himself that he admired the response. He wondered if it had been rehearsed.

"I totally understand. If mama ain't happy, then no one's happy, right? So, when might be a good time for us to get together for a chat? I'd prefer it to be in person and sooner rather than later." The president was off balance and trying not to sound desperate. He needed the meeting with Stowe, but he shouldn't have to beg for it. He was the president after all, and who turned down an invitation to meet with him at the White House?

Parker was ready with his answer. "We both know this is about control of the Senate. I haven't made up my mind yet, but you can help me."

Suddenly the president was less annoyed. He liked what he was hearing. "I'm glad to know that you haven't chosen a caucus and are open to your options. This is important to the country. How can I help you?"

"Can you have breakfast Saturday morning, say about eight?"

"Yes, that'll be fine." Jenkins was annoyed again. It was widely known that the president played golf almost every Saturday morning barring an overseas trip, bad weather, or a national security crisis.

Parker enthusiastically pushed his luck. "Great! Would you mind inviting the chairwoman, the majority leader, and the vice president?"

"They'll be here."

"Excellent. I know this will sound a bit unorthodox, but I would like you to also extend an invitation to the minority leader, as well as Wade Wilson and Miranda Cortez at the RNC. My campaign manager, soon to be chief of staff, Jason Tuttle will be with me."

The president paused after Parker finished speaking, and there was a heavy silence. Jason Tuttle stared at Stowe in disbelief and confusion. When the president finally began to speak, Jason began to breathe again. Parker was totally at ease.

"I was kinda hoping to spend some one-on-one private time with you, Parker. Give us a chance to get to know one another better. I can be a good friend to have in this city." The president was making one last attempt to regain control over the situation. Dangling his positional authority was an obvious power play by the chief executive and Parker found it a bit unbecoming. He chose his next words carefully.

"I'm honored, Mr. President, and I sincerely hope we can be friends. Since the whole country expects me to caucus with the Republicans, the fact that I just told you I've not made any decisions should, I hope, at least be encouraging to you. But a big part of my campaign was a promise of transparency. If I accept your offer and then choose to caucus with your side, the hometown press will skewer me. I'd be branded a traitor to my values and the people who elected me. They'd say I was paid off behind closed doors at the White House and that I lied about bringing accountability to Washington. I understand if you don't wish to entertain me in this way, but I hope you see that you have nothing to lose and everything to gain by making this happen."

President Marcus Jenkins ceded the field. "I guess we'll see you here Saturday morning at eight."

"Thank you, Mr. President."

CHAPTER 6

"The presiding member of the United States Senate is elected by the body and thus, in a system composed primarily of two parties, is referred to as the majority leader. The title reflects the simple majority of seats represented by the party's caucus."

The producer of the show didn't think the professor of political science at the University of Pennsylvania was playing well to the audience. He was too technical and heady. He was talking above the average viewer, and the producer could just see the ratings plummet. He keyed a microphone and said something to the host through her earpiece.

"Professor," she said, "can you use the graphic behind you to show what this all means?"

"Sure, Alisha." He moved next to a graphical representation of the Senate depicting one hundred seats, two from each state. "The current Senate is made up of forty-five Republicans, fifty-four Democrats, and one independent—Bob Lackey from New Hampshire." The graphic showed the seats held by Democrats in blue, Republicans in red, and the independent seat as half gray and half blue.

"And why is one seat half gray and half blue?"

"Senator Lackey, while an independent, has chosen to caucus with the Democrats, so when voting for leadership positions like the presiding member, he votes with them. The side with the most votes gets to run the Senate and chair all committees. It was in Lackey's best interest to side with them, and in return, they gave him the chairmanship of Small Business."

"So how did last night's election change things?"

A new graphic appeared next to him. "As you can see, the Republicans picked up two seats from the Democrats, and the Democrats lost one more to the independent candidate from North Carolina, Parker Stowe. There are still three technically undecided races, though all will likely go to the Republicans. If that happens, they would then be pick-ups from the Democrats who hold them now." The graphic changed to show forty-seven seats in red, forty-eight in blue, a single half blue and gray seat, three in yellow, and one full gray.

"So, for all intents and purposes, assuming that the three undecided races go to the Republicans as expected, they will hold fifty seats to the Democrats' forty-nine, is that right?"

"Assuming Lackey stays with the Democrats, yes that is correct."

"Which brings us to Parker Stowe. If he sides with the Republicans, they become the majority party with fifty-one seats."

"Yes. But here is the interesting thing. Although it is assumed he will caucus with the Republicans, he has not committed to doing so. It's being presumed only because they did not enter a new candidate after the Crockett debacle."

"If he sides with Democrats, what happens?"

The professor lit up. A toothy grin appeared on his face. "Well, the founding fathers anticipated such an occurrence where a majority consensus could not be achieved. In this case, the vice president, as the constitutionally mandated president of the Senate, gets to cast any tie-breaking votes. Where we currently have a Democratic administration in the White House, it means that the Democrats by default would technically retain control of the Senate."

"When will we know?"

"Officially, not until January after everyone is sworn into office and a vote is taken. Realistically, I suspect we'll know something in the next forty-eight to seventy-two hours. Once the three outstanding races are determined, Stowe will face an enormous amount of pressure to pick a side."

"Do you think there'll be another showdown like the 2000 presidential election? Will the courts be asked to intervene?" Alisha, like most TV news and commentary hosts, liked to speculate and create controversy. It kept people tuning in for the latest update, boosting ratings.

"Not likely. We haven't heard of any legitimate grounds to contest the election results in the outstanding races. Statistically speaking, the gaps are too large for the incumbents to overcome. I expect the three Democrats will be delivering concession speeches before the week is out."

Alisha Hollins seemed disappointed in the professor's last answer. Christmas wasn't coming early for her, or at least not today. This story could keep people hooked for the next three months.

As the program went to a commercial break, the president muted the TV and picked up the phone.

"Hey Allison, it's Marcus. I have a meeting with Rachael and Thach in about an hour. I'd like you to join us."

CHAPTER 7

As he turned onto the county road that led to Interstate 40 from the Stowe farm, Jason called Miranda Cortez. He had already sent a text while still at the house to a staffer about making the hotel arrangements. He would set up the Sunday morning rounds and the *60 Minutes* interview in the morning. None of them would balk at the opportunity to speak with Stowe, even if it meant bumping a previously scheduled guest.

Miranda answered right away.

"Hey, Jay! I was beginning to wonder if you forgot about me." Her voice was soft, her tone light and playful.

"Once you meet Miranda Cortez, she's impossible to forget. In a good way, of course." He was out of practice when flirting and always felt unprepared when delivering his compliments, no matter how much he rehearsed them in his head. She found it endearing when he fumbled his way through these moments with her.

"So, what's it going to be? Are we coming to y'all, or are you coming up here?" It didn't happen often, but occasionally her inner Texan crept through with a "y'all" or a "howdy."

"The uncomplicated answer is that we are coming up there and will meet with you, Wade, and Jack Archer at 8:00 a.m. Saturday."

"Okay." She paused. "…And the complicated answer is what?"

"We will all be meeting at the White House with the president, majority leader, and Rachael Zimmermann. But before you ask, I have no idea why. Parker set it up himself with the president when he called earlier this evening to congratulate him on his victory. I was there and heard the whole thing. The president seemed just as confused as you must be now."

"I don't like this, Jay. Where is Parker heading? I got the party to support him against Hall. If he breaks ranks, there'll be hell to pay for all of us. He'll never be re-elected, even if it means giving the seat back to the Dems. You and I will be lucky to get work on campaigns for a dogcatcher."

She wasn't saying anything Jay didn't already know, but he didn't like even an implied threat. "I understand, but it was all a surprise to me too. I'm sure he's not going to caucus with them. I don't know what he plans to do or why he set this meeting up."

Miranda paused for a second. She had a million questions. "Did he set up another private meeting with the other side?"

"Not to my knowledge, and he's not traveling anywhere until Friday night when we come up there. He has a small army of press camped out around the property, so anyone that comes to him will be well documented. Unless it is by video or phone, I'm sure there is nothing scheduled."

"Didn't you press him to find out what he's thinking?"

"Of course, Miranda. He just said, 'Be patient, Jason.' I even asked Veronica if she knew what he was thinking. All she could tell me is that before I went to the house, he was in his study reading. Like he was doing research. He's a different kind of politician, Miranda. We might not know what he's thinking, but he will never abandon his principles. Of that, I'm sure."

"This is going to create a firestorm."

"Up until your guy dropped out, he didn't expect to win. I never told you this, but he planned on ending his campaign and supporting Crockett. He was only days away from calling a press conference. We were running out of money, and Parker couldn't stand the idea of Rodger Hall being re-elected. He knew he was splitting the conservative vote, and if he dropped out, Crockett could win. The only reason he kept going after Crockett pulled out was because he felt obligated to give the voters an alternative."

"Maybe he just wants to see the look on everyone's face when he sides with us," she said, half joking, half optimistic.

"Not his style. My best advice is to come with open minds and without expectations. Truth be told, I doubt anyone gets what they want. Can we still get together for that drink?"

"Sure. How about Friday night?" She wanted to pick his brain one more time before the meeting Saturday morning.

"Sounds good. I'll call you when I get into town."

CHAPTER 8

March 27th, 1971 was an unusually bitter, cold day in Baltimore when a black sedan with Army plates pulled up outside of the Jenkins' modest rowhouse. Marcus watched from his upstairs bedroom window as two men in uniforms get out of the car and make their way to the walk. Before they disappeared under the porch, he had already made it halfway down the stairs. Pearl was standing in front of the door, shaking, with tears in her eyes, unwilling to answer the ringing bell.

Marcus got to his mother's side as she let out an unearthly wail, just in time to catch her as she began to fall to the floor. His father came running from the bedroom where he had been sleeping before heading out for the second shift at the mill. From the top of the stairs, Dwight quickly assessed the situation and told Marcus to get his mother to the couch and answer the door. He went back to the bedroom to get dressed and steel himself in private for the bad news that had just darkened his front porch.

Marcus' brother had died on the twenty-first, when the helicopter transporting him with the wounded was shot down. Ben was his hero, his role model. He sacrificed everything to help others.

It was the defining moment of his youth. He never felt more helpless in his life than he did on that miserable day when those men from the Army came to the house. A time when the inspiration of Martin Luther King Jr.'s dream, the tensions of the civil rights movement, and the humanitarian tragedy of a questionable war came together in a moment of determination and vision to fundamentally transform America.

Marcus Jenkins was bright, well read, and clean cut. He had never been in trouble with the law and kept away from drugs, avoiding most of the pitfalls many inner-city teenagers fell victim to. He regularly attended Mt. Zion Methodist Church with his family and could sink a very respectable 31% of the shots he took from outside the paint on a basketball court.

All of this was good enough to earn him a full scholarship at any number of schools, but his essay about his dream to be president got him into Yale. He wanted to show his fellow citizens a black man from Baltimore could become the president of the United States. In doing so, he intended to affirm the promises of the founding fathers that all men are created equal, and there can be justice for all.

Since his time at Yale, there had been few serious challenges to his agenda. Those that did arise had long been anticipated, strategized about, and ultimately overcome. No one had successfully outmaneuvered Marcus in a long time, and he was eager to learn more about Senator-Elect Stowe.

As soon as Vice President Allison Winter entered the Oval Office, the president was ready to begin. "I spoke with the senator-elect earlier this evening. I need all of you to clear your schedules Saturday morning and be here at 7:00 a.m. We are meeting with him, Jason Tuttle, Jack Archer, Wade Wilson, and Miranda Cortez."

"What's the agenda? Why so many people, and why the leadership of the RNC?" Winter was aware of the election numbers and what they could mean for her visibility if she were to become more active in the Senate. The next presidential election cycle would begin to ramp up next year, and she intended to announce her candidacy in April. A divided Senate where she would be the tiebreaker meant more publicity.

"Stowe told me that he had not made up his mind as to which side he intends to caucus. He also refused a private meeting with me. He went as far to imply that if we chose not to meet on his terms, it would seal the deal with the Republicans." This wasn't true, but Jenkins wanted the others to think he had no choice. "His terms were Saturday morning here at the White House, 8:00 a.m., and with the Republican players he mentioned."

"Let's be real," Rachael Zimmermann said. "There's nothing we can offer Stowe that the Republicans can't match. The fact that he is willing to meet with us at all is good. By doing it in this kind of forum, he removes the argument that any back-door deals were made. It's smart. This may be a sign that he wants to play ball in our court."

Mike Thach was more skeptical. "Or he's using us as a bargaining chip to get the best deal from the Republicans he can get. Putting us both in the room creates an open bidding forum and removes the ability for either side to peddle extras. We still lose in this fight, except maybe that we'll know everything the Republicans gave him."

"I'm not so sure that's his plan." Rachael pulled copies of a half-inch thick dossier on Stowe from an Italian-designed leather satchel on the floor next to her. She distributed a copy to everyone. In addition to a picture, demographics, and background information, it contained some documents that were prepared by Stowe himself.

Born the fifteenth of April, 1979, forty-four-year-old Parker Stowe has been married to his wife of nineteen years, Veronica

Leigh, who is forty-three. They have three children: daughter Samantha (13), son Amos (9), and son Burk (7). His parents William and Donna—seventy-seven and seventy-two, respectively—both still live in Wilmington, NC. He also has two older siblings: Bridgett, who is forty-six, and Creighton, who is forty-nine. There are no family scandals, and by all accounts, they are good people. As families go, they appear to be close-knit.

A graduate of Wake Forest University, he has bachelor's degrees in philosophy and economics. Shortly after her graduation, he and Veronica married and moved to Dallas, where he took a job with the Federal Reserve Bank. While working at the bank, he earned two master's degrees from Southern Methodist University, one in political science, the other in economics, and eventually received a PhD in economics.

While still at the Dallas Fed, Parker had written a prescient paper advocating for America to increase natural gas exploration and infrastructure development. Of note was the mention of the need to construct liquid natural gas terminals on the East Coast. By increasing production and infrastructure capabilities, natural gas could become a major new export opportunity for America to trade with Western Europe. This was happening at a time when much of Europe, especially Germany, was increasingly reliant on Russia to meet its energy needs. In it he pointed out that Western Europe's dependence on Russian natural gas exports could be used to deter a NATO response to an expansion of Russia's borders.

The paper focused mostly on job creation, tax revenue, and trade deficit implications, but found its way to the Pentagon. The projected impact of continued European demand for Russian gas could only serve to strengthen the Russian economy and increase its potential as a threat to its neighbors' sovereignty. Rachael had included Stowe's paper on the virtues of American natural gas. However, the most pertinent parts of the report on

Stowe began after he left the Federal Reserve and headed back to North Carolina.

In 2001, the Stowe family moved to Winston-Salem when Veronica got an amazing offer to join TechConnect Partners, a telecommunications consulting firm where her electronic data interchange background was a highly desired commodity.

Parker secured a position as an associate professor with his old alma mater, Wake Forest, and was promoted to full professor in 2011. His most popular course was one labeled in the catalog as The Ethics of Economic Policy in America. It was an amalgamation of his interests and background in economics, political science, and philosophy. He authored a textbook on the topic and spoke several times a year by invitation at various forums throughout the country on the subject.

Considered to be a fiscal conservative, his unconventional ideas on issues like the minimum wage and income gap tended to separate him from traditional Republican positions. On social issues, Stowe was all over the place. He was moderate on legislative policy, but his personal conduct reflected a more conservative set of values.

In a widely publicized quote, when asked by a reporter if his membership in an evangelical Christian mega-church would impact his stance on issues like gay marriage or abortion, Stowe responded, "Jesus didn't change lives by running for public office and writing laws. He changed hearts by the principled way He lived, and thus changed history. I'd rather lead by example than try to legislate morality."

Rachael concluded by saying, "Based on what we have gathered from his speeches and publications as well as his personal, academic, and professional backgrounds, we think he'll ask for the chairmanship of Health, Education, Labor, and Pensions."

She continued, "We think he'll use it as a platform to push his ideas on the minimum wage. It'll help him sell books and keep him in the press, once control of the Senate is decided. It also explains why he may want to work with us and not the Republicans. His ideas about the minimum wage were an attack point against him when Steve Crockett was still in the race."

"This is good stuff, Rachael." The president was always impressed with the thoroughness of her work. "The assessment answers all the big questions, including why he's made a place for us at the table. I like it."

Thach was more cautious. "Were there any other plausible, maybe less likely scenarios that emerged from the research we should be considering? His background in economics makes him a good fit for Finance or Appropriations, both of which are more powerful committees."

"I still have the analysts looking through his background, but right now nothing else explains why we have an invitation to the dance, so to speak." She was ready to call it a night and wanted to move the discussion along. "Either side can give him a chairmanship, so the key point is to figure out what else he thinks we bring to the table. We can meet again tomorrow to discuss any new developments."

"That's a good idea, Rachael. We'll have lunch tomorrow, here at noon." Marcus was done for the night too. "Let's also meet on Friday, say 4:00 p.m. In the meantime, we should all review the information on Stowe and see if any other theories develop. Meeting adjourned."

CHAPTER 9

Thursday morning came early, as mornings always did, for Miranda. Her inner clock woke her at four-thirty every morning, regardless of her schedule.

Early rising had been a bone of contention with her ex-husband, who was a light sleeper and thus forced to wake when she did. Even after all these years, she remembered how annoyed he would get when she got up before he was ready.

Miranda had attended an all-girls Catholic school, and the then all-female Wesleyan College in Georgia. Upon receiving her degree, she moved back in with her rigidly Catholic parents in Houston. Torn between her desires to be a strong, independent woman of the '80s and honoring her parents' conservative, old-fashioned values, she decided the only way to leave her parents' home was to get married.

Her looks gave her many choices as there was no shortage of suitors who sought her affections. At twenty-four years old, she ended up with a handsome man who was, of course, a good Catholic. His family owned a chain of popular Mexican restaurants and a bakery that supplied fresh tortillas and chips to many markets in the region, and he treated her like a princess. They went to the finest places, and he bought her the nicest gifts. He showed her respect and tenderness, and she grew to love him deeply. Her father gave his blessing when he asked for her hand, and after the customary marriage counseling with a priest, they wed. It was a grand Catholic ceremony attended by what seemed like half of Houston.

She divorced him four years later after he was arrested for drug trafficking, having used the bakery as a major cocaine warehousing and distribution point. He was sentenced to twenty years of federal time but was murdered in prison after serving only nineteen months.

She walked away with nothing, including an annulment, because the Catholic Church refused to grant her one. She had not gone back to church since. Miranda often wondered why, after all these years, she still thought of him when she first woke so early in the morning.

The Keurig machine brewed a cup of bold Columbian while she tied her sneakers and put on a pink hoodie. She grabbed the coffee, her keys, laptop, and a garment bag as she headed out the door. Her BMW X5 roared to life as she set out for the athletic club.

All-News Radio 880 was Miranda's listening choice as she drove to the club for her workout. It was just enough time to get caught up on the events that had unfolded overnight. Eastern Ukraine was still in turmoil as the Russian-backed rebels continued their push for separation. The Islamic terror group ISIS was threatening to behead another Western hostage and seize even more control over land in Iraq and Syria. And the Ebola outbreak in Congo was still raging out of control.

Miranda muttered to herself, "Well, there are three of the Four Horsemen of the Apocalypse: War, Death, and Pestilence." The next story referenced the drought in California and its impact on the price of dairy, fruits, and vegetables.

"And Famine brings up the rear." She said this out loud, though there was no one in the car to hear her. She didn't really believe the apocalypse was happening, but it was her way of poking fun at the news industry. The news media blew every event up to monumental proportions. They created artificial crises without regard for true significance in the context of world history. All done in the name of grabbing the largest market share of the listening audience to make a buck. It was absurd and just a little obscene to her way of thinking. If her marriage and subsequent divorce had taught her anything, it was that things were rarely as good, or as bad, as they seemed.

As she checked in at the desk, the handsome, young, six-foot-one, two-hundred-pound hunk of beautifully tan muscle flashed a perfectly white smile at her. "Good morning Ms. Cortez. You look great this morning, as always." It was their normal routine.

"Well thank you, Zack." She handed him her membership card and he scanned the barcode. It was such a shame he was half her age and had no interest in women. Not that she would have pursued him anyway, but she had the active imagination of a single woman in her early fifties. It was kind of like going to the museum. She appreciated the works of art but couldn't see them fitting in her house.

"Here you go." He handed her back her key ring and a bottle of water. As though in a perfectly rehearsed dance, he, in turn, took from her the garment bag she was carrying. "I'll call Kathy and have her take your clothes back to the locker room and steam them as usual. Your smoothie will be waiting for you here at the desk when you leave."

"You take phenomenal care of me. You know that, Zack. Right?"

"Yes, sweetie. That's why I get the best shifts and they pay me the big bucks."

"I'd brag to management, but I can't risk not having you here every morning. The thought of having to start all over again with someone else is simply dreadful." She slipped him a tip and headed to the mats to stretch.

After stretching, it was off to the treadmill for twenty minutes of cardio and a warmup. She watched the morning shows, catching commentary on items of interest to her. Today, she wanted to know what they were saying about Senator-Elect Parker Stowe. She was hoping no one had leaked anything to the press about the Saturday morning meeting. She wanted to break the news to Wade herself at their daily briefing.

Nothing new on Stowe so far from the press. Off to the weights for thirty minutes. At 6:00 a.m. she did a yoga class. At 7:00 a.m. she did twenty minutes of laps in the pool. By 7:55 a.m., she was showered, smartly dressed in a silk skirt-suit, and made up with her hair in a bun with light, flawless makeup. Precisely at 8:00 a.m., after giving Kathy her workout clothes to launder and giving her a tip, Miranda grabbed her green power smoothie and headed out the door.

With five minutes to spare, Miranda entered the conference room at the RNC Headquarters and took her usual seat at the table. She looked out the window and waited exactly four minutes for Wade to arrive.

"Good morning, Miranda," he said with a melodic cadence. Wade was a morning person.

"Good morning, Wade," she replied. "You seem particularly upbeat this morning." Telling him about Saturday's meeting would quickly change that.

"I just got word from my sources that Dowd and Henry will concede today. That gets us to forty-nine. That old fool Tapp in Arkansas is still holding out, but there's no real hope for him. I bet he folds tomorrow. Tell me some good news about Stowe.

Did you work things out with Tuttle? I'm assuming, since I didn't hear from you yesterday, that he's coming here."

"Oh, he's coming here." She looked directly at him.

Wade knew the look and became all business. "What exactly does that mean, Miranda? Let's not dance. It's too early in the day."

"We're meeting Saturday morning. You, me, and Jack Archer at eight with him and Jason." She paused as he waited expectantly. He knew there was more to come. She continued. "We're all meeting at the White House with the president, vice president, majority leader, and Rachael Zimmermann."

Wade stood up and walked to a window, turning his back to Miranda. He looked down and stared across First Street into the subway entrance as though it were an abyss. When he finally spoke, all he could muster was, "Why, Miranda?"

"I've been asking myself the same question, Wade. I asked Jason, and I honestly believe he doesn't know either. Stowe just told him to be patient. Jason even asked Stowe's wife, and it was news to her too. Whatever he's up to, he's playing it close to the vest."

"They can't give him anything we can't. He's got nothing to gain. Did you get the assessment from that analyst? He says that Parker will likely ask for Health, Education, Labor, and Pensions."

"I read it late last night. It makes sense. Even explains why he might be putting us in a room with the Democrats." She was leading him. Wade would eventually come to the same conclusion on his own, but she didn't have all day to wait.

Wade kept staring down at the opening on the other side of the street, watching people appear and disappear as they rode the escalators to and from the platform below. Even though he could not see the train, he knew it was there by the volume and speed of activity on the escalators. "It's the minimum wage thing," he finally said.

"Bingo. I think it's his way to get us to change our stance. I can't find another angle."

"What a mess. Out of the frying pan, into the fire. First Crockett drops chow in the bed and now Stowe's off the proverbial reservation. We—you and me, Miranda—have orchestrated one of the biggest turnovers of Senate seats in the history of U.S. electoral politics. And yet our own party will run us outta here because of Stowe."

Wade was right. A net gain of five seats in the Senate for a party, even during a midterm election, was a true rarity. It should label them both superstars. But if they had to give on the minimum wage, the cost would be high and their success short-lived.

"Stop contemplating a jump, Wade." She was trying to break the tension with some levity. Get him refocused and back to the table. "It's never as bad or as good as it seems."

CHAPTER 10

In early 1995, Major Jason Tuttle worked as an Army intelligence officer in the Pentagon, tasked with developing threat assessments now that Eastern Europe was no longer under Moscow's direct control. His unit was particularly interested in commodity prices, currency valuations, credit ratings, and the debt levels of foreign nations in the region. One of the major causes of conflict throughout history has been the possession or lack of natural resources. Control of things like oil, grain, natural gas, and even water—not to mention gold and silver—have been at the heart of wars for millennia. This is how Parker Stowe's paper landed on Major Tuttle's desk.

He met and interviewed Stowe as part of the intelligence-gathering process for the threat assessment. As the two spent time together, they discovered their mutual, almost lifelong involvement with the Boy Scouts. Because of his background in economics, his work at the Federal Reserve Bank, and connections in the oil and gas industry, Tuttle often had Stowe review some non-classified data for accuracy.

Jason regularly asked Parker for his perspective on projections that other analysts and scholars were making. He didn't abuse the relationship, but it was a good excuse to call Stowe and catch up with the world outside the Washington Beltway.

Two years after their friendship began, Stowe told Tuttle that he was putting together an expedition to Philmont, the national Boy Scout reservation and high-adventure base in New Mexico. He and two other adult leaders would be taking sixteen boys west for two weeks the following summer for hiking and camping in the New Mexico wilderness. When Stowe asked Tuttle if he'd like to go as a fourth adult leader, he jumped at the chance.

As a young scout, Jason had spent hours reading his *Boy's Life* magazines and had always wanted to go to one of the high-adventure bases. He would read the same stories and look at the same pictures repeatedly. He even bought a trail map of the reservation so he could locate where pictures were taken and events in the accounts of the writers took place. But his family was poor and could barely afford his uniform, so such an excursion was out of the question.

Besides being a means to fund his education, part of the allure of the Army to Tuttle was the opportunity to see the world and have adventures. He did ROTC at college, Airborne School in Georgia, and a tour in Germany. However, his degree in computer science, skills as an analyst, and leadership style made him more valuable at the Pentagon. Much to his displeasure, he spent most of his career with the military in Washington D.C. and not traveling the world as he had hoped. His time together with Parker in the mountains of New Mexico was all they needed to solidify their friendship, and the two forged a bond for life. Jason came to see Stowe as the younger brother he never had. Parker came to see Tuttle as the older brother he had wanted his own to be.

As Jason ate a banana and finished his corn flakes Thursday morning, he was contemplating why Parker was holding back from him. In all the years since their hike in New Mexico, they had been thick as thieves.

"He must have his reasons." He said it out loud, though there was no one to hear him. The house was empty except for Simon the cat.

Simon just looked at him and blinked slowly, as if in agreement. Jason suspected the only reason the cat was anywhere near him right now was the prospect of lapping any leftover milk from the cereal bowl. They tolerated one another, but it was no love affair. The litter box smelled, he shed on everything, and he constantly disturbed his sleep with his on-the-bed, off-the-bed movements.

Simon had belonged to Lilly, Jason's beloved wife, and he had been such a source of comfort and companionship to her in her final months that Jason could not abandon him. When Lilly was first diagnosed with cancer in 2003, Jason, who was then a Lt. Colonel, decided to retire after twenty-three years in the Army. Parker and Veronica were the first to jump in and offer to help in any way possible. Veronica got him his first private-sector job with TechConnect Partners.

Exiting the kitchen as Simon gladly indulged in his treat, Jason held his half-full cup of coffee and headed to his study to check his email before heading to the office. He had a lot to do. He needed to start closing out the campaign and settling the accounts payable. Parker would be in tomorrow to thank everyone and say goodbye to those whose jobs were finished.

It was customary, and there would be no hard feelings. With no more funds coming in, they had to cut expenses quickly.

He also needed to make sure all was arranged as Parker had requested. There was an email from him.

> *Jason,*
>
> *I know leaving here last night, you were confused and maybe questioning why I wasn't ready to discuss my strategy with you. Be assured that our friendship is intact and that other than Roni, there is no one in the world I trust more.*
>
> *As if it were not a big enough responsibility to be elected to this office, I am now carrying the burden of knowing what I do next will have a great impact not just on me or North Carolina, but on the nation as a whole.*
>
> *I am not fearful or without direction. I have a plan, but keeping it to myself, for the time being, will protect you and others if it fails. I must do what I think is best for the country. I don't want to be just another politician. I want to be a statesman. I want to remind people that it is who you are that defines what you do, and that significance is derived from character before it's defined by action.*
>
> *Know that I appreciate your trust, loyalty, and understanding. I would not be where I am or want to go where I'm going without you.*
>
> *Friends Always,*
> *Parker*

Jason powered down the laptop and put it in his bag. Simon sat in the doorway licking the remaining drops of milk from his whiskers, looking ever so much like a nap was in his near future.

"Don't sleep the day away, cat," Jason cautioned. "I need you to sleep tonight so I can too." Jason and Simon meant more to each other than either cared to express. He patted him on the head and went out the front door.

CHAPTER 11

There are screams of joy, screams of pain, and screams of anger, but the scream of sheer terror is unmistakably unique. For those who have heard it, it's one that's never forgotten.

Roni opened the back door to let the dogs out for their morning routine. Almost instantly, they took off running for the tree line in full bark and growl. She usually wasn't too concerned—they often spied rabbits, turkeys, and other wildlife out for an early morning forage. This morning, though, it seemed that they were chasing something much bigger, and it grabbed the attention of everyone in the house.

Roni ran back inside and hit the panic button on the alarm as she raced to the kids. All three were sitting at the table eating breakfast.

She yelled, "Get down on the ground," as she pulled Burk, who was closest, off his chair to the floor. Samantha had done what she was told immediately, and instinctively followed her mother's actions by pulling Amos with her. Together the four began to crawl further into the interior of the house and out of the kitchen.

By this time, Parker had arrived from upstairs, pistol in hand. The alarm was blaring, and he shouted to Roni, "What is it? What's out there?"

She was sobbing but in control. "I don't know!" She was shaking. He could see the terror in her eyes. "The dogs headed for the tree line, and something stood up, like a man. It looked like a bear, but I think it had a gun."

There was a knock at the front door.

"Senator Stowe, Mrs. Stowe, it's the State Police. Is everything okay in there?"

"Just a minute," he yelled. "We're all okay. My wife thinks she saw someone out back with a gun in the tree line. The dogs went after him. I'm sending my wife to the door to let you in. I'm armed. Don't shoot me." Roni moved to the front of the house, unlocked the door, and let the trooper into the house.

"Are you alright? Where's the senator?" The trooper was all business.

"Yes, we're okay. He's down the hall to the left."

Two officers entered the house. "Close and lock the door behind us." Their weapons drawn, they waited for her to secure the door again. Together they moved toward Parker and the kids in the hallway. Parker didn't look back at them. He just kept watching and pointing the gun at the back door. He could still hear the dogs barking.

One of the troopers moved next to Parker. "I got this, Senator. More officers are outside, and more are on the way. For your safety and mine, I need you to give me your gun." Parker did as he was told. Moving toward his family, he got out of the line of sight of the back door.

"You saw someone with a gun at the tree line?" the other trooper repeated.

"I think so," Roni said, still noticeably shaking.

The officer keyed his radio. "This is five-one. We have secured the family in the residence. Possible armed suspect in the tree line to the west. Family dogs were in pursuit."

"Ten-four, five-one. Backup has arrived. We hear the dogs and will check it out."

Parker, though grateful to have the police there, did not like being unarmed and thus unable to defend his family. He felt vulnerable and helpless.

"Is there a better place for us to be? Should we move to the basement?" Parker was sincere but did not want to take the trooper's focus away from defending the door.

"No. It's safer to stay where you are. There are officers outside clearing the grounds. As soon as it's safe, we'll move you away from the house until we can clear all the rooms." His radio came alive.

"This is five-eight. We got him."

"Five-one, this is five-five. All exterior doors of the house are secure except for the back door. Are we clear to approach?"

"This five-one. Clear to approach, five-five." The trooper covering the back door lowered his weapon and pointed it at the floor but did not stand or holster it. Four of his colleagues entered, weapons were drawn but also pointed toward the floor. The officers moved about the kitchen and then yelled, "Clear!" They proceeded from room to room, repeating the process until they were certain no one was in the house.

Parker helped Roni to her feet and headed to the keypad to silence the alarm. As he did so, he could hear his phone ringing in the bedroom upstairs. He couldn't care less, and went to join his family who had moved to the den. The kids seemed fine, but Roni was still visibly upset. Parker got her a bottle of water from the fridge. They could now hear both of their phones ringing from the upstairs bedroom. The sound of multiple helicopters could be heard above. Suddenly he remembered that the media was camped out a hundred and sixty or so yards from the front door. By now the helicopters were broadcasting live images of the house to TVs across the country.

"Sammy, run upstairs and get our phones for us please, honey. I bet those calls are from Popi and Nanni and Mema and Pepa 'cause they're worried about what they're seeing on TV. Are you okay to go up there and get them for us?"

"I am, Dad!" exclaimed Amos, and he bounced upstairs before Samantha could answer.

Samantha was on one side of her mother, and Burk was on the other. It was hard to tell who was comforting whom. If Parker weren't still charged up with adrenaline, he might have found the picture the three made on the couch to be an endearing family candid. But as it was, he was just glad everyone was okay. Now he wanted answers as to what was going on.

There was a knock at the front door, and two of the officers went to open it. Amos clamored back down the stairs, cell phones in hand.

"Can you guys please call your grandparents and let them know we're all okay? Tell them Mommy and Daddy will call them back after they finish talking with the police."

Amos gave a phone to Burk and they each called a set of grandparents as Parker had asked them to do. Samantha stayed on the couch with her mother as State Police Captain Alex Jefferies entered the room followed by the two troopers who had gone to let him inside.

"You folks okay?" he asked. "You've had quite a scare. Does anyone need a doctor?"

"We're all okay, Captain." Parker looked at Roni. "Babe, do you need anything?"

She looked at him. She was no longer shaking, and now noticeably less pale. "We're fine. Thank you. Was there someone out there?"

The captain smiled and spoke more to Roni than Parker. Years of experience taught him that in these situations, if he could get Mom to be calm, everybody else would generally be calm too.

"There was someone out there, but he didn't have a weapon. It was a freelance photographer in one of those specialized camouflage suits that snipers use in the military. What you thought was a gun was actually a camera with a very long, high-powered lens on it. Those dogs scared him good. We're going to charge him with trespassing, but that's about all I can do."

The color in Roni's skin had fully returned and marked a significant shift in her demeanor. Gone was the fear, replaced by anger. "What about the camera? Were there pictures on it? Isn't that some sort of invasion of privacy?"

"We do have the camera. He got a few shots of Mrs. Stowe letting the dogs out, but nothing else. Unfortunately, the camera is Bluetooth enabled and automatically sent the pictures to his partner's laptop. I'm afraid there's no way of keeping them out of the press at this point.

"I'm going to ask the U.S. Capitol Police to evaluate the security situation as technically your security falls to their jurisdiction. There's no specific threat, so the USCP won't likely get directly involved. Until the media circus outside ends, I'll keep two cars out front if for nothing else than to keep the talking heads from blocking traffic. We won't be too far away, Mrs. Stowe."

Roni managed to say, "Thank you, Captain," but she was still very much annoyed at the whole situation. Parker caught a glance she shot at him that said without words—'This is your fault. Fix it.'

"You're welcome, Mrs. Stowe." Captain Jeffries smiled again, trying to soften her. He had voted for Stowe, really liked him, and genuinely felt bad about what they just went through.

Parker thought for a moment and asked the captain to join him in his study at the front of the house.

"Captain, I genuinely appreciate your efforts. I never believed it would get this crazy."

"You're a good man, Senator. It makes me proud to be a North Carolinian knowing we're sending you to Washington. I sure hope you can change that place."

"Me too. I'll do the best that can be done," Parker replied. "I know the patrol cars being placed out front and all is unofficial, but if you can help me with something, I sure would appreciate it. You know why they're all camped out there and so interested in me right now, don't you?"

"Yes, sir. Everybody wants to know who you're going to side with."

"That's right. And I'm leaving for Washington tomorrow without my family for some meetings. I expect that I'll be resolving that question before the weekend is over." Parker smiled at Captain Jefferies and continued. "No matter what I do, I'm going to tick people off. I want to bring change to Washington, but I can't do that without knowing my family is safe. We both know you can't leave those cars out there forever, and I'm not going to officially be a senator until after I'm sworn in next January. I'm working on some longer-term security options, but I need to know you and your people have my back down here through Monday."

"I'll handle it. Don't worry. You have a lot of friends and support in these parts. Sheriff Arnold responded with some of his deputies and is outside right now. We'll work together and keep an eye on the family while you're gone."

"Thanks, Captain."

CHAPTER 12

Forbes Magazine listed Lionel Rockport as one of the twenty-five richest men in America with an estimated net worth of about twenty-seven billion dollars, give or take a hundred million. He was a secretive man and preferred to live as private a life as he could buy. Avoiding high-dollar political affairs, sidestepping red carpet events, and, with almost religious ferver, declining every request for an interview or comment sought from him furthered his objective of maintaining a low profile. He called a massive ranch in Texas home, but owning property all over the world, he rarely spent more than a few days in one location. Most people would not recognize him, and he liked it that way.

Rockport was unmarried and without children, though he had an extended family, many of whom he employed in one capacity or another. His only requirement of them was that they too avoid publicity and notoriety. If they or their children drew attention to themselves or the family, he was done with them. No exceptions.

He once employed a nephew whose son had the misfortune of dating a famous supermodel. While on vacation in the Caribbean, some compromising pictures were taken with her. The rather salacious images ended up on the cover of three national and two international tabloids with headlines like *Kat Brooks' Mysterious New Boy Toy* and *Kat Brooks' Connection to Secretive Billionaire's Family*. The nephew was excommunicated before the magazines hit the racks at the checkout counters.

Good publicity would be met with an equal consequence. A third cousin was once honored for a generous contribution to an ALS research program right around the time of the famous ice bucket challenge. She was discharged immediately from her position at one of his companies. Cut off from the Rockport fortune too.

The key to Lionel's ire was the public eye. Be generous but do it anonymously. If you screw up, keep it out of the news. He knew public opinion to be fickle. The people loved you one minute and hated you the next. Having money attracts people with needs. Meeting those needs makes you popular but draws more people with needs to you. Likewise, turning people away makes you unpopular. If you turn too many people away, you are labeled greedy and vilified. It's a no-win situation, and Rockport's solution was simply to avoid publicity altogether.

For those that knew him well, and they were few, Lionel Rockport was personable, kind, and even generous. He paid his people well but expected absolute loyalty in return. He did not consider himself particularly smart or wise, and he did not have great stature or even a commanding presence about him. The closest person to him was an administrative assistant who once asked him the secret to his success.

"I have a unique perspective," was Rockport's answer.

He got his beginning by identifying an opportunity created through the inheritance tax. Often the bulk of the value of a farmer's estate was tied to the value of the land, and owners were usually not flush with cash. People whose farms' or businesses' assets were not liquid could either buy enough life insurance or their heirs might be forced to sell to pay the inheritance tax.

Rockport established a small life insurance company in the Midwest and marketed specifically to family-owned entities like family farmers, equipment dealers, lumber mills, and trucking companies. His people were closing five out of ten appointments, and the money started flowing in the door, hand over fist.

Every insurance company needs a way to invest the cash generated from premiums. Rockport demonstrated a true knack for seeing opportunities others did not. He started keeping track of the people who did not buy life insurance from his salespeople, and the farms and businesses they owned. When one of these people died, he would then have a representative offer to buy the farm or business at a substantial discount in return for a quick, all-cash deal. If they refused, he would have a different affiliated company contact the heirs and offer to loan money to pay the taxes with high interest rates, using the business or farm as collateral. No matter what happened, his organization benefited. Through one affiliated company or another, Rockport's entities eventually did business with roughly sixty percent of the estates or heirs with whom the insurance company failed to secure a policy. In 1996, Rockport created a holding company for all his affiliated businesses and took it public. Now, Indiana-Fellows Holdings was worth more than forty-eight billion dollars. Among its assets, IFH owned commercial farms, lending institutions, insurance companies, pawnshops, fast-food franchises, hotel brands, and even a regional airline.

That morning, Lionel Rockport was in the middle of his second cup of coffee, sitting on the aft sun deck of his yacht as it sailed from the Chesapeake Bay to Rio. In his early sixties, Rockport preferred the warmer climates and tried to avoid the changes of season.

He would take the helicopter to the West Palm Beach compound when the ship was off the coast of Florida. It would sail on to South America, where he would catch up with it in a month or so. His phone rang, and he answered it as he moved off the deck and into his spacious cabin office.

"Good morning, Paul."

"Good morning, Mr. Rockport. I hope I'm not disturbing you. Is now a good time to talk?" Paul Harper was head of risk management at IFH. He had multiple teams of analysts that did nothing but predict the probable effects of various inputs on the portfolio assets. Any major risk needed to be identified early so a plan to deal with it could be devised. Most never crossed Rockport's desk. The election of Parker Stowe was one of the elite few that did.

"Now's fine, Paul. What do you have for me?"

"Our sources are telling us that Stowe will likely ask for Health, Education, Labor, and Pensions. It's the only thing that makes sense. There's some big meeting at the White House Saturday morning." Paul waited for a response but only received silence. He knew from experience that he should just keep going. "Our source believes Stowe wants the Democrats there to strong-arm a commitment from the Republicans to support minimum wage reform, in line with his book on the subject. This could be a game changer, Mr. Rockport. Depending on how the legislation is written, we could face major restructuring costs. Estimates are in the hundreds of millions."

"Thanks, Paul. I'll call you back." That was all Rockport said in reply as he picked up his copy of Parker Stowe's *The Ethics of Economic Policy in America.* The book began with a discussion of the constitutional basis for economic legislation focusing on Article One, Section Eight, where the scope of legislative power is defined.

At its core, Stowe argued that the purpose of economic legislation was not intended to inhibit or restrict commerce. It simply ensured unanimity and parity between the states and provided a way for the government to fund its obligations. He believed that the founders worked off two guiding principles: that businesses tend to thrive in predictable environments, and that thriving businesses create taxable commerce. It was a rather strict, literal, and conservative interpretation of the Constitution. Stowe began with a rather lengthy comparison of indirect taxes, which are voluntary or assigned to a transaction, such as a sales tax, and a direct tax, which are assigned to an individual, like an income or property tax. He pointed out that the founders were strongly in favor of indirect taxes and warned against the use of direct taxation, viewing direct taxation as a tool that tyrannical governments used to subjugate the individual. Direct taxation became popular during the industrialization of America to keep the wealthy from subjugating the poor. Stowe reserved judgment in favor of a balanced and thorough discussion of the pros and cons of each.

But the book was as much about ethics as it was about the tax code. The practical application of direct and indirect taxation was thus a central theme. Stowe argued that direct taxes were widening the gap between the wealthy and poor and shrinking the middle class, hurting more people than helping, and allowed wealth to buy influence. He argued money was neither good nor evil, but that its concentration had to be tempered to keep opportunity open to all. This discussion read to be a rather progressive, or liberal, point of view and left the reader asking, "How does a mess like this get fixed?"

Rather than attempting to tackle the massive issues of the tax code, Stowe shifted gears to the minimum wage. He laid out the historical evolution of the concept, beginning with the 1912 Massachusetts non-compulsory recommended minimum wage and of the Fair Labor Standards Act of 1938, which established a federally mandated minimum wage. He spent considerable time arguing about its ineffectiveness in closing the income gap.

He argued that it made low-income earners feel like their government was working for them, but it did nothing to lift them out of poverty. Just like a direct tax on business is passed along to the consumer in the price of the good or service, the increased cost of labor would be reflected in the price of the good or service. The wage earner made more, but would pay more for the goods and services purchased, resulting in no real change to lifestyle. Stowe even went further and argued that the only entity that gains from a minimum wage hike is the federal government. The government collects more income taxes when wages climb. The result made government debt that was issued years before cheaper to service. He concluded the minimum wage was just a means to artificially, but in a controlled manner, inflate prices and revenue without adjusting interest rates. And then he made a proposal that would address the income gap:

> *If there is a true need and desire to regulate the gap between the richest and poorest of Americans, then the minimum wage is not the best way to accomplish this purpose. I propose that instead of setting a standard that must be debated and adjusted periodically by a legislature that is prone to demonizing those with a differing opinion, we come to agree that all who contribute should benefit without limiting those who innovate and create opportunity.*
>
> *It is in this spirit that I suggest that the greatest in an organization should be able to earn as much as he or she can negotiate, but not more than forty times that of the least within the organization. This means that any corporation paying the current federal minimum wage of $7.25 per hour or $14,790.00 on an annualized basis cannot provide a compensation package to anyone in the corporation worth more than $591,600.00. If the organization chooses to*

*compensate an individual beyond $591,600.00, they may
do so without restriction, but must proportionally increase
the amount that the lowest wage earner makes to maintain
the maximum forty-to-one income ratio.*

Stowe went on to say that the forty-to-one ratio was debatable
and only used for illustrative purposes. It established a true
means to regulate the income gap without the use of the tax
code and with no inflationary effect on the prices of goods and
services offered. It promoted fairness without stifling innova-
tion. He also noted that it would do nothing to change the
current value of personal fortunes and would not likely change
the amount of tax revenue received by the government, only
broaden the base of participation. The only organizations that
would suffer were those that through poor governance or
corporate greed had allowed the top few to benefit without
regard for most employees or other stakeholders.

He concluded that the debate over the minimum wage may
continue to be relevant as a tool to fine-tune the cost of servicing
government debt but should become less of a political issue as
more incomes adjust to the success of their organizations.

Lionel pulled a pad from his desk and began to imagine
opportunities that might arise from the implementation of
Stowe's ideas.

CHAPTER 13

Roni and Parker snuck the kids out the back of the property and off to school. They were an hour late, but by then the administration at Forest Park Prep already knew what had happened earlier that morning. Headmistress Graft assured them she would keep an eye on the children and told the Stowes not to worry. She was a fan of the senator-elect and viewed the enrollment of the children at Forest Park as being akin to winning the fundraising lottery.

Roni had taken the entire election week off from work, and Parker had been on sabbatical from the university for over a year. They had intended on spending the day as though on an extended date. But instead, they were on their way to an early lunch and then off to meet with a private security firm.

When Jason arrived at the office that morning, he called Parker as soon as he heard about the commotion at the house. When nobody answered the first four times he called, Jason was about to jump back in the Lincoln and drive to their home. Thankfully, Amos answered the phone on Jason's fifth attempt. After hearing all was okay, Uncle Jason asked Amos to have his father call him back as soon as he was able. When Parker finally returned the call, Jason had already arranged a meeting with some people he knew from the Army who were now in the private security business. They would meet with them at the Stowe-for-Senate election headquarters later that afternoon in downtown Winston-Salem.

As they headed off the school grounds in the Suburban, Parker said, "I'm sorry."

Her first instinct was to say something like, 'You should be.' However, enough time had passed, and Roni had a grip on her emotions. "Thank you, but I know it's not your fault." She didn't quite believe the words she was saying but reminded herself that Parker was not the enemy. He had been ready to die defending her and the children.

"I made us public figures. I made this kind of thing more likely to happen."

"Are you trying to make me angry again?"

"No. I don't want to fight, but I also don't want stuff, especially this kind of stuff, between us. I hate that you were scared for the kids. I hate that you felt threatened. I know that given how it turned out, you feel embarrassed. I want you to know that I'm glad you were there. I'm proud of what you did, and I'm sorry that you had to go through any of it."

She looked away from him out the passenger window. "You're an ass, you know that?" She grabbed her purse and pulled out a tissue. Her eyes were wet, and she was sniffling, trying not to break out into a full cry. "I had this under control and promised myself I wouldn't blame you. Now look at me. I'm crying all over again. Why couldn't you just let me be? I'd have gotten over this eventually. Now I really am mad at you, even though you were so brave this morning and so sweet to me just now. Oh, you drive me mad sometimes!"

Parker just sat there and let her get it out. She needed to be mad so they could move past the morning drama. He wanted to know they were okay before he left for Washington tomorrow afternoon. His world did not function well when all was not right between them. Being his best for her now meant he could be his best for the nation on Saturday morning.

"I know, but you love me anyway for reasons I still don't understand."

"Because you let me be me." She smiled as she said it, and he knew she was done with the anger. "I do love you. You know that, right?"

"With all that I am, I know it. I love you too."

As they came to a stoplight, Parker checked his rearview mirror. The same car had been following them since they left the school. At first, he believed he was being paranoid. The car would change lanes, drop back, or place multiple cars in between them. But no matter how many random turns he made, the car always seemed to reappear in his rearview mirror.

"What do you say to lunch at the University Club? It'll be a little more private and intimate." He knew that the university would be a good place to hide. At least once a week before the campaign, he and Roni met there for lunch. The staff all knew them well. Parker said nothing to her about the car following them.

"Okay." Roni sounded almost enthusiastic. "We haven't been in so long. It'll be good to see everybody."

Parker made a U-turn and headed back towards the campus. He took note of the sedan and its occupant as they passed him going in the opposite direction. It was a younger white guy in his twenties or possibly late teens. He was artsy looking, not threatening at all, giving Parker the impression that maybe he was just another photographer looking for a candid shot to sell to the papers. He checked the rearview mirror. Sure enough, the sedan made the U-turn about four or five car lengths behind them.

When they got to the club, Parker used the valet. He quickly greeted Peter with a twenty-dollar bill and told him to park the Suburban upfront where he could keep an eye on it. He quickly moved to the other side of the car, eager to rush Roni inside. Parker noticed the sedan pulling to the curb on the opposite side of the street as they entered the building.

Charlotte greeted them with a big smile. "Congratulations, Senator and Mrs. Stowe. So good to see you! It's been so long. Will it just be the two of you today?" She was an attractive young lady with thick, blond, curly hair. She was never inappropriate, but Roni always thought she was a little too flirtatious with Parker.

"Yes, Charlotte. Just the two of us," Roni replied. "Sorry it's been so long, but with the campaign and everything, time has just gotten away from us. It's good to be back and see all of you."

"Well, if you're ready, I have a table right by the window up front."

Parker was quick to inquire, "If you don't mind, after the hoopla this morning at the house, I'd rather not be seated by a window, Charlotte. Is that possible?"

"It sure is, Senator." She flashed him a big, white, toothy smile and batted her bright green eyes. "I bet that must have been just awful. We saw it on the news with the police, helicopters, and—"

Roni had enough. "Yes, it was terrifying. Thankfully there was no real threat. I hate to rush you Charlotte, but we have an appointment at one downtown."

"I completely understand, Mrs. Stowe. Right this way."

"I'm going to run to the restroom," Parker said. "Go on without me to the table. You know what I like, so go ahead and order me something."

Roni looked at him funny but went on to the table, with Charlotte leading the way. She hoped Parker was feeling alright.

When he got to the bathroom, Parker called campus security. He did not want to make a big deal of things, considering all the publicity that morning. But he didn't want to take chances with his wife either.

"No, I did not see a gun or weapon. … Yes, I suspect the guy is just paparazzi. … Please don't let my wife know what's going on, if possible."

As he hung up the phone, Chief Gus Moffatt already had a plan in the making. Before he was Senator-Elect Stowe, he was Professor Stowe. Campus police were a special breed, being both sworn officers and a private security force employed by the university. They often had to balance enforcement of the law with protecting the privacy and reputation of the institution, its faculty, staff, and students. The campus police chief viewed Parker as one of his own.

He dispatched a uniformed officer in a marked car to the University Club with instructions to go inside under the auspices of eating lunch. The officer's real mission was to protect the inhabitants of the club from any unwelcome person. Nobody needed a gunman, however unlikely, to perpetrate another mass shooting on a college campus. The officer knew he would be the last line of defense should a suspect make it in the building. Pulling into the lot of the club, the officer spotted the unknown subject's vehicle across the street, just as Stowe had reported. It appeared empty. He had strict instructions not to investigate the vehicle. As he walked to the door, he chatted up the valet for just a minute, all the while surveying the area for any suspicious characters fitting the vague description Parker had given the chief. He then entered the building, acting as though it was just a routine meal stop.

Chief Moffatt had already contacted the manager at the club and asked him to call the station when the Stowe couple requested their check. He told the manager it was out of an abundance of caution, given the circus at their house earlier in the day. And just for good measure, he was sending over an officer to hang out until the senator and his wife left.

In the meantime, three plain-clothes officers, looking like students, entered the immediate area on foot. A half-dozen more uniformed officers casually assumed posts inside the main entrances of the surrounding buildings. When everyone was in place, four marked patrol cars positioned themselves at strategic points along the exit routes should a car chase ensue.

The description Parker gave of the suspect was so vague, it matched more than half of the males in the area. Being lunchtime, there was heavy foot traffic. Unless this guy decided to reveal himself, he would in all likeliness evade detection.

Though twenty-four and already possessing a degree in criminal justice, Officer Meghan Fowler looked the part of an upperclassman when dressed in street clothes. She was looking at her phone as she approached the red Ford Focus. She texted the license plate number to the chief, just another student sending messages back and forth to her boyfriend. She took pictures of the two barcoded stickers on the window, a sure indication the car was a rental, which she also sent as she walked past the car.

The chief became noticeably more agitated. The record check on the sedan's plates revealed that the car had been stolen the night before. The report had come from a club valet station in Durham, about thirty miles away. This was no paparazzi. It was a real criminal threat to the safety and security of the campus. He was sure that Stowe was the reason for the guy being there, but that did nothing to assuage his concerns about a possible gunman on campus. He now saw only bad options. He could use the senator as bait and hope the suspect revealed himself by either returning to the car, or God forbid, trying to assault him. He could scare the suspect off by letting him know they were onto him, but that would allow him to evade capture and strike again in the future. He could also put the campus on lockdown, close buildings, and send phone alerts out, but that could also trigger the unknown subject to attack or flee. In the end, Moffatt could not risk having a newly elected U.S. senator assaulted on campus, and he could not place the lives of any faculty, staff, or students in jeopardy. He decided to scare the guy off.

Chief Moffatt ordered one of the marked patrol cars to slowly move up the street as though he were doing a regular check for parking passes. When he got to the sedan, he stopped, clicked the trigger on the microphone attached to his chest, and acted like he was running the plate for the first time. He waited the appropriate amount of time for a response, keyed the transmitter again with a "ten-four," turned on the flashing lights of his vehicle, and approached the Ford Focus as if inspecting a dead body.

Officer Fowler watched a guy matching the description as he stood up, put a cell phone in his pocket, and picked up a knapsack that was sitting on the bench next to him. He nervously looked at his watch and started to walk down the path toward a large academic building across the quad. Fowler thought he seemed normal enough, but maybe because nobody else had anything, she decided to follow him.

As he was sitting on the bench, he saw the flashing green lights of the patrol car come on next to the Focus. Derick looked up from his phone, and though every instinct was telling him to run, he looked back down at his phone and worked on controlling his breathing. They found the car, big deal. He couldn't keep it forever, and there were plenty more to take when needed. *Breathe in deeply through the nose. Slowly exhale out the mouth. You look like you belong here, act as if you do. Surely there is a class starting soon.*

He looked around the quad and noticed a fairly large number of people going into what appeared to be a large academic hall. He slowly stood up, put his phone in his pocket, and picked up his bag. He checked his watch. It was 12:17 p.m. *Relax, you're on the way to class.* He began strolling down the path toward the academic hall, unaware he was being followed but paranoid just the same.

He entered the building and followed a stream of co-eds through a set of double doors that put him at the top of a large lecture hall with seats for more than a hundred students, though he doubted it would be full. He decided to get as close to the other set of doors with a red exit sign over them, providing an escape route if necessary. He took a seat four rows up from the lecture floor and two seats in from the aisle. He wondered what today's lecture would be. He still had no idea that Officer Fowler was watching him from behind and to the left. He unzipped his bag and reached in it, brushing the textured grip of the loaded nine-millimeter Glock with the back of his hand. He pulled a notepad out and placed it in front of him on the desk. He zipped up the bag again as he secured a pen from another compartment. The class turned out to be Accounting 101.

Officer Fowler found a seat in the hall and watched her subject prepare to take notes. Her instincts told her something was off, but if he was following Stowe, how could he be this ready for class? She stayed and watched him take notes for twenty minutes before deciding she was chasing a rabbit and left him to his lesson.

After an hour and a half of a mind-numbing, monotone discussion of the various elements and ways to calculate liabilities on the balance sheet, Derick exited the lecture hall with at least fifty other students. He worked his way to a bus stop and disappeared into the city of Winston-Salem.

CHAPTER 14

Mike Thach was in his seventies and four years into his fifth term as a U.S. senator. He had spent twelve of his twenty-eight years in the Senate as the minority leader, and the past ten as majority leader He cut back-room deals, sold access and influence, and had enough dirt on everyone to strong-arm them when necessary to get his way. He was loathed by the opposition, and even a few in his party harbored a secret disdain for Thach. He attacked his opponents' character instead of debating the issues, especially when the facts didn't support his position. He was a notorious hypocrite, but the people of Illinois had a history of loving their scandalous, if not outright corrupt, politicians.

Thursday morning found him at the Athletic Club of Washington D.C., where he met his son for breakfast. He and Mike Jr. were fixtures there and were treated like royalty. Over French toast, they talked about the recent election, the grandkids, the weather, but nothing that could get them in trouble if heard by others. This was a ritual of sorts, and after years of practice, they played their parts as if in contention for Oscar nominations.

From breakfast, they headed to the hot tub, a great place to discuss things of a more controversial nature. The bubbling jets and the acoustics of an echoing room made overhearing conversations difficult. The water provided an extra layer of security as microphones were hard to conceal in a bathing suit and most electronic listening devices are averse to wet, chlorinated environments. They were alone, and finally ready to discuss the Stowe situation. Thach used his son as a go-between when items were too important to ignore but too hot to play with directly. In this case, he could not risk being in open conflict with Rachael Zimmermann, though he despised her.

"What's the word on the street?"

"Our friends in union management like the concept of income gap reform but want an angle where they can be given credit. They fear if reform happens without their influence, membership will decide the union is no longer necessary. If we decide to play ball with Stowe, they want a seat at the table and some credit at the finish line."

"No surprise there. Next."

"Our corporate friends are against the idea, outright. Some are threatening to cut support for the party in general, and any candidate who supports it specifically. They can shift the cost of a minimum wage hike to the consumer but have no angle to mitigate a proportioned income gap mandate. I don't think Zimmermann can buy their support, even if we back off on cap and trade. The socialists, on the other hand, are warm to the idea even if they dislike Stowe."

Junior continued. "The minorities will firmly support the move. Most minimum wage jobs are disproportionately held by members of their communities, and they can't find a downside in this for them. If Stowe moves it forward, they will openly support him regardless of which side he takes."

Senior nodded in understanding. "Makes sense. Who else?"

"The academics are generally supportive. They see initial volatility in the stock price of some of the large multinationals but overall see it as good for the marketplace. It should increase liquidity, stimulate spending, and lift the economy in general. Some think tax revenues will get a Clinton-era boost, and we may even end up with a surplus. There are inflationary risks, but the Federal Reserve can manage them. The lawyers are a mixed bag. They generally like the idea and see a new niche of specialization arising from all this with a boatload of fees to be billed. There is money to be made in litigation as well as corporate restructuring and contract negotiation."

"The only significant negatives so far are with the rich corporate elite," said Senior. "They're mostly Zimmermann's people, not mine. What about the environmentalists and the LBGTQ crowds?"

"I don't know if the income gap thing is enough to push them past their other issues with Stowe," Junior responded. "Stowe has connections to oil and gas as well as banking. The environmentalists will likely oppose us working with him at all. The LBGTQ group is still questioning if Stowe had anything to do with Crockett's outing and don't like his evangelical connections."

The elder Thach stared into the steam rising off the surface of the water. The twists and turns of the vapor mimicked the processing of the information his son imparted to him.

"I don't see how I can keep my role as majority leader. The Republicans will offer him Health, Education, Labor, and Pensions. He'll get a commitment from Archer to bring his legislation to the floor for a vote, where he'll get enough support to get it passed. I bet more than half our side will vote for it, with what you just told me. The Republicans will have to swallow the pill to keep the Senate, so Wade Wilson will do Stowe's lifting in the House. He doesn't need us other than to pressure the Republicans into taking up the cause. He's got to go if I'm to stay as majority leader."

Senior's last words hung in the thick, humid air. Junior simply nodded in agreement. He looked Senior in the eye and said, "Plan A, B, or C?"

Assassinate.

Besmirch.

Coerce.

"All of the above, if necessary."

Rachael Zimmermann believed in being a voice for the little guy and thought she should be paid handsomely for the privilege. Unlike many of her fellow Democrats, she was very careful not to demonize corporate America or the uber wealthy. Without them, she didn't get paid. When she was in her teens, she once had a conversation with her father about the role of the litigator in seeking justice.

Rachael liked the idea of big judgments and settlements. They paid for her lavish lifestyle and first-rate education, but far too often she had difficulty seeing the fairness. Individuals could get obscene judgments, blaming companies for making coffee too hot, but victims of securities fraud would only be compensated for a fraction of their loss, if at all. It seemed like the only consistent winners were the lawyers.

Arthur Rosen responded that the law was not about fairness, only conflict resolution. If it were fair, all persons who commit the same crime would get the same punishment without respect to circumstance. There would be consistent guidelines for assigning punitive damages in civil cases. The law simply gave people a way to work out their problems without resorting to violence. Even criminal proceedings were just a structured means of dealing with those who had broken the social contract. The law could not be fair because some things just couldn't be undone. How did you make the family, let alone the victim of a murder, whole with a legal judgment?

The second piece of wisdom Arthur passed along to his beloved daughter was his rather unique twist on an old adage. He told her that at some point in her life she would certainly hear the saying that all lawyers were parasites. Arthur explained that all parasites live off a host, but not all were bad. In the case of the lawyer, the host was the one who paid the bill. "Don't kill the host," he cautioned. "Know that those who learn to provide some benefit to the host are the ones who are most likely to live happy and long in symbiotic existence." Rachael took his perspective to heart.

Rachael was now pondering her father's advice over a cup of coffee in the back of the black Cadillac Escalade that shuttled her from one end of Pennsylvania Avenue or the other. As an activist and a lawyer, she liked Stowe's ideas on the income gap. They made a lot of sense and could do a lot of good for the bulk of her party's constituents. But a change of this magnitude would cut into the very heart of the party's financial support, the "host" she relied on to survive.

She had spent years cultivating the wealthy and pulling them into the party by working specific areas of interest to them. With wealthy women, the message was protecting your liberty and health. With wealthy LGBT+ people, it was more acceptance and legitimacy. With second and third-generation wealth, it was usually the arts, or the environment, or anything to assuage them of their affluence guilt. She did meticulous research and tapped into the desires and interests of her target audiences and got them to contribute generously to the party. She kept the money coming in by making slow progress while never actually completing the job. Now, perhaps, the reckoning was upon the party. On one side of the ledger were money and power, on the other were ideological integrity and the votes of the loyal masses.

The numbers were clear. To comply with the Stowe proposal, the executives with compensation packages in excess of one hundred million dollars would have to raise their employees' base wage to more than two and a half million dollars on an annualized basis. Companies would have no choice but to slash wages at the top and increase income at the bottom. Rachael always said she did what needed to be done for the plight of the little guy, but if that were true, her path would be distinct and unencumbered. Instead, she kept trying to find a way to hold on to all that she built while still championing life's underdogs. It was abundantly clear that her values were at odds with her circumstance and, no doubt, about to be tested.

Her only solace was that just three blocks away, the Republicans must have already come to the same conclusion regarding Stowe's impending demands. Wade Wilson was probably having a complete breakdown as he pondered even the slimmest possibility that Stowe might side with the Democrats.

Miranda and Wade bantered back and forth all morning before ultimately concluding that Stowe's proposal might hurt the highest earners in the party, but it would hurt the Democrats more. The super-wealthy more often affiliated with the Dems than with the Republicans.

The demographics were in their favor. A greater number of people earning over five hundred thousand dollars per year leaned Democrat. As incomes rose from that point on, the percentage of Democrats to Republicans in those higher income brackets continued to increase. The only reason that the average incomes of the parties showed the Republicans to be higher was that the Republicans owned the middle-class income earners, those making in the low thirties to the one hundred thousand level. But because the Democrats claimed stake to the vast majority of the lowest income earners, those making twenty-five thousand or less, the average income of a Democrat showed to be lower than that of the average Republican. Even though most of the super-wealthy were Democrats, there weren't enough of them to offset the masses of poor who made up the bulk of the party. The statistical average hid the ugly truth that the Democrats were the party of the uber-rich and the poor in America. The Republicans were the party of the middle class.

For the first time in years, Wade considered that the wealthiest congressional districts in the country might be put in play in the next election. Sixty-five percent of households making five hundred thousand or more lived in Democratic districts. Stowe's income gap proposal could split the wealthy social activist wing of the Democratic Party from their poorer, but vastly larger voting base.

Republicans didn't have to necessarily unanimously support the legislation. They just didn't need to stand in Stowe's way. They could let each congressman or woman vote their conscience to represent their constituents and let the Democrats rip each other apart. They might finally get a chance to get out from under the stigma of being called the party of the rich. By noon, the two had a strategy, and Wade began to regain some of the cheerfulness that he exhibited earlier that morning.

CHAPTER 15

Chief Moffatt arrived at the University Club shortly after the patrol car pulled alongside the sedan and alerted their suspect that they were on to him. There was no way to know if the plan worked and the threat had been scared off. The chief was reluctant to simply let the senator and his wife stroll outside without a better plan of protection. The trick was to pull it off just short of alerting Mrs. Stowe and the entire campus of what was happening.

Approaching the valet, he said, "Hey, Peter. Please move the Stowe's vehicle around to the front by the doors."

"Sure, Chief. Is everything okay?"

"Didn't you see all that craziness at their house this morning? I just don't want that kind of circus here."

Peter had no clue about the issue at the Stowe house earlier in the day. He'd partied the night before and slept well into the morning. He just shrugged his shoulders and went to fetch the keys as the chief moved inside the club.

Parker saw the chief as he entered, and they nodded to each other. Parker and Roni were finishing up, and he asked her if she minded closing out the bill while he said hello to the chief.

"Don't be long," she said, mindful of their one o'clock appointment. Roni was always organized and punctual.

"Yes, dear," he replied as he winked at her.

"Hello, Senator. This is Officer Pierce." The chief made the introduction and kept going. "The car is stolen, and we can't locate the driver. This may be a real threat."

Parker furrowed his brow. "What's the plan?"

"We alerted him to our presence and likely scared him off. You didn't plan lunch here until the last minute, so he couldn't have arranged alternate transportation to get off campus. His car is secure. It'll be hard for him to follow you once you're back in the city. You need to arrange for security. If you don't mind telling me, where are you going next?"

"To the election headquarters downtown. Ironically, our one o'clock meeting is with a private security firm."

"Good," said the chief. "I had Peter pull your car around to the front. Pierce and I will walk out with you and provide a little more cover. I'm going to follow you to your office. I'd be happy to share what we know with your security firm. We're ready to go when you are."

"Let me get my wife," was all he said. Parker went back to the table where Roni was waiting.

"Is everything okay, Parker?" Roni was concerned. She thought Parker looked a little pale and remembered he'd spent all that time in the bathroom when they first got to the club.

"Not really. The chief is concerned because they located a stolen car parked across the street from the club. He doesn't want us taking our time getting to our car and is going to provide a little security for us." Parker just wanted to get in the car and away from campus as fast as possible.

Roni didn't press the issue. "I'm ready, let's get outta here," she said and grabbed her purse.

The exodus from the University Club to the downtown office went smoothly. In the car, Parker brought Roni up to speed regarding the suspicious sedan and his call to campus security. She was mad at first. She did not like being kept in the dark and the deteriorating situation was testing their promise to keep communicating, no matter how difficult things became.

Sitting in the conference room with Jason Tuttle were three lean, clean-cut, ex-military types, two middle-aged men and one woman. All were people Jason had personally worked with in the intelligence community. Although his unit's work was mostly theoretical, from time to time it led to operational interventions, especially in the era of state-funded terrorism.

They were not mercenaries. They were not political. They saw themselves as guardians and expert advisors in devising and assessing security protocols, processes, and methodologies. If you needed someone or something protected, they were your people, provided it wasn't immoral or illegal. When Parker, Roni, and Chief Moffatt entered the room, they all stood for introductions.

"Hello everyone. I'm Parker Stowe and this is my wife, Veronica. This is Chief Angus Moffatt of the Wake Forest Campus Police. He's here because we may truly have a threat."

"Call me Roni," she said as she shook Chief Moffatt's hand.

Jason stepped forward and introduced the members of Bull, Alvaro, and Deegan: Advisors in Security Services. "These fine people are Andrew Bull, David Alvaro, and Valery Deegan." Then, speaking directly to Chief Moffatt, "I'm Jason Tuttle, the senator-elect's campaign manager."

The conference room was small and nondescript. They spent about an hour discussing the day, listening to Chief Moffatt discuss the events on campus in detail.

"It appears that the situation has evolved from this morning's concerns about privacy to something a little more insidious." Bull was the default spokesperson for the group. "I'm going to reach out to that state police captain and see who he's talked with at the Capitol Police Department. They need to open an investigation on this guy in the sedan at the college. I wouldn't be too concerned except the car he drove was stolen. It was an amateur move to be detected when tailing you, but everything else appears to indicate someone with more advanced skills."

Roni asked, "What could he possibly want? Parker's not even in office yet. He ran a positive campaign."

"It may not be related to anything but Parker's relatively newfound celebrity," said Deegan. "Some people go after public figures just to draw attention to themselves. By his age, it could be a disgruntled former student that failed a class the senator taught. The target might even be you, Mrs. Stowe. Why this guy is interested in your family will be important in catching him, but right now we need to focus on keeping all of you safe."

"I agree," added Parker. "I'm leaving for Washington tomorrow with Jason and need to know my family's being looked after. The state police said they'd work with the sheriff to keep an eye out at the house, but they have limits. I'd feel better knowing someone was with them all the time."

"Let's do this," suggested Bull. "I'll go to Washington with you and Jason. Val and Dave will stay here with the family. Val will be primary on Mrs. Stowe. Dave will have the kids. This won't be cheap, Senator."

Roni and Parker looked at each other. "How much?" asked Roni.

"Eight hundred per day per person, plus expenses. Figure three thousand a day." Both Roni and Parker noticeably winced.

"Okay," Parker said. "Dave, Val, and Roni can start making the necessary arrangements for things here. I suppose you'll have to talk to the kids' school and so on. I want to talk with you and Jason about this weekend." He stood up and motioned for Jason and Bull to follow him down the hall to his office.

They took seats around a small round table. "Bull, I want to thank you for making this possible in such a short time. The trip to Washington will only last the weekend, but it's a jam-packed schedule. If all goes according to plan, I'll be at the office tomorrow morning to say goodbye and thank the staff who are no longer needed now that the election is over.

"It's about a six-hour drive to Washington, and I'd like to get there before seven. That means we're on the road no later than one. We are staying at the Willard and have an appointment at the White House at eight Saturday morning. I suspect we'll be done by noon, if not sooner.

"I'm holding a press conference at five in the ballroom of the Willard. That's followed by a *60 Minutes* interview at eight. I plan to eat in the room between the press conference and the *60 Minutes* interview. Sunday morning I'm scheduled to make the rounds with the networks. Jason has the details. I want to be back home Sunday night before seven."

Bull was taking notes. "I have a security clearance that will allow me to enter the White House grounds. You won't need me inside with the Secret Service around, but I'll try to arrange a meeting with them about your security while I'm there. They don't usually get involved with members of Congress. This guy from today in the sedan at lunch might be enough to get them interested."

Jason waited patiently until he could offer his information. "Everything is set up. Do I reserve another room at the Willard for you?"

"No. I'll stay in the suite with the senator and bunk on the couch, if it's okay. It will allow me to stay close if I'm needed and save some money too."

"Very well." Jason continued. "There's a studio not far from the hotel where he'll broadcast live to the networks. He's not going in person to do any of the shows as there's not enough time to shuttle him from one to the next."

"If I've got this right, you're only going to be in three places when you're there—the Willard Hotel, the White House, and this broadcast studio."

"Correct."

"Who else besides Jason knows your itinerary?"

"Jason, you, and I are the only ones with the complete picture. The press knows about the scheduled events, but that's it. It was all arranged today."

"If he's after you, his best chance to attack will be between now and our departure to Washington tomorrow. After that, it will become increasingly more difficult to do something."

"You're the expert," replied Parker. Bull went to join his colleagues and make preparations. Jason and Parker were alone.

"I got your note this morning. Thank you." Jason was probing. "Are you ready to tell me what you're up to?"

"Not yet. Be patient. This security issue is an unexpected wrinkle."

"They're good people, but you can't afford them forever."

"I hope by Monday I won't need to." Jason looked directly at Parker. He was now even more perplexed than when he left the farm the previous night.

"What do you mean by that?" Jason queried. "I don't understand how this just goes away."

"Do you have plans with Miranda Cortez while we're in Washington?" Parker was trying to change the subject.

"Not yet. We talked about having drinks and maybe dinner tomorrow night if you don't need me. I was hoping to sneak away for a few hours. Why?"

"I think you two make a nice couple." Parker smiled. Jason did not.

"We're not a couple, and you're changing the subject."

"I'm not off subject as much as you protest. What I do this weekend will have a profound effect on national politics for the next two years. She has a vested interest in helping one of those sides. You have an interest in her. If you know too much too soon, you may feel torn between loyalty to me and your relationship with her. I don't want to place that burden on you."

"I'd never betray you. You know that, Parker." Jason was insulted.

"I know, Jay. This is why I'm not going to discuss my plan with you right now. I'm not afraid you'll betray me, I'm afraid you'll cancel your plans with her. You deserve to have someone in your life besides that cat."

"You're not seriously considering siding with the Democrats, are you?"

"It's a possibility if the Republicans force my hand. I don't want it to turn out that way, but let's just say for now I'm still undecided. Go out with Miranda and talk about anything and everything except politics." He paused then gave his friend a wry smile, "Why not start with religion?"

They both laughed hard at Parker's joke, and Jason stopped the inquisition. Jason loved that his friend put his budding relationship with Miranda before the politics of his position. He admired Parker's sense of empathy and how he genuinely cared for the wellbeing of others before his own. A truer friend he'd never had.

CHAPTER 16

The lunch meeting at the White House brought to light no new ideas or angles Stowe might have for giving them a seat at the table. They generally agreed they were there for Stowe to use as leverage. The gaggle discussed the problem that Stowe's position on income gap reform posed for them with their wealthy constituents. No matter who controlled the Senate, they would still have to deal with their donor class problem. The upside on not controlling Congress would be that they could give their legislators the freedom to vote in line with the district interests they represent. It provided cover for those representing wealthy districts to vote against it. Zimmermann was quick to remind everyone that the next election cycle was just two years away and they needed funds to retain and gain seats.

After the cadre disbanded and he was alone, Marcus ticked off his achievements as president so far. Landmark legislation in the areas of healthcare and banking were passed. He began to wind down unpopular military conflicts and opened lines of communication with countries that for decades were labeled enemies. And with much controversy, he had issued an unprecedented number of executive orders to deal with intractable problems like immigration and the environment.

Marcus did not feel like a success. The country was not lauding him as a great leader. He flirted with the integrity of the Constitution to get some things done and set some bad precedents along the way. If future administrations were to follow his ways, a showdown between the Legislative and Executive Branches was inevitable. America was more divided along religious, racial, ethnic, and economic lines than ever. Civility in government seemed at best ceremonial. The concepts of sharing, transparency, sacrifice, trustworthiness, and fairness were all but abandoned and had been replaced by demagoguery. Worse yet, the national debt tripled under his administration.

His legacy might be a track record of results, but the immense cost to the country in actual dollars, social unrest, and governmental dysfunction threatened to be what history would remember as his bequest to the American people.

With degrees from Yale and Harvard Law, he had made friends along the way among the trust fund elite rebelling against the conservative ways of their parents. Many, like himself, could not comprehend fighting endless wars against people fighting for economic equality and to end bigoted colonial oppression.

Marcus Jenkins did not believe in communism. To do so, he would have to abandon much of what he believed about his older brother Ben. However, he would have to admit Ben was fighting for the wrong side when he died. He also understood that mid-20th century American institutions were corrupt and structured to favor the white, the wealthy, and the male. As proof, he cited statistics about the disproportionate numbers of minorities that fought and died in most of the conflicts since the Second World War. He touted the data showing they were less educated, made less money in equal paying jobs, and incarcerated at much higher rates than their white counterparts. He wanted to change this, to help people, to level the playing field. He was failing because he highlighted the dividing gaps instead of strengthening the ties that bind.

When he started, Marcus wanted to be something different, something better. And while he achieved the first, he realized that he sacrificed the second. The more he thought about Stowe's proposal, the more he believed he could change his legacy and be something more than what he'd done.

Six years into his presidency and the country was different, but it wasn't better. The rich were richer, the poor were poorer. The government was bigger and functioned worse than ever before. He could blame the Republicans, or even well-intentioned people in his own party who made bad decisions, but shifting blame did not change reality. He could justify his actions by touting his results, but he needed to come to grips with the fact that the country was deeply fractured, and he was largely responsible. As they say: "The buck stops here."

<hr>

Rockport finished reading Stowe's work late in the afternoon. He could see how the work horrified Paul. Nevertheless, it fascinated him. He looked at his notes. Could a corporation avoid the gap ratio by outsourcing the front-line labor? What about utilizing a payroll agency? Would the labor structure of a subdivision or subsidiary roll up to the parent? How would foreign labor structures and costs apply? What about domestic help? The library of questions and issues that would need to be resolved was colossal. No, Lionel Rockport wasn't scared—he was excited. The challenge was worthy of his complete attention like no challenge he had experienced in a long time. He got on the phone and started putting his team to work.

"Paul, it's Lionel. Just finished Stowe's book. Interesting stuff."

"Interesting is an understatement. It could put us in a real jam if it were instituted tomorrow." Paul's total comp package was more than seven hundred and fifty thousand a year.

"Maybe not. It all depends on how the final legislation is put together. Right now, it's just an idea. I have a list of data I want put together. There's always opportunity, we just need to uncover it."

"I already have some preliminary…"

Rockport cut him off. "I'm sending you a list of what I want. I'm sure what you have already put together is on the list. We have time to get things in order. Nothing in Washington moves quickly. Stowe doesn't even take his office for another two months. Relax, Paul, this is going to be fun."

"If you say so." Paul did not view this as fun. The holidays were coming up and he had year-end plans with his family. Rockport had no wife or kids, and his understanding of the demands of a family at this time of year was limited to his recollections of childhood. "I'll get a team focused on this first thing tomorrow. What's the deadline on this?"

"Let's touch base this time next week. And one more thing, Paul, get me in a room with Stowe. I want to meet this guy."

———

Chief Moffatt brought State Police Captain Jeffries up to speed. Captain Jeffries said he'd call the local troop and get them to coordinate processing the car with the crime lab. He gave Moffatt the name of the detective he spoke with at the USCP and warned him that the USCP detective didn't seem too interested. They agreed it didn't help their cause that the guy from the farm event turned out to be an over-achieving journalist.

As Chief Moffatt worked his way through assembling the incident report, he noticed that the only officer who seemed to have identified a possible suspect was Fowler. He called her into his office just before the shift change.

"You wanted to see me, Chief?" Fowler asked as she stuck her head through his open office door.

He looked up from his laptop with his reading glasses resting halfway down the bridge of his nose. "Yes, come in, Meghan. I was just reading your report from this afternoon on the guy you followed."

"Sorry, Chief. I guess I was wrong, but my instincts told me something was off about him. I should have stayed in the area of the club."

"You did the right thing. It bothers me that the subject just disappeared. He couldn't have planned to be on campus if he was following Stowe. The senator wasn't supposed to be here today. Most people who don't belong on a college campus stand out. This guy didn't. Why?"

She paused for a moment. "The senator said he thought the guy driving the car was young. Right age to be a student."

"That's exactly what I'm thinking." The chief was looking directly at her. "It would explain why he blended into the campus so well."

"So, we need to be looking for a white male in their late teens or early twenties. About thirty-five percent of the campus." She giggled as she stated the obvious.

"If he didn't plan to be here, then what would make him stand out if he fit the demographic? Clothing?"

"Maybe," she said. "I don't know. Most college-age kids are fashion conscious. If he's a college student, then his clothing will likely provide camouflage. If he's not a student, then maybe he stands out, but it's doubtful." She thought a moment longer and added, "Book bag. If he's a student, he'd have a book bag or knapsack. If he's an outsider, he might not."

The chief marinated on the revelation for a moment. "We don't have an image of the guy in the car. I've requested traffic cam footage from the city, and maybe we'll get lucky. In the meantime, I want you in the office tomorrow reviewing the security footage from our cameras in the area. Look for a white male, late teens or early twenties, without a bag and maybe dressed differently. Do you remember what made you think the guy you followed was our subject?"

"No." She shook her head. "He had a book bag and was dressed like most of the young bucks on campus. I'm glad I didn't make a fool out of myself and tackle him."

"Who knows, he might have liked being roughed up by a pretty girl." The chief's attempt at a joke and compliment made her blush. It was inappropriate, but the chief was like a father to her, and she let it slide. She realized she hadn't even been able to tell if the guy was cute, though she did remember he had great hair.

CHAPTER 17

The television was on and blaring when Derick entered the apartment. Dirty dishes lay scattered around the table, and a mostly full gallon of milk sat on the counter, uncapped. All the lights were on. She'd had a bad day.

The patio door was still ajar from where she went out to smoke a cigarette. An Afghan lay on the floor next to the couch, presumably from when she got up and stumbled into the bedroom to sleep the day away in a pharmaceutically induced haze.

He found the bottles of pills on the counter next to a nearly empty bottle of wine. There were antidepressants, anti-anxiety meds, sleeping pills, and a host of other yellowish-orange prescription bottles. Collectively, they vaguely resembled a small plastic city rising from the corner of the breakfast bar. He checked them to make sure she hadn't taken too many.

The bedroom door at the end of the hall was ajar. He went in to make sure she was still breathing. Her sweatshirt was off, and she was lying half-naked on top of the bedspread. She'd said the drugs sometimes gave her hot flashes, and she would break out in a cold sweat. There was a tee-shirt in her hand, which she had probably intended to wear but passed out before she finished putting it on. To say she was okay would be to overlook the obvious signs of severe mental distress. She was in the midst of a breakdown. For now, however, she was alive and at peace with herself. Shut out from her pain and in a deep sleep. He covered her with a blanket from the chair and left her alone to rest.

As he set to putting the place back in order, Derick began to shake, not just out of sadness but out of anger, continuing to wonder how this all came to be, and not for the first time. They'd had it good once and now he wanted to run, to get away, to wake up from this nightmare and start over. He didn't care where it was as long as it wasn't here. The feeling of being trapped and helpless was overwhelming. He wanted to feel powerful and in control, but he couldn't leave her. Not now. Not yet. Maybe she'd get better. Maybe she'd be admitted to an institution. His anger and own pain began to be compounded by a new sense of failure. He reprised his deficient efforts over and over in his head. Stowe had been right there.

"I should have shot him when he dropped the kids off at school," he muttered to no one. "I missed my chance."

———

Alisha Hollins went off-script on her nightly news broadcast for a late-breaking report.

"Senator Tapp from Arkansas has called a news conference where he is expected to concede his bid for reelection to his Republican opponent, Elliott Sparks." The image on the screen switched from Alisha behind the anchor desk to a ballroom at the Little Rock Hilton. When Senator Tapp approached the podium everyone settled in for the obligatory campaign obituary.

This, of course, would be followed by a victory speech from Elliott Sparks and would give the network plenty of time to get their experts lined up and ready for analysis. The news provided a perfect segue way into the story about Senator Parker Stowe, and the news conference from Washington scheduled for Saturday evening. The machinery of speculation was operating at a fever pitch, and there was no shortage of talking heads prepared to share their opinions.

Jason Tuttle stood up from his chair and took his dishes to the sink. Simon shadowed him, hoping to secure a stray piece of pot roast lost in the congealing pool of gravy remaining on the near-empty plate. The rotund cat sat on the floor, meowing at Jason.

"If you can get up here, you can have it, cat." Simon's front feet were hidden beneath the cat's ample girth. Pleased to have Jason's attention, Simon stood on his hind legs, leaning against Jason, ready to climb him to get to the plate.

"No cheating. If you're too big to jump up to the counter, maybe you don't need the extra calories." Simon looked at him with disgust but did not give up. He meowed again and now walked between Jason's legs, purring loudly, rubbing his head along Jason's calf. Jason shrugged. The kids were out of the house, Lilly was gone, and he had no one to look after or spoil but Simon.

"You know I don't like you," he said as he placed the plate on the floor. He stroked the furry beast, who suddenly lost interest in affection. As Simon immersed his snoot in the plate and continued to purr, Jason smiled.

He called his son at UNC to make sure he was still planning on coming home for the weekend. Simon needed to be cared for, and there was no one else lined up to do it. After he secured multiple assurances, he packed his bag for the trip to Washington. He straightened up a bit, read his Bible, and went to bed.

Parker and Roni finished tucking the kids in for the evening and met in the hallway outside their rooms. For what seemed like the first time all day, the house was quiet. Roni was physically and emotionally spent.

"I'm going to bed. Goodnight." She wasn't mad at him, only tired. She was done with a day that had turned out to contain everything except quality time spent reconnecting with her husband. She was disappointed that their plans had been so drastically undone. It wasn't Parker's fault, but she was too tired to start over with him at nine-eighteen in the evening. He hugged her and kissed her cheek.

"Good night, my sweets," he replied and went downstairs.

No sooner had he finished drinking a glass of water than his phone dinged, alerting him he'd gotten a text.

"You're coming back up here, right?"

Bingo! Parker got a sheepish grin on his face and almost skipped back upstairs.

"When did you do this?" she asked.

"While you were with Burk," he replied. "Amos fell asleep quickly, and I felt bad that our day got interrupted."

She had tears, the good ones, running down her cheeks. "Come here." She beckoned as she stood up in the tub. The bubbles from the bath clung to her body, making her glisten in the candlelight. They covered her so as to preserve her modesty but tantalize his imagination. She kissed him as she unbuttoned his shirt. "Get in with me. It'll be like old times."

He finished undressing as she poured him a glass of wine from the bottle in the ice bucket. The water was still quite warm as he stepped into the tub to join the love of his life. Stan

Getz was playing his tenor saxophone in his sultry, jazzy way on the old iPod. The room was filled with scents of lavender and honey.

"Sorry again about today," he said.

"It's not your fault. Quit apologizing. I'm over it, except maybe the three grand a day."

"So maybe now's a good time to let you know what I'm thinking." He posed it as a question, but it was certainly a statement.

"Well, you do have my undivided attention." Her mood had significantly improved with the wine and other effects. She was playful, genuinely interested in conversing and connecting with him. Gone was the feeling of being tired, and she realized that what she needed was relaxation, not sleep.

"I like your undivided attention, Mrs. Stowe." It felt good to flirt with her. It reminded him of their early life together when their love was new and exciting. He craved the playfulness of engaging in a battle of wit, innuendo, and compliment. The mystery was no longer in the meeting of flesh but in the dance of connecting on a more intimate, emotional, and spiritual level. A level where thoughtfulness and tolerance forge enduring bonds. There was no accusation about—or defensiveness of—past events. Nor was there any jealousy over things that had stolen time and attention away from the other. It was about looking forward and creating a vision for tomorrow. These times were so important to them and their marriage. He could not let the events of the day steal it away.

She smiled at him. Her brown eyes were bright in the candlelight. "Thank you for all of this. I love how you know what I need before I do. Now tell me your plan while I am finding you so incredibly attractive and before I decide politics are boring again."

"You sure know how to sweet talk my secrets from me, my love," he cooed, and laid before his wife and best friend the plan for the events of the weekend.

CHAPTER 18

Roni was always about the details.

"Pack your dark blue suit with the faint pinstripes. Wear a white shirt and a red, white, and blue tie. Don't forget your American flag lapel pin and North Carolina tie-tack. Also, make sure you have the hotel get the wrinkles out of everything and shine your shoes before the press conference." She was a planner, and he wished she were coming with him.

"Yes, dear. What do you think about jeans and this cream Henley under my brown tweed jacket for the *60 Minutes* piece?"

"Scholarly, hip, relaxed, and real. I like it. You know you're going to need people to do this for you, right?"

"What are you talking about, Roni?"

"Someone to manage your image."

"Nonsense. I have you to keep me from making bad fashion choices. I got this far without anyone managing my image. Half the problem in Washington is that politicians start letting others manage their image instead of leading by their conduct. If you don't act poorly, you don't need image management. The way I speak and treat others reflects my character. If I have a bad character, I should not be in any position of authority regardless of how I look."

"Okay, Professor." She admired his principles but hated his lectures. "Save the ethics lesson for the lectern at the university. Now come down off your soapbox and pick out your suit for the Sunday morning circuit."

She got like this every time one of them went on a trip without the other. If Parker was on the road, it was all about organizing him. If she was the one traveling, it was the detailed list of where things were in the house, the schedule of kids' events, and a host of other things to deter him from calling her twelve times a day. It was a bit over the top sometimes, but mostly, he saw it for what it was: love.

He finished packing and glanced at the clock. "The kids are going to be late for school."

"They're not. Remember, we all have shadows now. Dave's taking them in the Suburban. You can take my car to Washington. If I need to go somewhere, I'll take the truck."

"Thanks, but I think we'll take Jason's Lincoln. Three grown men in the Lexus for six hours isn't going to work. Will you drive me and Bull to the office?"

"Sure."

"So that means I have more time than I thought?" He looked at her wantonly.

"Yes, but not that much time." She knew her husband well and exactly what was on his mind. "Go get cleaned up while I get the kids out the door."

He frowned and went to shower and shave.

Paul Harper pulled into the basement parking garage of the downtown Fort Worth sky rise at seven Friday morning. He liked to arrive before the staff to allow himself to get settled and arranged. He was notorious for calling meetings before nine o'clock, and most of his senior team arrived between seven-thirty and seven forty-five. At least three out of five days a week, arriving at eight o'clock would mean you were already late for an impromptu assembly called by Paul.

The assignments and invites were sent by email the night before. He was printing a few copies for those who did not check their email before heading in. They would be ill-prepared for the gathering, which started in twenty-two minutes.

All of them were top-notch and the teams they led produced impeccable work. They were young, tech-savvy analysts and all held advanced degrees in business or finance. The crew represented some of the finest minds produced by the millennial generation and were now assembled in a conference room with a magnificent view of the County Courthouse. Paul was pleasant, but all business. There would not be small talk about their lives outside work, the weather, or the outcome of last night's game.

"I'm glad to see you all here bright and early on a Friday morning. Thank you for being prompt," Paul began. It was one minute past eight. "I received several requests directly from Mr. Rockport yesterday. Each of you has been given an assignment in the email I sent last night. As always, I expect you to be thorough and timely. I want your completed work back to me before I arrive in the office Wednesday morning. Don't put this off to the last minute as getting some of the data might require you or your teams to reach out to a few of the portfolio companies. Those of you with salary data need to be precise and round up to the nearest whole dollar. Any questions?"

There were a lot of questions, but nobody would ask them. If anyone had a question, a more private encounter had less chance of conjuring a public humiliation. They scattered at eight-fourteen, and the whole floor, some hundred people, were nose down in their cubes by nine.

The senator-elect's car arrived at campaign headquarters promptly at nine. The media had vanished from the edge of the property once word of the news conference in Washington spread. There were still some freelance photojournalists hanging around, but the local sheriff had them in line. Bull had already worked out the most secure ways to get in and out of the building. Val was there too, and the presence of the private security force allowed the Stowes to relax and enjoy the occasion.

Roni insisted on being at the farewell party. For the next three hours, they expressed their sincere thanks and appreciation to the small group of paid staff who had seen them through to victory. The food was inexpensive but delicious. It was a catered lunch from a popular BBQ chain owned by the father of one of the clerks. And though neither the Stowes nor Jason or the security detail were drinking, there were a few cases of beer for their treasured guests to enjoy.

At ten minutes past noon, Parker and Roni made the rounds to each of the staff. They personally thanked them, told them to enjoy the party for as long as they wished, and said their goodbyes. By twelve-thirty, Val was driving Roni home in her Lexus and the boys were on their way to Washington in Jason's black Lincoln.

The coffee in the pot was still warm. Derick poured himself a cup and surveyed the room. He felt generally optimistic about the day ahead. The note she had left thanked him for cleaning up after her and apologized for her condition the night before. It said she was feeling better this morning, and she wanted to take advantage of the sunny, fall day, so she had decided to walk to her appointment with the therapist. Next to the note was a plate displaying a rather large blueberry muffin from the bakery down the street.

There was no clutter or mess on the counter. Her dirty coffee mug and plate from breakfast had found their way to the sink. The doors were all locked, and he could still smell the air freshener he used the night before to cover the stale cigarette smoke.

It reminded him of how his mother used to make him breakfast when he was a kid. His father hadn't been around much, and his mother lavished her affections on her only child. She would make him these elaborate hot breakfasts with scrambled eggs, fruit, biscuits, and bacon. He was spoiled and wished he could return to that time. He hated that he could no longer ask momma to kiss his troubles away.

Derick felt the hopelessness of his circumstances and being unable to see a better future. The money problems were getting worse and only being compounded by the pills and booze. Neither one of them could get a good-paying job. She had the degree, but no experience. Not that it mattered anyway because she could barely function in her condition. He had dropped out of college two months into his junior year. Without a degree, his prospects were slim, and his options limited.

The job at the distribution center would keep a roof over their heads and some food on the table, but it was a hand-to-mouth existence. He could join the Army or Navy. But that would mean leaving her alone, and he couldn't. Not in her condition. Not like this. She was sick, and leaving might just kill her.

He looked at the row of pictures resting on top of the laminated pressboard shelf. They'd seen good times. She would get better. He fought back the tears and then suddenly became angry. First angry at himself for wallowing in his own self-pity, then at Parker Stowe, who had stuck him with this dismal lot in life.

Miranda spent most of the day taking care of herself. During the busy election season, she had little time for anything. Her normally flawless appearance was in serious need of some maintenance. She wanted to look perfect for her trip to the White House and her date with Jason.

After making sure Wade didn't need her, she booked a day at the spa. The full works. As a consultant, she was always on call, but it also allowed her to flex her schedule when necessary or desired. In this case, it was a little of both. For the last two years, she and Wade had worked tirelessly to deliver a referendum on the policies of President Jenkins and the rubber stamp of Mike Thach. Except for the anomaly of Parker Stowe, they had almost completely dispatched a monumental defeat upon the Democrats.

It had been three months since her hair had been professionally managed.

She was looking forward to shedding the fizziness of ends that were splitting and letting an expert remove the graying roots. She wanted a massage in the dimly lit room where it smelled like a spring day and the sounds of nature took her to a place far away from the trenches of political warfare. Thoughts of a facial and body scrub with those wonderful salts, minerals, and oils that left her skin soft, smooth, and fragrantly fresh appealed to her sense of being a woman. She desired to feel attractive and sexy. She knew just how to make that happen.

Jason Tuttle had captured her imagination. His gentle and kind ways were disarmingly genuine. He became shy, even a little awkward, when given the slightest of compliments, but not embarrassed. When she spoke with him, she didn't feel like she was being judged. He listened and wanted to know her. There were never strings attached to an offer of assistance from him.

It was this gracious humility about him that she found so magnetic. Her late ex had certainly been charming, but not even he had attracted her the way Jason was now doing. She might fall for him. This both terrified and excited her at the same time.

CHAPTER 19

The Lincoln pulled up to Miranda's townhouse at twenty-eight after seven. Jason knocked on her door precisely at half-past the hour. He felt a goofiness about him that only surfaced in dating situations, which is why they were rare events. He felt awkward and clumsy, in contrast to the strong leader implied by his resume.

Jason was normally well equipped for almost any situation. From his background in scouting where the motto "Be Prepared" seeded a desire to gain skills, knowledge, and experience long before they were needed, through his development as an Army officer where that desire was forged into a mindset, came a confidence that helped him manage most every situation with poise and grace. The word preparation could no longer be separated from who Jason was. However, the discipline of preparation escaped him when embarking on romantic endeavors. His dating experience was limited, refined and tailored for the affections of a single woman, his wife.

"Good evening, Miranda," he said as she opened the door. Miranda looked stunning. Her black hair was shimmering and in sharp contrast to her olive skin as it danced on her bare shoulders. Long eyelashes framed her soft brown eyes. Her red lips matched the color of her dress and shoes.

"Hi, Jason."

"These are for you." He handed her a bouquet he'd picked up on the way from the hotel.

"They're lovely." She smiled and pushed her nose into the bundle of blooms. "And smell good too. Would you like to come in for a minute while I put these in some water and grab my coat?" It was more of a command than a question.

He followed her to the kitchen, where she asked him to retrieve a vase for her. "I'm a little vertically challenged and don't want to climb on the step stool in these heels." She began to trim the stems at the sink. Jason placed the container on the counter next to her.

"You have a very nice place. Have you been here long?"

"Thank you." She smiled and looked up from her cutting. "I think it's been about five years. It works for me and my life-style. Low maintenance, three bedrooms, one of which I use as my office. I travel so much that it doesn't make sense to have more." She filled the vase with water and arranged the flowers. "The house will smell incredible when we return."

Jason was an astute listener. It did not escape him that she said, "when we return." It knocked him off balance. She brushed past him, and he became enrapt by the fragrance of her perfume. He felt his heart racing in his chest. Suddenly he had a desire to be anywhere but there, alone with her. It was the closest thing to fear he allowed himself to feel. He followed her down the hall to the front door, where she grabbed her coat.

"Here, let me help you with that." Jason held the coat as she slipped it on. Instinctively, he lifted her hair out from under the collar and then realized that was a very personal thing to do.

"Oh, I'm sorry. Please excuse me."

"For what?" she asked.

"I moved your hair. It was instinct." Jason's wife used to ask him to help her with her hair when she donned a coat.

"Then you have good instincts, Jay. I just had my hair done today and would hate to have the coat take all the bounce out of it. Are you okay?"

"Not really." He looked right at her. "It's been a while since I've been on a date. I guess I'm out of practice." He forced a sheepish smile.

"Well, Mr. Tuttle. I did not know I had such an effect on you. So far, you're doing better than most. Let's go eat, I'm starving."

He took a deep breath and felt himself relax. He walked her to the car and opened the door for her.

⬥

By the time they were seated at Mario's Italian Bistro, Jason had settled down and was operating in his normal cadence. Maybe it was because there were other people around, but he no longer felt the pressure of being on a date and was enjoying himself.

"What do you think Hector and Mi-Hi make of their daughter?" Miranda had just finished telling Jason about her family and he was probing for more.

"They wish I'd have had kids and raised a family. I tell them that's why they have Heriberto. This is not the life they'd have picked for me."

"Did you want kids?" Jason asked, knowing it could be a touchy subject and prepared to abandon the topic if necessary.

"When I was younger." She had not told him about her previous marriage. It was their first date. "Let's talk about you for a while. How did you get involved with Parker?"

Jason had been asked the question a million times throughout the campaign. During the next twenty minutes, and in between bites of chicken parmesan, the story unfolded before her. She already knew some bits of the story from her research on Stowe, but it was delightful to hear the details from a first-hand source.

"What works the best between you and him? I mean, y'all come from such different backgrounds." She saw an opportunity to gain insight. Ever curious, she couldn't resist the opportunity to fish. He knew what she was doing, but he didn't mind.

"We're like iron on iron. We sharpen each other. We learn from each other. We are better husbands, better fathers, and better men because of our friendship. We share our faith and a purpose. Our passions have taken us down paths that have often crossed, and we help one another on the journey."

The way he answered was unexpected. She had never seen the side of Jason that spoke in metaphor. The answer was powerful and stirred something emotional in her. At the same time, it was vague and elusive, leaving her wanting for more detail. It was as if he described the exact type of relationship she wanted to have with a best friend, but she could not define it any better than he did.

She decided to press him. "That sounds amazing. I think most people define their relationships differently."

"How so?" asked Jason. He caught her before she could ask another question of her own.

"I'm not saying it is right, but I think a lot of people define their relationships in terms of obligations and benefits. Like I'm obligated to have a relationship with a family member, or I want a relationship with her because she can help my career."

He smiled for the first time in what seemed like forever. The next question he asked well before he had thoroughly thought it through. "So why do you want a relationship with me?"

Miranda blushed. She'd gone fishing, but she was now the one on the line. Jason saw what he'd done and quickly back-stepped. He wanted to know the answer, but not at the expense of her dignity.

"I'm sorry. I didn't mean to embarrass you." Jason was sincere in his apology. "My natural sense of curiosity can lead me astray. The way people think fascinates me, and sometimes I get carried away. Please excuse my selfishness."

"That's why I want to know you. That, right there." She blurted it out and surprised herself.

"I'm not sure what you mean, Miranda."

"You have a way about you that I want for myself. You are humble and caring, and open with people even when they don't deserve it. You apologized to me when I should have been apologizing to you. I shouldn't have been poking around your relationship with Parker when we're supposed to be out getting to know one another. But to answer your question, I want to spend more time with you because I think it's the way I'll learn to be more like you."

Now it was his turn to blush. He didn't turn away from her, but he broke eye contact and looked down at the flame of the candle. He nodded and smiled as he returned his gaze to her face.

"Now you understand how it is with Parker and me. In a sense, we want to be more like each other."

Miranda felt the impact of the revelation. It was like a wave of understanding washed over her. What it left behind changed the way she would see her relationships forever.

"Forgive my boldness," she said. "In light of my newfound wisdom, I know why I'm here." Now she wanted to level the field. "May I ask why you're here?"

All Miranda's well-developed protective guard and sense of invincibility were gone. For reasons she could not fully reconcile, she admired and trusted him. Despite her vast list of life accomplishments, all she wanted at this moment was some validation that she was worthy of his friendship.

"Why wouldn't I want to get to know you better? You captivate me and challenge me. We are here, in this place, together for a reason and a purpose. It's like reading a good book that you can't put down because you must know how the story unfolds. I want to discover how I fit in your story, and you in mine."

Not exactly what she was looking for in a response, but she liked what she was hearing. "So, it's just allure and curiosity?"

"Yes. For now, anyway."

"And nothing else?"

"Well, it doesn't hurt that I find you incredibly attractive too." It was out of Jason's character to make such an overt reference to a woman's looks. It brought back the feelings of awkwardness from earlier in the evening. "Parker is also worried that I spend too much time with the cat."

She let out a giggle. "You have a cat?"

Now, Jason was eager to change the subject. Miranda knew he was widowed, but he did not want to discuss Lilly and her relationship with Simon. "Yes, I have a cat. It's a long story for another time. So, what did you want to know about Parker?"

"Do you have a better sense about what his plan is for tomorrow morning?"

"None. He said I'd find out with everyone else. Whatever it is, he's holding it close."

She decided to take a calculated risk. "He didn't have to entertain the Democrats. We're prepared to give him whatever he wants."

"I think he knows that." And then it dawned on him. "Parker is not a career politician. Do you know how it is that he decided to run for election?"

"Only what I've heard in the press." She had no idea that he'd had an epiphany. "Kind of the same old stuff: bring change to Washington, restore civility, champion integrity. Talking points."

"He ran because of his students. They challenged and encouraged him. They raised money for him and volunteered. They believed in who he is, how he thinks, and the values and principles by which he leads his life. He created a following by being uncommonly good at being common.

"It's different with Parker because he's different." Jason continued. "He's not motivated by power or money. Titles mean nothing to him. Character is of greatest importance. He doesn't seek to transform by regulating the way people act, but rather by developing how they think. Parker's first rule of life: 'If you want something different, you first have to be something different.' The system is predictable; Parker is not."

"So, what's he going to do, Jay?"

"Nothing that either side will have anticipated. It will be unexpected."

⬧

As he walked her to her door, the awkwardness returned. He wanted to kiss her but wasn't sure if it was appropriate. He thought it had gone well. They'd had a good time, and he wanted to do it again. She unlocked the door, and when she had stepped through the threshold, she turned to him, and the moment had arrived.

"Would you like to come in for a bit?" Her offer was sincere, not obligatory, and most definitely not tawdry.

"That would be nice, but we have quite the early meeting tomorrow. I really need to get back to the hotel. I had a great time with you and would like to go out again, if you're up for it."

"I had a great time, too. I'd very much like to do it again. How long are you in town?" Miranda was smiling from ear to ear.

"I'll be here until after the Sunday morning shows are finished. Parker wants to be home for dinner."

"How about tomorrow night? I know it's a little soon, but I want to see you again, alone, before you head back home."

"It'll be late. Parker has called a press conference for tomorrow in the early evening, followed by an interview with *60 Minutes*."

"Come over after it's done. I'll have something for us to eat here. Just don't stand me up." She leaned into him, and they kissed briefly. "I'll see you at the White House in the morning."

"Yes. In the morning."

———◆———

"She didn't suspect you knew?" Parker asked again.

"No. It was just a hunch." Jason had found Parker awake in the suite when he returned to the hotel. Bull was in the other room watching the eleven o'clock news. "Are you really going to do this?"

"The train's already left the station, Jay. We have a half-dozen stops to make between now and home. The only outstanding question is who's going to get on board along the way."

CHAPTER 20

The Stowe family were members of a large, non-denominational, evangelical Christian church in the suburbs of Winston-Salem. Parker viewed the rituals of religion as man reaching for God, and though he respected tradition, he was not one to place ceremony above substance. How and where he practiced his faith was less important than actively being in relationship with God. He embraced Christianity because it is the only religion with the unique perspective of God reaching for man. Viewing Christ as the bridge between man and God, Parker tried to live his life as a relationship builder.

The separation of church and state is codified in the First Amendment of the Constitution and has long been the basis for probing the religious affiliations, practices, and beliefs of political candidates. Fearful that a leader might be beholden to spiritual teachings in contradiction of established law, it has become almost expected that candidates be questioned about their spiritual traditions. Parker was questioned about his often. The answer was always the same, "I'm a Christian. I believe all of humanity carries the same stain of sin. There is nothing I can do to atone for my sins, but God has made a way for me to have a personal relationship with Him through the perfect sacrifice of His Son, Jesus Christ."

The evangelical wing of the Republican Party loved this answer and lauded him for unashamedly proclaiming his faith. The far left-wing Democrats were highly suspicious, always looking for a way to stigmatize and stereotype him. During the election, they tried to use his affiliation with the church as a basis to paint him as a zealot who hated homosexuals and would try to legislate morality.

When he was pressed on the issue of abortion, he found a way to couple his beliefs with the law by looking to his Bible, saying, "To my fellow believers and friends on the Christian right, Christ did not come to write policy or change the law. He came to change the hearts of people who would listen.

"While I personally believe that the practice of abortion is used far too often and mostly for the wrong reasons, making the practice illegal is not the answer. The answer is to strengthen the institutions that support our communities and families. Living a life of compassion and support for others will do far more for the cause of life than making abortion illegal ever will.

"And to my critics who wish to paint me as subjugating women and wanting to control them, nothing could be farther from the truth. The only person I work on controlling is myself. I believe, at our core, we have more in common than we do not, and maybe we can start by agreeing on a simple premise. The world is a better place when everyone focuses on self-control before attempting to control the choices of anyone else."

It was a well-crafted response that left neither side able to claim a victory or seethe in defeat. What gave it impact, though, was Parker himself. There was no posturing. He was simply stating his personal conviction. The message was carried by the sincerity and kindness intrinsic to his relational style.

When dawn arrived on Saturday morning, Parker was already up, making coffee and reading from his Bible. Just as Miranda started most days exercising at the gym, and Jason started his days with fresh-pressed orange juice, Parker tried to start most of his days strengthening his spirit while sipping his favorite brew. He tried to spend at least twenty minutes looking for insight on how he could do a better job of leading himself and others. A cornerstone of his friendship with Jason was their shared faith, and this morning the two of them were reading and praying together before heading over to the White House.

Pennsylvania Avenue was a short trip along 15th Street NW from the Willard Hotel. They could have walked, but Bull had secured them a rather hassle-free entry onto the White House grounds via car.

Parker had toured the White House as a teenager on a class trip to Washington. One of his classmates was a distant relative of the Bush family and had been able to secure a more intimate visit than the average citizen. When he was a teenager, the structure so impressed him with its tall, white columns and cast-iron chandelier adorning the entrance at the pinnacle of the circular drive.

Now, as they drove onto the compound, it seemed smaller than he remembered. This morning, its grandeur was dwarfed by the weight Parker felt upon him. The people he would be seeing had expectations of him: plans, schemes, and promises they'd made. Parker would be the key to fulfilling them or the instrument of their demise. He wasn't afraid of disappointing them. He feared that the pettiness of party politics and self-interest would blind them.

The Roosevelt Room, across the hall from the Oval Office, was given its name by President Nixon to honor both President Theodore Roosevelt, who added the West Wing in 1902, and

President Franklin D. Roosevelt, who remodeled the West Wing in 1933.

The room was typically used to host larger delegations and for staff meetings. The table had enough room for sixteen, but this morning there were just nine place settings prepared on the end closest to the fireplace. Parker was disappointed. He wanted a smaller space in which to execute his plan. The arrangement provided only a modicum of the intimacy he desired for the elected elite and their party representatives to converse in such a rare and informal gathering. No one would be posturing for the cameras. Just nine power players coming together to discuss what the Senate of the United States would look like for the next two years.

As he and Jason entered the room, Jason took notice of the numerous flags and service ribbons adorning one of the walls while Parker's eye was drawn more to the heaviness of the Queen Anne and Chippendale-style furnishings accentuated by portraits of the room's namesakes. The room was too formal and stifling, especially since it lacked windows. Parker wondered if he could have pulled off getting everyone out to his farm for this gathering. Wade Wilson, Miranda Cortez, and the current minority leader, Jack Archer, were already present, drinking coffee from china adorned with the presidential seal. They said their good mornings and made formal introductions. Parker had never met Minority Leader Archer. Jason had only met him twice many years before while serving at the Pentagon.

Because it was such a small, informal affair on a Saturday without other business at the White House, the group would have the privilege of placing orders rather than selecting from a menu of choices. Jason ordered oatmeal and fresh berries to help his body deal with the cholesterol he'd consumed the night before. Parker ordered the eggs Benedict at the sugges-tion of Jack Archer, who was known for his not-so-subtle wit.

The two newcomers were served coffee in matching china cups and, for a moment, Parker found himself wondering how many place settings of the china existed. Parker, like Jason, had a natural curiosity that made conversing with him easy but filled his head with tons of useless trivia. Sometimes his ability to converse on a cursory level about almost anything fascinated Roni. More often it just annoyed her. When she felt his affection for useless factoids was manifesting prideful arrogance, she would suggest that Parker try out for *Jeopardy!* or move in with Alex Trebek. Parker had long ago learned this was Roni's way of telling him to move on to something or someone else. He missed her and wished she was with him.

At eight after the hour, Vice President Winter, Mike Thach, and Rachael Zimmermann entered the room. All shook hands and greeted one another with introductions made. This was all a formality, as everyone knew all the players in the room by research, if not having previously met them in person. Five minutes later, President Marcus Jenkins came into the room. The welcoming ritual was once again repeated, only this time the focus was solely on him.

The table was arranged with four chairs on either side of its length and one at its head. Though it was customary for the president to assume the seat at the head of the table, today he opted to sit next to Majority Leader Thach and DNC Chairwoman Zimmermann. The opposite side of the table was reserved for the Republicans. At the invitation of the president, Parker was seated at the head. This suited Parker just fine, though it did not escape him that his physical position was indeed the dividing point between the opposing party lines. It made eye contact with all rather easy and enabled him to look directly at Jason if necessary.

The president invited the group to take their seats, and they all assumed their positions. Wade sat across from Rachael, furthest from Parker. The majority and minority leaders faced one another nearest to him. Miranda was seated across the table from President Jenkins while Jason and the vice president faced one another. The irony did not escape Parker that either by design or chance, the Democrats were seated to his left and the Republicans to his right. It made him think of the Old Testament story of Solomon and the two women fighting over the baby. He hoped God would give him the wisdom of Solomon, but he felt like the baby.

"Thank you all for coming this morning," President Jenkins offered to start the meeting. "I had the opportunity to speak with Senator-Elect Stowe earlier this week. At his suggestion, you were all invited here, so I will forego the formalities and turn the proverbial microphone over to the senator-elect."

Parker stood as the president took his seat. "Thank you, Mr. President. If it pleases the group, I'd like to offer a prayer of thanks before we eat, or if there are objections, we can have a moment of silence."

The Democratic contingent had already gathered with the president in the Oval Office when the others had arrived at the White House. The president had laid out the game plan, including a review of the seating chart to them. Thach thought it inappropriate that he should relinquish his place of power at the head of the table, but Zimmermann agreed that esteeming Senator-Elect Stowe with the seat of honor could only help their cause. They also agreed that this was Parker's show. No harm could come from extending him every courtesy possible. More than once, Thach had to be reminded that his position as majority leader depended on the vote of someone who was not generally inclined to align with their party's brand of politics.

The group offered no protest, and Parker commenced with a brief prayer. "Heavenly Father, thank You for the food we are about to eat. Please bless it to the nourishment of our bodies and bless the hands that have prepared it. Grant us ears for Your voice and hearts for Your will. May our conduct be pleasant in Your sight and be a blessing unto You. Amen."

The staff brought forth the plates of food, and after everyone was served, Parker stood. "I appreciate that you have come this morning, especially on such short notice. I'd like for us to just sit around the table, not as the president, or the minority leader, or the chairperson, but just as Americans." He removed his suit coat, and sat down at the table, loosened his tie, and unbuttoned his shirt collar. Parker looked around the room. Jason followed his lead first and removed his jacket, loosened his tie, and generally became more relaxed. Jack Archer moved quickly to join them, followed by the remaining guests. Mike Thach was not on board. It wasn't until the president removed his tie that Thach got in line.

"We all know why we're here," Parker continued. "Everyone wants to hear which side I'll choose to caucus. That can wait a little while longer. The truth is that I don't know yet how that question will be answered. A lot will depend on what transpires here, this morning, in this room. For now, let's loosen up a bit, relax, and get to know one another. Let's move beyond the dossiers that our research teams have built on us. I'll begin."

Wade Wilson looked to Miranda, who he hoped had a clue where Stowe was going. Miranda shrugged her shoulders. Of all the people at the table, Jack Archer had the most to gain. With the title of Majority Leader rolling around his head, he would do handstands for Parker if he thought it would secure his vote.

Parker took his seat and kept going. "The most influential moment in my life happened when I was about twelve or thirteen. I was on a trip with my father and brother in the mountains and we got caught in a fierce snowstorm. We pulled off the highway and found a room in a boarding house, as all the hotels and motels were already full. Then, two college kids looking for a room arrived at the boarding house. With no other choices available, reluctantly, they handed the landlady their last thirty dollars. We were on the way out to eat, so my father invited them to join us for dinner. They politely declined the invitation but my father told them he would buy their dinner. Over the meal, they thanked my father profusely. As we said our goodnights in the foyer of the boarding house, my father gave the boys a twenty-dollar bill, 'Just in case.'

"As we got to the room and were preparing for bed, I asked my father why he had helped those boys. He said, 'I did it because I hope if the two of you were in a similar situation as those boys, someone like me would do the same for you.'"

When Parker finished, he looked at Jason who nodded his approval. It assured Parker he was connecting with the group. Parker finished by saying, "Now you all know something about me that I don't share with just anyone. Who wants to go next?"

There was an uncomfortable silence as each of the other participants reviewed stories about themselves, struggling internally to find the proper balance between disclosure and discretion.

"I'll go next." Jason finally broke the stillness in the room. "When I was a young man, I wanted to be a traveling evangelist or missionary. We didn't have much growing up. My family was poor. One of the only books in the house was the family Bible. My mother used to read it to me every day until I was old enough to read it myself. I was, still am, mesmerized by the places described in the stories. I would dream of visiting them one day. I thought that my love for the Word and desire to travel would be best served by combining the two in a career."

Miranda was especially interested. For a moment, she forgot her current circumstance and simply asked, "So why didn't you follow that course?"

As Jason continued, he noticed that the president, vice president, and minority leader seemed almost as engaged as Miranda. Rachael Zimmermann, Mike Thach, and Wade Wilson all seemed preoccupied with other thoughts. He proceeded with his story.

"Two things happened that changed my course. The first was a revelation that I have an intense dislike for fish. This almost eliminated the possibility of being a missionary. Most of the world's population lives near a coast of one sort or another. Fish is a, if not the staple source of protein in the diet of many developing nations. Being a picky eater and a missionary are not compatible lifestyles.

"The second thing that happened was I met an Army recruiter who convinced me that having my education paid for by the military would be easier than putting myself through seminary. He showed me how the Army could pay for my college degree and be a source of income. He told me I could pursue a degree in theology and become an Army chaplain. Needless to say, I ended up joining the Army. While at camp my first summer, I met the daughter of my commanding officer. I switched my focus to the Army and hoped that it would fulfill my desire to see the world since preaching was being traded for the love of a girl."

"And how'd that turn out for you, Lieutenant Colonel?" The president was honestly interested.

"Which part?" Jason turned to the President and smiled. "I'd make the same choices again. Doing anything different, I might have missed out on some truly amazing things. It's not what happens to the plans we make that's important. It's what we do with the opportunities we receive that makes all the difference."

"Well said, Tuttle." President Jenkins smiled. He had warmed to both Jason and Parker. It had been quite some time since he'd had the opportunity to connect with people outside his inner circle. The president was shielded from most by security concerns. But even when security was not an issue, the schedule of the chief executive was so managed that almost every interaction was handled to maximize efficiency and to fulfill a specific purpose. Rarely did he engage someone where the affair was not scripted or directed by a protocol. He was being reminded what it was like to take part in a relationship for the simple enjoyment of connecting with another person. He began to develop an appreciation of what made Parker Stowe such a refreshing anomaly in the otherwise polarized and predictable political environment that confined him.

"Thank you, Mr. President," Jason said. "Ms. Cortez, what story will you share with us that few know but will tell us about who you are?"

"Nothing like being put on the spot." She smiled and played along. "Why don't I share a story from my marriage?" From the wedding date to the arrest, divorce, trial, and subsequent jail-house murder, everyone in the room knew the dirty details of her early adult life as a married woman.

Miranda took a sip of water and cleared her throat before she continued. "As I'm sure you all know, I had the misfortune some thirty years ago of being married to a charming man who turned out to be a key player in a rather large cocaine operation. I learned many things from the experience, but rarely do I talk about that time in my life. I am ashamed of having ever been associated with such people.

"The truth is they were, like all people and especially my ex-husband, multifaceted. While he secretly helped to poison the country for profit, he was extremely kind, caring, and generous with me. He was very respectful to both me and my family, especially my father. We went to Mass on Sunday without exception and participated in all the rituals of the Church like good Catholics. I loved him."

She again paused for a sip of water. "But even before we were married, I lived a life of respect and tradition. I dated in accordance with my father's wishes. I went to educational institutions that only served women. I sought to please my parents and everyone else by living life according to the rules. I also vividly remember leaving the Federal Building in Houston with my lawyer after being interrogated by the FBI for the third time, and I truly believed my life was over."

Unbeknownst to Miranda, her ordeal had Rachael Zimmermann captivated.

"To make things worse, the Church refused my request for an annulment. The bishop said I had an obligation to forgive him and a duty to honor my vows and stand by him. I couldn't understand how a person like me, who followed all the rules and did everything right, still ended up alone, broke, and now shackled forever to a notorious drug dealer.

"I went to my father, ready to blame him for sheltering me from the real world and setting in motion all the events which led to my misery. As I poured out my troubles and wept, all he did was hold me, listen to me, and cry with me. When I finally told my papa the Church would not grant me an annulment, he said, 'Get divorced anyway. I'll pay for it.' When I told him I wanted my old name back, his family name, he said, 'You are my daughter, always. What's mine is yours.' And when I told him I was sorry, he said, 'What for? You did nothing wrong. I am proud of you for trying to get up after being knocked down so hard. Who you are is not defined by what happens to you. Your character is forged in your values and tested by the trials of life. You are being tempered. You must be made with great strength and are surely of great value. You certainly are to me.'"

Rachael Zimmermann was connecting with her tale of betrayal. Her husband Stanly had been caught in an affair with some C-list actress at his father's studio in Hollywood. She believed there were many more. Leaving him was not an option as his family's connections had been a key to her success both in running for office and afterward as a fundraiser. She felt trapped in her situation and almost wished her husband would die so she could be free of the arrangement without the complications of a divorce. When Rachael had gone to her father, he told her to suck it up. It wasn't the end of the world. He said, "You're not the first woman to have a cheating husband, and you won't be the last. Find a way to turn it to your advantage. You now have leverage." How she wished her father had just let her cry.

"What was the biggest life lesson that came from it?" Rachael asked Miranda.

"There are so many." Miranda paused and reflected for a moment as the rest of the table adjusted their postures. Some picked at their food while others took a sip of something to drink. "For me, it became the beginning of a quest to let my character shape my circumstances more than letting my circumstances shape me. The true irony of the story is that my only regret now is that I divorced him. I did it out of anger and shame, two things that are contrary to who I am."

"Surely you believe he got what he deserved?" Mike Thach was eager for an open conflict, hoping it would end this love fest. He wanted to move the discussion towards the business at hand. There was little doubt in his mind that Stowe was using them, making this whole exercise rather pointless. His term would be up in two years, and he was contemplating calling it quits anyway. He'd played lapdog to the president and chairwoman's agenda for the last six years and had no interest in kissing the backsides of the Republicans too.

"That was a little uncalled for, Mike. Don't you think? The man was murdered in prison." Rachael Zimmermann did something rarely seen in Democratic circles. She openly admonished one of their own and in the presence of the opposition.

"It's okay, Rachael," interjected Miranda. "What happened to my ex had little to do with me. True, he deceived me, but who am I to judge what he deserved? How I feel about him and what I believe about what he did are two very different things."

The president shot a look at the majority leader that would have killed him if it had the power. He said, "Mike, you be next. Share a story with us." Everyone at the table understood it to be the command that it was intended to be.

Thach knew the pot was stirred. Now he'd turn up the heat. "When I was a kid, I was bullied. Really picked on by the other kids in the neighborhood. At least once a week, I got beat up. I was told to not hit back, but rather tell the teacher when I was punched. That only made the next beating more severe. To add a greater injustice to the insult and injury, it was me that eventually got sent to the school counselor. Twice a week, I was supposed to share my feelings with an adult stranger because I was deemed to have socialization issues."

Parker, Jason, and Wade were the only ones with true compassion for Thach. Miranda was indifferent at this point, working hard to just ignore his oppressive aura of self-impor- tance. The president, vice president, Rachael, and Jack Archer all had varying degrees of contempt for Thach. They worked with him only out of necessity and always felt the onus for maintaining civility in his presence. His callous way of leading by threat of force and cutthroat style of negotiation made him a useful tool, but those same characteristics made him rather personally dislikeable. Thach seemed to rather enjoy feeding America's thirst for an audacious one liner. Jack Archer had been smartly insulted too often by Thach to have any empathy for the man and rather enjoyed the thought of a young, obnoxious Thach getting the snot knocked out of him.

Thach was out to show Zimmermann and Jenkins that he was right. Stowe was just using them as pawns in his game with the Republicans. He was in a hurry to get to the "I told you so" moment. That meant teaching Parker Stowe sooner rather than later there would be no holding hands and singing Kum-Ba-Yah in front of the fireplace this morning.

"Kids can be pretty cruel, Mike," Parker offered in an attempt to connect with Thach's memory.

Thach would have none of it. "Not the point of my story, Parker. But building on your tale about doing unto others, and Jason's subject about seizing opportunities, and even Miranda's matter about shaping one's circumstances, I do have another brick of wisdom to add to your wall of life lessons. Do unto others *before* they can do unto you."

The Democratic contingent listened in horror as Majority Leader Thach showed his proverbial ass. The bull was loose in the china shop. They could only watch as he tore the place up.

"I sharpened my tongue and paid a couple of dropouts in my neighborhood to protect me." Thach was on a roll. "Then I got into a war of words with the loudest mouthed, jock bully at that school during lunch. I mercilessly insulted and embarrassed him in front of everyone. And then on my way home, knowing that boy would hunt me down to deliver the beating of a lifetime, I let him chase me into an alley where my paid thugs whooped him so bad his face was black and blue. I was never bullied again."

The Republican side of the table was secretly rejoicing at the gift delivered to them by the hand of the majority leader himself. There was no way Parker could possibly consider letting the Democrats retain control with that kind of mindset in the wheelhouse. They didn't need to convince Stowe to come to them. Majority Leader Thach would push him to their side.

The president boiled with controlled anger. He just couldn't find the words to repair the damage. Rachael was as pale as a ghost. Already faced with the looming fracture within the party over the Stowe income gap initiative, it was obvious now that she would also be contending with an unchained, self-centered Mike Thach. Vice President Winter lost any hope of getting some positive, cost-free press and now just hoped Thach wouldn't hamper her presidential bid.

Parker spoke first. "Well Mike, I guess that was one way to deal with the problem. It was certainly effective in achieving your desired result."

"More than effective," Thach smirked. "The best part was, from that day forward, I owned the school. The weak wanted my protection. The strong wanted to avoid my wrath." Mike was in the zone. He'd just sent the message to Parker he'd been eager to deliver since Wednesday morning. *Title or not, Stowe, I've got power.*

"It was a very Darwinian solution to a difficult situation. Survival of the fittest and all. Very cunning. It was fortunate you had the resources to buy the strength of those older boys. How do you solve problems when you have nothing to trade? What if the other side can offer more?"

Rachael winced at the question, hoping Thach would shut up and show some humility. Mike caught the inference but just kept going. Only now he was sending a message to his Democratic colleagues.

"I learned long before I stood up for myself in that lunchroom how to avoid losing situations. I pick my battles and don't get into contests I can't win." Thach was looking away from Parker when he responded to him and down the table at

Jenkins and Zimmermann. He was showing them why this whole breakfast thing was a bad idea.

"It must be a hard way to lead. You need to keep lists of all the people you've overpowered throughout the years and track their resources to make sure they can't mount a successful retaliation. All that plus looking out for the next generation of would-be challengers sounds like a job for the Defense Department!" Parker looked at President Jenkins with a smile.

Mike felt a flush of embarrassment. However, he was a practiced politician at the pinnacle of his profession. It would take more than a little barb at his leadership style to rattle his cage.

"You're right, Parker, it is difficult to lead the Senate. One hundred accomplished men and women, each a skilled leader in their own right. Only those elite few with exceptional abilities get to hold the title of majority leader. You have no idea what it takes to get fifty-one, let alone sixty to break a filibuster, or even sixty-seven or more remarkably talented people with their own agendas to move in one direction. It's like herding cats. I make no apologies for using a plate of tuna or a switch stick to get things done. Now with all due respect, we've been here over an hour, and I'd like to get to the business at hand."

CHAPTER 21

Being as quiet as possible, Derick hesitantly entered the apartment. He never knew if she was awake or sleeping, and into what disaster he might stumble. Always bracing himself for the worst, he found that a quiet entrance sometimes gave him a chance to assess the situation before directly interfacing with her. Everything was peaceful. The apartment was, more or less, still in order. He walked down the hall and heard the water in the shower running as she sang along to the radio.

He huffed a sigh of relief as he went to undress and wait for her to finish in the bathroom. Hopefully there would be enough hot water left for him to enjoy a shower. His schedule had him working three twelve-hour shifts from eight in the evening to eight in the morning, Friday, Saturday, and Sunday. Most weeks, he picked up another shift, giving him his forty regular hours plus eight hours of overtime. Thirteen dollars an hour wasn't bad for the work. But even with the overtime, it was less than thirty-five thousand dollars a year before benefits and taxes. Her medical bills alone were going to be over five thousand dollars between deductibles, co-pays, and co-insurance.

She had multiple diagnoses, including adjustment disorder, acute situational depression, and bipolar disorder. Usually, when she was up this early and grooming herself, it meant that she was on the high side of her bipolar disorder. He was convinced that the medications the quacks had prescribed her were the cause of her bipolar moods. If it weren't for the cocktail of antidepressants, her mental disorders would be limited to acute situational depression and adjustment disorder. He knew how she was before. She just didn't have good coping skills. So long as the medications kept her from being institutionalized or committing suicide, he'd learn to deal with the drug-induced highs and lows.

It appeared she was not cutting a single but intended to sing the whole album. So much for a hot shower. He went back down the hall to the kitchen to pour himself a cup of coffee.

He desperately wanted to be in bed and asleep before ten. He'd have to be up again at six and back on the job by eight that evening. Putting his head down on the small round table, he felt his fatigue. His body lifted slightly as his lungs filled with air. He could hear the faint beating of his own heart with his ear pressed against the hard surface.

Was this going to be the new normal? He could hear the beats come quicker as his anger began to surface once again. At first, Derick had wanted to kill him. Now as he thought about the prison his life had become, he wanted Parker Stowe to live in a world like his. A world where everywhere he looked, memories reminded him of what was. An existence without hope, filled with fear, sadness, and anger. So angry that life stole from him, cheated him, and betrayed him that it consumed him.

Derick rose from the table and went to the kitchen counter next to the sink. He bent down and pulled out the bottom drawer of a cabinet, revealing a hidden space underneath. The Glock was where he had left it, wrapped in a cloth. Next to it was a maroon three-ring binder. In another life, the binder had housed biology notes, but it now contained his collection of articles and information on the Stowe family. He removed the binder and replaced the drawer just as the water stopped running in the bathroom. He scurried back down the hall and placed the binder under the bed. With just enough time remaining to slip out of his boxers, he grabbed a towel before the bathroom door opened.

They passed each other in the hallway. She had a towel wrapped around her head.

"Morning, sport." She sounded perky. Definitely on a high. "Want some breakfast when you're done?"

"No thanks. Just sleep," was all he said as he closed the bathroom door behind him.

———

Officer Fowler awoke Saturday morning grumpy and in an unsettled mood. She'd spent the entire day on Friday reviewing camera footage and had not been able to find a viable suspect. Lots of white males fit the age description, but all looked like college students who belonged on the campus. Three were without bags, but one of those was making out with a girl who he'd clearly not just met. She eliminated him. The senator had insisted the person of interest was by himself in the car. She was able to trace the movements of the other two using views from multiple cameras and determined that the timeline of their paths was inconsistent with the timeline of their guy.

Standing before the bathroom mirror, she turned to the side and looked at the profile of her body. Well pleased with her tight abs and flat tummy, Meghan worked hard to maintain her well-toned physique. She brushed her teeth, put on a running bra and shorts, drank a tall glass of water, and began stretching on the floor of her living room. She wanted to think about her run but kept obsessing about how to identify her unknown subject.

After ten minutes of stretching, she put on her black running shoes with neon pink laces that matched her shorts. She grabbed her iPhone, earbuds, and a key from the table by the door. It was bright and sunny but also chilly outside. The apartment had been warm, and she'd forgotten that it was November. Meghan put the earbuds in, started the music, and began her run. Before she had taken nine strides, it hit her. She realized what stood out about the dude she'd followed to Accounting 101 on Thursday.

Special Agent Edgar "Ed" Cosby and Andrew Bull went way back. They'd been at Annapolis together and, on a bet, challenged one another to become Navy SEALS. The very best of the best. SEALS are a brotherhood of men where life-long relationships are forged on a foundation of values like loyalty, trust, and excellence. After military service, Cosby sought a second career with the Secret Service. He was well respected by his colleagues for having thwarted a sophisticated terrorist plot aimed at kidnapping First Lady Jenkins.

When Bull had called him two days earlier, Ed was happy to put together a small meeting with the United States Capitol Police to discuss the Stowes' security. Detective Amy Cobb was already with Ed when Bull was escorted to a small conference room in the West Wing.

Ed began. "Bull, you're the only one who's been on the scene. In your opinion, how real is the threat?"

Cobb butted in before Bull could answer. "I'd like to know that, too. I got a report about some photographer at the residence from a State Police captain. Then another report came in from the chief of campus police about an incident involving a stolen car and an unknown subject at the university.

"The two incidents appear, at this time, to be unrelated. I agree that the first situation at the farm seems to be benign. The second threat is real. There is an unsub, late teens, early twenties, Caucasian, with dark hair. The senator thinks he followed him and his wife from their children's school after morning drop off. I have no doubt he was being followed. Since the subject vehicle turned out to be a stolen rental, prudence leads me to conclude malicious intent."

"What did you make of Chief Moffatt? He sounded like a hick, sexist redneck on the phone, calling me 'honey' and 'sweetie.' Is he as dumb as he sounds?" Cobb had decided she didn't like Moffatt almost immediately. She had a hard time believing he could find his ass in the shower, let alone be able to determine a real threat from a false alarm. In her mind, he was a glorified rent-a-cop.

"He's alright. Competent. A little old-fashioned, and he's got to be close to retirement. Don't let his communication style and old Southern ways fool you. He's smarter than he sounds. However, Stowe is a professor at the university, so Moffatt sees him as one of his own."

Bull understood why Cobb fell sideways with Moffatt. She was a professional, urban, minority female in her early or mid-thirties with little time for what she perceived to be a sexist, racist, rural, white man. Bull assumed she'd just not had enough exposure to things unfamiliar to her own stereotypes to accurately separate the mannerisms of a different generation or culture from true bigoted beliefs. Bull, however, had spent years in countries where women were treated like cattle and people were persecuted. He'd seen populations slaughtered en masse for being of a different ethnicity, religion, or sexual orientation. He'd spent considerable time in places where he was the minority in almost every respect of the word. Becoming good at distinguishing what he should and should not take offense often became a matter of life and death. Bull found it ironic that he made a living using a gun, but he truly believed that forcing change was always less effective than being change.

"Are you thinking 'professional plot' or 'lone wolf with an axe to grind'?" Cosby saw the USCP presence as a courtesy, not a necessity at this point. The USCP could have reached out to the Stowes when the first reports were filed. They only came to the meeting to protect their jurisdiction and budget.

"Hard to tell at this point, Ed," Bull said. "We got elements of both. He was smart enough to use a stolen rental without a GPS and left no fingerprints for the techs to find. Moffatt had a significant force looking for the guy, yet he evaded them. Both these elements suggest a professional. On the other hand, the unsub seems young, and he screwed the pooch tailing Stowe. The only thing I'm for sure about is that there's an active player on the field."

"I checked with the FBI and other intelligence agencies." Ed was thinking out loud. "There's no chatter on Stowe as a target. I'm thinking this is personal. Are we sure Stowe is the target and not his wife?"

"It's a possibility, but one with low probability given her career and background."

"This guy's not even taken office yet." Detective Cobb re-entered the conversation. "It's probably personal. What about a disgruntled student?"

"We're exploring that possibility with Moffatt," Bull replied. Cobb grimaced at the mention of the chief's name. "The problem is how far back to go. Stowe hasn't taught a class for over a year. From what he told me, his classes are not difficult, and he's rather popular."

Cobb appeared satisfied but wanted to float one more possibility. She'd been around D.C. and the members of Congress long enough to know she was not out of line asking scandalous questions but had risen to the rank of detective by being discreet. Stowe wouldn't be the first politician to get caught with his pants down with the wrong person. "What about his personal life? Any affairs, a previous marriage, or maybe a kid out of wedlock that you don't know about?"

Bull looked at Cosby and then back at Cobb. "None that I'm aware of. He and the missus are tight. They met in college and appear real solid. I've been with him almost forty-eight hours and not witnessed anything that would suggest he's hiding anything. I doubt he's having an affair. But our unsub may be from a relationship before he met his wife. If it's an unknown or unwanted kid from that time in his life, he would now be in his early to mid-twenties. The publicity of the election might have caused some unresolved daddy issues to surface."

CHAPTER 22

Wade Wilson could taste victory. Not wanting to waste the negative atmosphere created by Thach, he decided to speak up for the first time all morning. "Parker, as much as I've enjoyed the past hour… maybe now is a good time to talk about your plans." Wade was not exaggerating. He had enjoyed the conversation, and his words came across as sincere.

Miranda wished Wade would not push Stowe. She saw what Jason had foretold about Parker's way; he wasn't going to be forced anywhere he didn't want to go. Not by Wade, and certainly not by Thach.

Rachael now looked across the table at Wade, thinking to herself what an opportunistic bastard he could be. Not that he was doing anything she wouldn't had the situation been reversed. It didn't make her like him any better. "Do unto others *before*…," echoed in her ears.

"Jack, why did you run for office?" Parker was looking to his right at the minority leader, purposefully ignoring the others.

"A lot of reasons I suppose, but mostly to help people."

"Which people?" Parker acted like they were the only two in the room, and they were having an intimate conversation.

"At first the people of Utah, but in reality all Americans."

Parker persisted. "Help them how?"

"Make the government smaller, reduce taxes, and strengthen defense. Support liberty and freedom and oppose those that would take it from them."

Parker sensed Jack's discomfort. "Thank you, Jack. All that sounds good, but I'm trying to see how any of this helps people."

President Jenkins watched this exchange with great interest. Maybe not all was lost after all.

"Lower taxes leave citizens more money to buy the things they need and want. Smaller government means less waste by bureaucrats, and a strong national defense provides the security for people to pursue happiness and prosper. I thought you were an economist and conservative, Stowe. I'd thought you'd know these things."

"I do, and many more things too, Mr. Archer. I know that the government is the nation's largest employer. A smaller government would mean fewer jobs. I'm not sure our current economy can support more people out of work. Does higher unemployment sound like helping people? If a piece of pork legislation keeps fifty people in your home state working, is the project it supports considered waste to those people or just the rest of the country? I'm no liberal, but it seems to me that you need to rethink your definition of helping people."

The silence in the room was so stark, so heavy and complete, that in the instance when Parker finished speaking, the scene could have been mistaken for a life-size diorama of the Roosevelt Room. No one moved, and if anyone was breathing, it was so shallow it went unheard.

The Republican side of the table had not seen that coming. For the first time in forty minutes, they were as uneasy and unsure of their position with the senator-elect as they had ever been. Parker looked at Jason, whose face told him he needed to change course and get out of lecture mode. He'd made his point, and it was now time to move along.

Even Mike Thach, who was still licking his wounds after his tryst with Stowe, was taken aback by his exchange with the minority leader. It seemed to reflect a rather congruent, if not sympathetic position to the one held by many in the Democratic Party.

Rachael Zimmermann had leaned forward as Stowe took aim at the minority leader. She rested her hand on the President's shoulder to keep from falling into her plate. He turned to her with a look of confusion and renewed optimism; neither of them knew what just happened, but knew it wasn't bad for their cause.

"It was my hope when we began this morning to get to know each of you better. I wanted to help each of you get to know one another better." Parker still had control of the room. "I thought we were off to a good start. Minority Leader Archer and Majority Leader Thach, I'm sorry for insulting you. It was not my intention, nor is it consistent with how I want to lead myself. I desire to have good and positive relationships with both of you. Please forgive any disrespect.

"I am not naïve about the complexities of governing or the challenges facing our nation. We cannot legislate our way out of these problems. We must lead ourselves out of them. That means why we do things and the way we do things need to be just as important as getting things done. If we are doing the right things for the right reasons and in the right way, we shouldn't need to use incentives or threats to get them done.

"Likewise, a vision for smaller government is but a dream without a clear understanding of the purpose for a smaller government. I believe that unto everything there is a purpose. We all have a sense of it, but all too often our desire to do good is substituted for actually being good. As the elected elite, we have a duty to first define that purpose for ourselves, and then collectively for the nation. We all have a vision about where we want to go, but it appears that few know from where they start."

"What is, then, the purpose of this breakfast?" Mike Thach was still raw but more open to humoring Stowe, now that a Republican Senate was not the foregone conclusion he once believed it to be.

"I'm glad you asked, Mike." Parker was back on track. "The purpose is to enter a relationship with all of you. What I choose to do is of little consequence without the context of the relationships through which the work will be done. I wanted you to experience my friendship without the expectation of material benefit. I wanted to show everyone that regardless of party affiliation or title, I have a sincere desire to know you as people."

President Jenkins seized the reins. "I can't speak for the rest of the folks at the table, but I would like to be your friend, Parker."

"Even if I put the Republicans in charge of the Senate?"

The president smiled. "Yes, even if you give them control of the Senate. I like you, Stowe. I can work with you. If you side with them, I hope they're smart enough to put you in charge." The president's remark drew laughter from everyone but Jason and Parker.

Miranda noticed it before the others and suddenly stopped laughing. Her cheerful demeanor immediately changed to one of gravity. Like a shockwave traveling outward from a blast, each person stopped laughing, realizing what Parker intended on doing, that the president had unwittingly stumbled across his intention.

Parker stood. "If you want something different, you first have to decide to be something different. Like most Americans, I want something different, something better. I'm no longer content, and neither is a growing number of our fellow citizens, with the way our government functions. It increasingly divides us into groups, white and black, rich and poor, straight and gay, industrial and environmental. It starts here in Washington with Republicans and Democrats, conservatives and liberals. What's worse is the example given to all Americans about how to work with those who are not in our group and have different opinions.

"I believe if we act differently, the country will operate differently. It's time to stop managing our problems and lead the country through them. I have a possible pathway to do it.

"Should I caucus with the Republicans, I will be offered the chairmanship of whatever committee I want. I'm sure my new Democratic friends are willing to also offer me the chairmanship of my choice. There is nothing that one side can offer that the other side can't match. Except making me the majority leader."

Thach, now red in the face and boiling at the presumptiveness of this freshman senator to claim his job, jumped to his feet.

"I told you he was a phony. This whole 'let's be friends' nonsense was nothing but a load of crap. He staged a power grab for himself." Mike could suck it up for two years working with Archer as majority leader. But to be replaced by this nobody senator-elect who should never have won his race in the first place was too much for him to take.

"Please sit down, Mike, and let him finish." Jack Archer also did not like what he was hearing. He had as much to lose as Thach.

"Thank you, Jack," Parker continued. "There is no point in being a majority leader by forcing myself into the position. If I can't be elected to lead the Senate by both sides because the members believe in my leadership, then I don't want it."

"What are you proposing, Parker?" the president asked, even more intrigued by the anomaly standing before him.

"The way I see it, if I pick a side, I'm going to be blamed by the other party for keeping legislation from passing. That makes me a built-in scapegoat. If I'm going to shoulder that burden, then I want to be responsible for what bills come to the floor. There is a history of this body, under leadership by both parties, of debating issues in the media and not on the floor of the Senate where it belongs. The majority leader can kill a bill before it ever sees debate and good ideas are being suppressed to fulfill party line agendas. There is little bipartisanship because, ultimately, the majority leader controls what is—or is not—brought before the body.

"Furthermore, under this same construct, committees are chaired exclusively by the majority party. The business of these committees is thus, once again, controlled by a single point of view and we are not getting the best that can be gotten. The majority has little incentive to work with the minority and simply strong-arms votes with crumbs when a three-fifths or two-thirds majority vote is required.

"According to the rules of the Senate, only a simple majority is required to determine leadership positions. Assuming straight party line votes on leadership positions, I am the deciding vote each time. I bet I can create a simple majority to back me as majority leader by ensuring members of both parties hold an equal number of committee leadership positions. No single senator will hold more than one chairmanship. Regardless of who's in charge, they'll have to work with both sides of the aisle. To make things even more interesting, it is very unlikely I will let seniority determine chairmanship or let parties determine committee majority seating.

"I think I can bring a coalition together to form a non-party line majority with me as its leader. But even if I can't, the worst-case scenario for me is that the senators all fall in line by party again. Then we're right where we are now."

Gone were the concerns of how to manage a Stowe agenda fueled by income gap reform. Suddenly Rachael Zimmermann and Wade Wilson were faced with a complete reformation of the power structure in the United States Senate. The status quo was being upended. Stowe could do what no one had successfully done in almost two hundred years. He could split the two-party voting block for Senate control by appealing to the centrist majorities of both established parties. The practice of polarizing may have finally led to the fracture of a government managed by the monopolies of the current two-party system.

"Well played, Stowe." Thach was now fully geared in bully mode. "How do you intend to keep us from allying against you? What makes you think I can't get some of Archer's people to come to my side?"

"Maybe you can, Mike. And maybe Jack can get some of your people to come to his. Even if that happens, I still achieve my goal: a government that is working together across party lines, regardless of which side of the aisle their representative sits. Oh, and before you start talking about rules, we all know the incoming Senate adopts the rules every two years, and they can and do rewrite them.

"I have nothing to lose by trying to do something more for America. I am taking this to the people this afternoon at a press conference. I'm doing the circuit of talking-head shows tomorrow morning, and I'll be on *60 Minutes* tomorrow night. If you want to stand with me at the press conference tonight, there is room for all of you on the podium. I am not your adversary. I want to work together to achieve something better. Something for which we can be proud of having taken part. I am an advocate for the people of America who are desperately screaming for better leadership than they are getting.

"I'm not going to pretend I can fix all that's wrong. Truthfully, I'm not that smart. All I want to do is demonstrate there is a different way to look at the challenges before us and see who wants to follow an uncommon path."

CHAPTER 23

"What are you doing here, Fowler? You're not on duty today."
Willy Peters and his wife had six kids, and money was tight. He
always worked odd shifts on the university police force to pick
up some extra income.

"Working a hunch on my own time," Meghan said. "I remembered something and want to check the video." She was
still in her jogging gear as she had decided to finish her run
before heading to the station.

"You know you can't work and not be on the clock." Willy
was a sergeant and a by-the-book kind of guy. "Clock in or get
on outta here."

"Yes, Sarge." Meghan wasn't going to argue with him and
would clear the hours with the chief later. It was technically the
beginning of the pay period, and she wasn't burning overtime
hours. She slid her identification card through the time clock,
and yet another reader to open a door with a magnetic lock.
The door lock clicked as the magnetic action released, and she
pushed through to the protected inner area of the station. The
building was empty except for Willy up front at the desk. In
the squad room, the officers shared a few terminals so they
could fill out reports and such, but only the chief and other

ranked officers had assigned workspace. She sat at one of the terminals in the small farm of cubes and got to work. After twenty minutes of searching, she found the footage she wanted. It had poor resolution because it was too far away, but she was able to make out the gross movements of her target.

Sure enough, as she remembered, he put his phone in his pocket and then checked his watch. Why not confirm the time on his phone that he'd just had out? Unless, of course, the phone was just a prop he was using to look unassuming while he was actually observing what was going on around him. Now she needed to find out who he was and what he wanted with Senator-Elect Parker Stowe.

Agent Cosby cupped his chin between his index finger and thumb as his elbow leaned on the armrest of the chair in which he was sitting. As he pondered the probabilities of a wayward child being the issue, he concluded that it was as good a theory as any. Who the threat was and why they were a threat were always secondary issues to the mission of protecting the elected. Nobody cared about who or why unless there was a public incident. It was his agency's duty to make sure there wasn't one, at least not one that was successful. Identification and subjugation of threats was more the purview of the FBI.

"Bull, what's your arrangement with the family?"

"Three people including myself working per diem plus expenses. They're not poor, but they can't keep this up. He was hoping there'd be enough evidence to warrant a protection detail."

"I think there's enough to be concerned about," Cosby acknowledged. "In the meantime, Detective, maybe you should get your agency up to speed and provide uniformed officers, at least until they leave tomorrow. The FBI may be better equipped to handle the investigation."

Detective Cobb took some notes and nodded her agreement. She liked the idea of handing the investigation off to another agency. Never having to speak with Chief Moffatt again was fine by her. But she knew the senator-elect's security would never be relinquished to the Secret Service. Even if it were possible or even desirable, her chief would not allow another agency to so visibly assume a function of his department.

***

President Jenkins was rarely impressed with people. Parker Stowe might be one of the few exceptions. There was something so disarming and real about him. He didn't cozy up to people. He was not impressed with the title or position but respectful of both. His judgment appeared reserved, not severe. When others ran afoul of him, it was their behavior and not the person that received the criticism. He didn't seem like a blamer or finger pointer. He talked more about where he wanted to go than he looked back at past mistakes. Marcus found himself inspired by Stowe, not envious or threatened, Stowe stood in stark contrast to Thach, who was a useful tool to push things through the Senate or stop them from being considered, but always at the cost of cooperation, respect, trust, and general civility.

While this didn't often concern the president so long as his agenda was being moved forward, with his time in office in its setting years, he found himself surrounded by a legacy of hollow victories. Worse yet, there were several scandals in the wings, the investigations of which had been buried by Thach. Under a Republican-controlled Senate, those scandals might just mire his remaining years in office and taint an already controversial legacy. He had almost resigned himself to the inevitability of waging war with Congress. Stowe's ideas now offered him hope for a different conclusion.

Thach put himself and his self-interests first. Stowe had a courageousness about him. Not like that of a warrior in battle, but more like a Martin Luther King Jr. He acted in ways contrary to the anticipated and expected. However, his path always seemed designed with a purpose. His confrontation with Jack Archer was not an attack on Archer himself. It was a masterful example of how the politics of achieving an arbitrary goal regularly trump common sense.

Marcus Jenkins was fast coming to the realization that he'd achieved most of the goals he had set out to achieve. Now he found himself questioning what purpose those goals were meant to serve. He was not inclined to believe everything said about him. But in the privacy of his thoughts, Marcus was very honest with himself. Some things were done for the good of the country, others for the good of the party, and some were done for self-elevation. There were practical things accomplished, and creative things too. There were also a lot of wasteful endeavors. Worse yet, there had been rewards and favors doled out to loyal supporters along the way.

Despite promising to be different, he'd just delivered a lot more of the same old stuff wrapped in a different package. The country wasn't necessarily worse for him being president, but it sure wasn't better either. He knew it too, and it saddened him. It was the same kind of sadness he'd felt when he lost his brother. A sadness that was driven by the promise of an unrealized future.

Supporting Parker Stowe he might deliver an enduring achievement by providing an example of how people could cooperate to make things better. Somewhere along the line, President Jenkins made what he accomplished more important than who he was. Aligning himself with the likes of Mike

Thach should have been a blaring warning that he had sold out. Perhaps he was being given another chance to demonstrate the choice of character over the power of opportunity.

These were the thoughts in his head competing for a voice. In an uncalculated moment, Marcus Jenkins the man simply stated, "I'll stand with you, Parker."

CHAPTER 24

Before Paul Harper rose to the heights of leadership at IFH, he began life in the small, southwestern town of Lewisville, Arkansas. The town was the seat of Lafayette County, which borders Louisiana to its south. One county to the west is the Texas border. Just over ten thousand residents called the county home during the decades of his youth. Since he'd left in the early part of the nineteen-nineties, the population had been on the decline, and only about seventy-two hundred souls remained.

Lewisville was split almost evenly among blacks and whites and was home to almost thirteen hundred people. It was a small, rural American town where most of the roughly five hundred households each earned less than thirty-five thousand dollars per year. A college scholarship was the ticket out for those that could get one. Few ever returned once they learned to navigate the much more exciting world outside the fishbowl from whence they came.

Growing up, Paul's father ran a feed store that had been in the family since the end of the nineteenth century. His family lived better than most in the community. They were not wealthy, and certainly not wealthy in comparison to his current standard of living. He got what he needed, and he never went to bed hungry. That is more than could be said about many of his classmates. The second of four children, Paul was not the only one of his siblings to escape the doldrums of Lewisville. While his older brother had made a life for himself with his high school sweetheart running the feed store with his father, his younger sister had married the son of the local Baptist minister, and the two of them left to be missionaries in Guatemala. His younger brother has been in and out of trouble with the law. At present, he was doing a five-year stint in prison for unlawfully distilling and distributing alcohol in the notably dry County Lafayette.

The most famous resident to come out of Lewisville was Charlie McClendon. Before Bear Bryant became the legendary head coach of Alabama, Charlie had played for him as a University of Kentucky Wildcat for two years. He then went on to an illustrious coaching career for Vanderbilt and Louisiana State University. All the kids in Lewisville knew McClendon's story as their hometown hero. Paul had decided early in his youth that football would be his ride out of town too. As quarterback for the Lafayette Cougars, he led the team to an impressive nine-win and two-loss season in both his junior and senior years. Paul earned his way onto the roster at Texas Christian University in Fort Worth with excellent grades and his skills on the field.

Leaving his hometown, Paul was confident in his athletic prowess and his academic achievement. However, he quickly became aware that at TCU, he was surrounded by a lot of smart people and discovered his football skills were well matched by those of his teammates. He was no longer a big fish in the small pond of Lafayette County. The security of being the big man on the high school campus was quickly replaced with feelings of self-consciousness.

At home, he'd had his pick from any number of good-looking and popular girls to accompany him to a school dance or the banks of the Red River for an afternoon of teenage horsing around. At TCU, he wasn't even ordinary.

He had that Deep South drawl that made him sound like just another dumb redneck from some backwater bayou. His clothes were from Walmart and not the fashion labels found at the mall stores in Dallas and Houston. The 1974 Ford F150 he bought third-hand couldn't hold the attention of the socialite girls. They were driving their 1992 convertible 325i Series BMWs and Volkswagen Cabriolets. He was miserable those first few months at school and came very close to dropping out after he finished the fall semester.

But upon returning from Thanksgiving and after the football season came to an inglorious end, Paul met Floyd Rockport. Floyd was an immensely popular guy for two reasons. He had money, and wherever he went, Floyd brought the party. It didn't matter what you were into, Floyd had access to it. Upper, downer, narcotic, hallucinogenic, or all-natural, whatever the taste, Floyd was the man. He had a flair for the flashy and drove a 1988 fire-engine red Porsche 911 Turbo. It was rarely seen two weekends in a row with the same girl in the passenger seat.

Near the end of an off-campus party, Paul began the half-mile walk back to his dormitory when he found Floyd in the alley behind the house with two guys. The gathering didn't seem to notice or care about him as he stepped into the shadows and walked toward them. At some point, Paul realized this was not an assembly of friends. He stopped just in time to watch the larger of the two men land a solid blow to Floyd's gut with a fist that looked to be the size of a softball. Floyd dropped to his knees and emptied the contents of his stomach on the ground. While still coughing and spitting, Floyd was gasping for air when the other guy kicked him, causing him to fall face-first into his fresh vomit.

Paul located the broken shaft from a garden tool lying in the alley. He caught the smaller guy across his chest, knocking him backward onto the pavement. The big guy was also caught by surprise but reacted in time to bear the brunt of the blow with the six-inch bicep of his left arm. He wrenched the pole out of Paul's grasp. Before Paul could fully process his new situation, the big guy swept low, landing a painful hit to Paul's left knee. The hit shattered Paul's kneecap and any remaining hope he had of being a star quarterback.

He passed out. Paul had no memory of how the fight ended. When he regained consciousness, the two guys were gone, and Floyd was kneeling over him, begging him to just tell the cops he got jumped and mugged. He told him not to mention that he was there. Floyd promised to catch up with him later and make it right by him.

It wasn't a stretch for Paul to play dumb. He couldn't point the assailants out if they were riding next to him on a bus. Telling the police he couldn't remember much about what happened, the story they got was the muggers wanted money, and when Paul didn't have any to give, they assaulted him with a kind of club.

The detectives believed he knew more than he was revealing. Paul couldn't explain the blood and vomit on the ground near where they found him. The doctors didn't find any drugs or alcohol in his system when he was brought into the emergency room, so the police had no leverage. Without any witnesses to the assault, they had little to investigate so long as Paul was being elusive with his answers.

Very early in the morning on the third day of his hospital-ization, a nicely dressed man and his incredibly attractive assistant came to visit Paul in his room. The man introduced himself as Allen Duff, a local attorney with the Rosen Law Firm. He explained that his client was an interested party who wished to assist with Paul's recuperation. He told Paul that his client greatly appreciated his discretion in keeping Floyd Rockport's name out of the investigation. He was thankful Paul was there to help. Paul asked Mr. Duff who exactly his client was, to which Mr. Duff politely responded that his client was someone who valued a great level of privacy and obscurity. To the extent that Paul had helped protect those items thus far and in return for continuing to do so, his client was prepared to go to great lengths to help Paul secure his future.

The folder Mr. Duff handed to Paul contained a multi-page confidentiality agreement. Upon execution by Paul, all his medical expenses would be covered, and his tuition paid through graduation. In addition, Paul would receive a thousand-dollar per month stipend until he started his first job after graduation or until he began work at Indiana-Fellows Life Insurance Company as an underwriter with a starting salary of forty-five thousand dollars per year.

Paul was still in a lot of pain, and focusing on the document was rather difficult, but he captured the highlights. He wanted to be a lawyer, not an underwriter. Although he was still an undergraduate, he knew enough to be concerned about the enforceability of the document. If the document should come to light, he might face a criminal charge of obstruction of justice. He thanked Mr. Duff and told him that he was open to some form of agreement, but that he wanted to have his attorney review the documents. Eventually, an arrangement was reached. He added tuition to law school and a job in the legal department of the Indiana-Fellows Life Insurance Company for eighty thousand per year into the agreement.

Lawrence Rockport, Floyd's father and brother to Lionel, ran the legal department of Indiana-Fellows Life Insurance Company. He became Paul's boss upon graduation from law school.

After the incident in the alley, Floyd withdrew from TCU to enter rehab at his father's insistence. Upon completing the program, Floyd enrolled in a very small, private college in New Hampshire. His ability to get in trouble was more limited, and it was easier for the family to monitor his activities. Floyd finished his degree in marketing and shortly thereafter went to work at IFLIC in sales. Successfully beating his affection for drugs and alcohol, he fueled other desires, like his desire for female attention. Floyd spent most of his twenties ruining the lives of young co-eds hoping to land a wealthy husband. Lawrence worried about his son constantly. He encouraged Paul to keep an eye on him with the hope that some of his more measured ways of approaching life would help moderate Floyd's propensity for the excessive.

Unfortunately, Floyd had a greater impact on Paul's comportment than Paul influenced Floyd's behavior. Paul felt like an interloper in a world where he did not belong. When Floyd offered him legitimate entry into the social world that matched his newly earned income, the two of them embarked on a self-serving conquest of the fairer sex. For Floyd, it was all about the pursuit of happiness. For Paul, it was a quest to prove he had what it took to be a player in a big world far away from Lafayette County.

Eventually, a young socialite with the right pedigree and a genuine disregard for Paul's roots persuaded him to settle down and start a family. She was a good mother to their son and a good partner in managing their home and social calendar. But by the time Ezra was six, Paul once again felt like an actor in another person's story. He was playing a part he could authentically sell to the audience, but inside, it felt like he was wearing a costume. He recited lines and went through motions that weren't natural to him. He longed for something more familiar, more real, more comfortable.

Paul had his first affair two weeks after Ezra's seventh birthday, and he was now turning twelve in February. Since his initial foray into the world of infidelity, the count was a cool half dozen women with whom Paul had cheated on his wife. The only thing the women had in common was that they were common. They were all unremarkable, middle-class women with no ties to Paul's world. There was little probability any of them would ever enter it or cross paths with him once he decided to move on to the next.

Today, on this bright, Texas Saturday afternoon in November, Paul was heading to the office, ostensibly to do some work. He told Regina, his wife, that after Ezra's soccer game, he'd have to check on the team at the office. They were working on a big research project for Mr. Rockport, and he might be very late. At least part of this was true. Paul did intend to go to the office. He would check on the team and some emails, but then he would catch a cab to a North Side motel, where he'd meet Becky.

Becky was fifteen years his junior. A country girl from Weatherford, she worked as a bartender at one of the many joints that were within walking distance of the Stockyards. She booked and paid for the room, which left no paper trail that could lead back to him. Paul always gave her more than enough money to cover the cost. Becky wasn't a prostitute. She'd have booked the room anyway just so that she didn't have to drive back to Weatherford at three in the morning. It just happened that after she took Paul back to her place for the first time, she had already paid for it. He'd insisted that he give her money to cover the cost. She saw it as gentlemanly and kind, not tawdry, or as a way for him to assuage his guilt.

And it wasn't like he just rushed in and jumped into bed, expecting to be serviced. Mostly they sat and talked, drank a few Bud Lights, and watched an afternoon game. He didn't put any demands on her and only called when he'd be in town, maybe once or twice a month. She believed Paul was from Oklahoma, in farm equipment sales, and visited Fort Worth periodically to pick up one thing or another from a distributor. She didn't care. She had to be at work by six, and there were a few times they didn't have sex at all. He never stayed the whole night though sometimes he hung out in the room after she left. She knew it was casual. She wasn't looking for a husband or a boyfriend. She just wanted someone who'd treat her well and required low maintenance. He fit the bill, and besides, he covered the cost of the room.

Paul purposefully left his iPhone on his desk and made his way to the elevators. While descending to ground level to catch a cab, his pocket began to vibrate. This phone never went home with him. It was one of those prepaid deals that couldn't be traced back to him, only a select few had the number. Paul reached into his pocket, expecting to see Becky's number on the screen. He assumed she was wondering where he was. Instead, the caller ID showed "caller unavailable." He let it go to voicemail.

CHAPTER 25

"What the hell was that all about, Marcus?" Thach was fit to be tied. The Democrats were holding their postmortem in the Oval Office. "If you get on that stage with Stowe this afternoon, you'll blow any chance we have of pulling together a coalition of senators to back me to lead the Senate. I can do this. I've got a lot of leverage."

"You have nothing. You're a bully and a jerk, Mike. You showed your ass in there. You won't be able to swing a single Republican to switch sides, and we already have the only other independent. Stowe will never cast the deciding vote in your favor.

"You still don't get it. We got it all wrong. Stowe isn't using us as leverage with the Republicans, he is using the Republicans as leverage with us. He's offering to share control of the Senate. He could have easily taken his position of choice and sided with the Republicans. Making a bid for the Senate leader isn't about power for him. It was a message for us, me and Rachael, that he'll share the Senate, but that your brand of leadership no longer has a place in the equation."

"Are you writing me off, Marcus? I'm the only thing standing in the way of investigations into your administration. Do you really want to make an enemy of me?"

"I can't speak for Rachael and the party, just me. We got a lot of things done, Mike, and we assumed we would be lauded for our accomplishments and hoped our transgressions would be overlooked. I may be proud of what we've done, but we broke a lot of norms in the process of doing it. The consequences of which are now catching up with us. We've poisoned the well with our tactics. We've set some bad precedents and sowed a lot of ill will."

"Nonsense! We got things done for the American people."

The president looked at Thach with great skepticism. "Come on, Mike. There are no cameras or microphones in here. Be real. It's just us talking. We got things done for a select few. We paid back favors to our rich donors and strengthened our voting base with handouts. We worked for our Americans, not all Americans. The country is more deeply divided than ever, and it started right here with my ambition and your methods. The logjam existed because everyone in this town is always focused on agendas that benefit themselves and their friends. If we did things the right way from the start, there would be no need for backroom deals and strong-arm tactics. Parker Stowe intends to show the country a different way, with or without us. He is focused on leading, not legislating. Those that get on board will share the spotlight in a band of heroes. Those who do not are likely to be episodic characters in his story. Mark my words, history will treat them as the villains."

"Stowe is a flash in the pan." Mike was pleading his case to an unsympathetic president.

"Parker's been underestimated all along his journey. I bet on you, Mike, when you were the winning commodity. You're not that guy anymore. I'm switching horses."

Miranda pulled Jason aside as they were exiting the Roosevelt Room. "I didn't see that coming."

"I said it would be unexpected. I didn't know for sure until I got back to the hotel last night and asked Parker."

"You suspected? Nice to clue me in," she said in jest, mostly.

"With Parker, you never know. I didn't want you up all night working up a strategy on speculation. This, you and me, is going to be complicated if we can't separate business from our personal interests. I can't be your inside guy."

"Relax, Jay. We can talk about it tonight after the interview is over. You're still coming, right?"

"Yes, but it'll be late. Close to ten, maybe."

"No worries. I had a good time last night and am looking forward to tonight. See you then."

Wade approached, looking annoyed. He was polite, but there was a coldness to his body language. "Are you riding back to the office with us, Miranda?"

"I'm ready when y'all are. Let's go."

"You'll hear from us later today about the press conference, Jason. We need some time to digest all this and decide how we're going to proceed."

"I understand, Wade. If I haven't heard from you by two, I'll give you a shout." Jason watched them move to the exit and was glad he was not riding in that car. He imagined it would be a tense trip back to the office. They would almost assuredly be on stage with Parker at the press conference. Some power was better than no power.

When the meeting concluded, Parker excused himself rather quickly. He felt an urgent need to relieve and refresh himself. As he exited the restroom, he met Bull, Agent Cosby, and Detective Cobb in the hall. The four of them approached Jason in the foyer where he was waiting. Bull made introductions, and Jason exchanged contact information with Cobb and Cosby.

"When can we expect to know a determination about a security detail?" Jason was even more concerned now that Parker had announced his intentions. Broadcasting them to the country in less than seven hours would only serve to increase the ill will aimed directly at Parker.

Expressionless, Cosby replied, "Likely by day's end." He made eye contact with Cobb. She understood the urgency by which she needed to get her chief up to speed and inform him of Cosby's intention to make a play for jurisdiction.

Cobb smiled at Stowe.

"Based on the incident at Wake Forest two days ago, we'll have uniforms assigned to you until you leave Washington. We're also going to contact the FBI and get them to investigate the situation. You're in good hands, sir."

"Thank you, Detective, and thank you, gentlemen, but I'm more concerned for the safety of my wife and children than myself." Parker was especially anxious while being so far away from them.

Agent Cobb responded, "We understand. They will be considered in the assessment."

Parker went on to explain the rather controversial plan he just finished disclosing to the meeting attendants. "As you may have already deduced, my intentions will likely cause considerable animosity."

"I'm glad you said something now, Senator. It should expedite a decision." Cosby was ready to put the resources of the Secret Service in motion but needed to get things at the White House wrapped up and talk with the director.

"I appreciate it. Thanks again."

The group shook hands. Parker, Jason, and Bull returned to the hotel. The car ride was short and silent, as was the trip up the elevator. There were of course things to be discussed, but privately. They suspected that word of the plan would be leaked ahead of the press conference. By which side or player, it didn't matter. Some foreknowledge might help build public interest in watching. Increasing the number of people who witnessed Parker's plan debut on the national political stage could only help.

Bull did his customary sweep of the suite while Parker and Jason set up their laptops. It was time to begin the process of drafting the speech for the conference. Parker finally broke the silence.

"How'd you think it went?"

Jason looked up from the computer, smiled and shook his head. "Not as good as it could have gone, but not as bad as it probably feels. You have the respect of the president. Zimmermann wants to like you. You have an enemy in Thach."

"I should have been better prepared for him." Parker lamented his encounter with the majority leader. He hadn't intended to go nose to nose with him, and now everything would be more difficult. "He represents everything I hate about this town. I let him get under my skin and pull me down to his level."

"That's how it feels, Parker. Not how it is." They had a lot of work to do in the next few hours. Jason wanted to help Parker quickly gain the perspective he needed to be most effective. It's not that Parker wouldn't find it on his own, but time was currently working against them. The hour of the press conference would arrive quickly.

Parker sighed and grimaced. "I know. Too late now, anyway. What was your take of Miranda, Archer, and Wilson?"

"Miranda likes you."

Parker interrupted. "You mean she likes you, and it's transferring to me by association."

"Maybe, but her opinion isn't going to move the players one way or the other." Jason had no desire to discuss Miranda with Parker. "Let's focus on Archer and Wilson. They're like the kid that was hoping for a bicycle at Christmas and got clothes instead. It's not what they wanted, but it's more than they had before. You could have been gentler with the minority leader."

"They'll get on board, but not because they want to."

"Exactly."

"I'm going to call Roni, and then let's get to work on this speech."

Jason's assumption about the car ride back to the RNC headquarters was more accurate than he would have guessed.

Wade's volcanic anger was spewing forth from his mouth without discrimination. He tore into Archer for being led like a lamb to the slaughterhouse. He turned on Miranda for having ever suggested that they support Stowe. He even went as far as to lament not putting up another candidate after Crockett pulled out of the race. This was all followed by a final few minutes cursing Crockett and his inability to keep his pants on.

By the time they got back to the office, Wade had taken a shot at anyone involved in the Crockett for Senate organization and every person attending that morning's breakfast. Jack and Miranda just let him have his tantrum as they settled themselves in the conference room. They'd seen him like this a few times throughout the years. Although his behavior was extremely unbecoming, they also knew once he got it all out, he'd be better able to focus. They needed him calm and collected to begin the process of putting the pieces back in order.

"Why didn't we see this coming, Miranda?" Wade had already shifted gears.

"I don't know, Wade." Miranda wanted an apology for having to endure his brashness but knew it wouldn't come. She focused on the question. "It's probably because we all expected him to think and act like one of us. Like a professional politician. We put ourselves in his shoes but looked at the situation from a perspective of how things are done. Stowe looks at situations from the perspective of how things should be."

"I hear you, Miranda, but I'm not sure I'm following." Jack was humble enough to not be afraid to ask for clarity. This trait sometimes brought ridicule upon him, and the popular opinion of the intellectual elite was that he was short on gray matter. The truth was that he genuinely wanted to understand what others were saying.

"We assumed he would choose to caucus with one side or the other and be happy with a standing committee chairman-ship as a reward for doing so. We assumed that he would be motivated by control, influence, money, and title. You know, power, because that's how Washington works."

"What you're saying is that because Stowe is not motivated by any of these things, we just had no clue what he was going to do. That's why we missed it."

"You got it, Jack. Parker Stowe doesn't think like us. He's not motivated by the same things and makes different choices. Most people in his position will grab whatever they can for themselves, sometimes even justifying it as being for the greater good. I get the impression he would truly sacrifice his own life to be the right person for others."

"This is where you lose me, Miranda."

"He's the kind of person who would rather be remembered as an example of the kind of person others want to be than for passing a piece of landmark legislation that holds his name. His voting record will always reflect his values and principles.

No party. No compromise. If we want to know what he'll do, we first need to understand who he is."

"Who is he?" Wade cut to the core question.

"I think he was trying to show us that this morning, Wade." Jack Archer rarely came to the wrong conclusion. "That's why he wanted all of us to share a story, and he went first. We were all so focused on what he was going to do. We should have been focused on getting to know who he is."

Wade contemplated this statement. The pause caused a gap in the conversation long enough for Miranda to fetch herself a cup of coffee. Pride almost got the better of him. He was tempted to dismiss Jack's assessment, but he quickly realized Jack was most likely right. Wade had the revelation that chief among the people he'd berated should have been himself. Pressuring Stowe to move past the personal stories was a mistake. Being honest with himself, Wade had no idea what he was going to share with the group when his time came. Pushing Stowe to get down to business was motivated as much by the opportunity presented by Thach as it was by his desire not to have to share a personal story of his own.

Miranda decided to break the silence. "At this point, it is fruitless to cry over miscalculations. We need to decide how to move on from here."

"This is Jack's field of play. It's his call." Wade was not about to tell Jack what to do. Jack would let him know how he and the party could help.

Jack Archer may have had a stunted sense of purpose, but his convictions were well defined. And while his intellect was often misjudged as primitive, his ability to assess the character of a person was chief among his strengths. He did not take offense at what Parker said to him at breakfast. He just wished it had been pointed out in a less public, more intimate setting. Nevertheless, what Parker said was accurate. His purpose, maybe the purpose of the Republican Party, was ill-defined and in bad need of an overhaul.

"For the next two years, Stowe will be the deciding vote when ranks hold on party lines. I don't doubt that if push comes to shove on who will lead the Senate, he'll side with us. What we're really talking about is control of the rules and the flow of bills that come to the floor for a vote. Ultimately though, the power is his anytime something controversial is brought up and the Senate splits along party lines."

"If I'm hearing you right, Jack, you want to force the vote. You trust that Parker will side with us and make you the majority leader." Wade believed this, too.

"Yes and no," Jack replied, much to the confusion of Wade. "Yes, I believe he sides with us if it means me or Thach. No, I don't want to force the vote. What is the downside to encouraging the party to support him as majority leader?"

"You mean besides losing control of the rules and flow of bills?" Wade was being sarcastic.

"Jack may be on to something, Wade," Miranda put in. "If we're in control and bury a bill Stowe likes, all he has to do is switch sides, put the Dems in control, and it will come forward anyway. He calls the shots, title or no title. Giving him the title only makes his control more official, not more effective.

"Think about the genius of his plan. He will probably be successful in gaining support from most members to back him as the leader of the Senate. Almost all of them will get committee chairmanships. That's ninety-six votes. If we follow the current construct, one party is entirely shut out of leadership... like we are now. Half the power is better than no power."

Stepping aside in support of Stowe just made sense to Jack, and he was not going to fight to be a figurehead. "And by elevating him, we show support for his goal of shared government. This is something the country wants. The president has already decided to stand with him. We will end up looking like the obstructionists if we oppose him. And for what? The title for me isn't worth it."

"This only works if all Republicans vote for him." Wade saw the logic but didn't like the concept. "Are you sure we can get everyone on board?"

"I will publicly put my support behind him at the press conference." Jack made his decision. "If you as the party chairman do as well, then it will place a lot of pressure on the members to fall in line. Combine that with the 'some power is better than no power' argument and they'll get on board. The country wants what Stowe is selling."

Wade frowned and shrugged his shoulders. "I'll make the call to Tuttle while you and Miranda prepare a statement."

"The president is outright supporting Stowe. Zimmermann is refusing to throw the weight of the party behind me." Senior Thach was speaking to Junior. They had met at the club after Senior's visit to the White House and were currently in the hot tub. "She didn't go as far to say the party would support Stowe, but she refuses to stand opposed to the president. She said she would let each senator decide to vote their conscience."

"How can I help, Dad?" Junior was always ready to help his old man, usually with no questions asked.

"I need to know where we're vulnerable from within the party. How many senators are likely to break ranks if given the choice? I then need to know who we might be able to coerce from the Republican side."

This time, however, Junior was ready to confront his father. "Dad, maybe you should rethink fighting this battle. Even if you win, what do you really gain? You may be the figurehead, but in reality, Stowe is still the swing vote on anything that splits along party lines. You can twist some arms for a title, but for what? The Democrats will still be the minority party. It'll be a hollow victory. Stowe will still control leadership with his single vote. He will achieve shared power with or without you."

"You too, Junior? You sound like Zimmermann and Jenkins."

"I'll do whatever you want me to do, but I don't see any gain in this." Junior wanted to reassure his father that he still held significant power. It was his only chance of talking him out of pursuing this folly. "You don't have to support him, but you have enough power to make his life miserable. Get your supporters to block his initiatives. There's always the filibuster. You can spend the next two years marginalizing him and criticizing every move he makes. Same as if he were a Republican."

"This guy's a problem, Son. He can do a lot of damage to the status quo, even if we successfully block him. He doesn't care about being re-elected. He has no party allegiance and is the majority deciding vote. He'll control the flow of bills.

"Reach out to our friends on Wall Street and see what they're thinking. They can't like his ideas for income gap resolution. Maybe we can get our large donors to pressure some votes by threatening to pull contributions." Thach knew Stowe was not motivated by being re-elected, but almost every other elected official was. Campaigns are expensive, and the funding sources are a major leverage point. "If Zimmermann won't do her job, I will. Where are we with ABC?"

Junior once again visually inspected the room and lowered his voice. "We can't 'C' him. You and the Republicans tried that earlier, and it didn't go so well. Our people can't find any leverage. Your best bet is 'B.' Ruin his name and image. I've had a story planted about his suspected role in outing Crockett. With his evangelical background, we'll paint him as a gay-hating fascist. That will change the narrative and force some of the moderates on the Republican side to rethink supporting him. At the very least, it'll make Archer's job more difficult."

Senior nodded and queried further, "and 'A?'"

"That's already partially in motion. Words from our people inside the FBI is that a credible threat already exists. That may work to our advantage. Are you sure you want to actively pursue this line? His replacement will undoubtedly be Republican."

Thach Senior didn't even pause. "Yes. I can stomach Archer for two years. Stowe is a real threat to the Washington way of life."

CHAPTER 26

Floyd left Paul a voicemail and put his cell phone back in his pocket. The exploits of his younger years, while fun, had created some obligations he felt he was ill-equipped to deal with himself.

In the weeks leading up to his departure from TCU, Floyd had made the acquaintance of a young woman from Florence, North Carolina. She was the only child in a well-to-do family whose wealth was made in the timber and furniture industries. It was a family that was very Baptist and very conservative. Despite her upbringing, or maybe because of it, the young lady had tested her independence at college and got involved with the likes of Floyd Rockport.

His disappearance shortly before the Christmas break of her freshman year broke her heart. It was, however, only the beginning of her troubles. She found out she was pregnant just before New Year's. The baby had to be Floyd's as he was the only man she'd ever known in that way. She had no idea where he was or how to contact him. She was alone and scared, fearful her parents wouldn't understand. A grandchild born out of wedlock would ruin their respectable lives.

She went to Planned Parenthood the following week to inquire about an abortion. She set an appointment for the procedure to take place three days later. Unbeknown to her, a friend of her mother from the church was in a group of protesters across from the clinic. The woman recognized her as she exited the building and called her mother. She feared what her parents would do, but when she told them of her situation, she found only love and compassion, no condemnation. Together they formed a plan. At the end of July, they welcomed a healthy baby boy into the world and their family.

When the boy was eight, his grandparents died suddenly in an automobile accident on Interstate 95 traveling to Florida. The family money was mostly tied up in the business, which neither the young woman nor her son were able or prepared to take over. Compounding the difficulties of the loss was the insufficient insurance to cover the taxes due on the estate.

The surprise on Annmarie's face when Floyd Rockport, the father of her child, entered the room was so distracting that the attention of all present turned to her. No one knew she was confronting a ghost from her past. He was there to present an offer from Indiana-Fellows Investment Group to purchase her family's business. Without knowing their history together, the gathering assumed her reaction was a mixture of grief and stress resulting from weeks of loss and uncertainty.

Floyd thought she looked vaguely familiar, and after a few minutes of trying to make the connection, he put the pieces together. Annmarie Harris was the freshman girl, Ann, with whom he'd been messing around for a short while before leaving TCU nine years earlier.

By this time, Annmarie had regained her composure and abruptly excused herself from the meeting before it ever began. After years of searching without success and then trying to forget him, Floyd Rockport had resurfaced in her life. She had no idea what to do.

She exited the conference room and went down the hall to her father's office, where she started to cry. At the age of twenty-seven, she felt hardly prepared to bury her parents and settle their estate. She also was the single parent of an eight-year-old boy. She spent the next hour crying, struggling with her loss, and pondering the thought of telling Floyd about his son.

Floyd was self-centered but not selfish. He often was quite generous and worked off the principle that by helping others get what they wanted and needed, he would get what he wanted and needed. He hated conflict and confrontation. He would lie about anything to avoid entering either type of situation. Floyd was secretly thankful when Ann left the room. It set aside his fear that he would have to explain his disappearance from her life in front of a room full of strangers. But he knew she was ultimately the decision maker, and he couldn't completely avoid her. The circumstances surrounding the sale of the company were not a secret. Somebody would be buying it regardless of their past relationship.

When her lawyer found her, Annmarie's tears had dried. Her mascara had left black lines on her face, and there was a pile of used tissues in the trash can beside her father's desk. She assured him she was okay and calmly explained the whole story to him. When she finished, she asked the lawyer what she should do.

"In regard to the purchase of the company, it's a fair deal," the lawyer said. "Don't let your history with Rockport cloud your judgment. You need to sell the company, pay the government, and settle your parent's debts. This can be an opportunity to build a new life for you and your son. In the end, you'll walk away with a sizable pile of money, at least five million dollars. As far as telling Floyd Rockport about his son, you should consider what purpose it will serve. You and the boy might both be better off not getting involved with him."

———

Annmarie followed the lawyer's advice, or at least part of it. The company was sold to IFIG, a sister corporation to IFLIC, and both wholly owned subsidiaries of Indiana-Fellows Holdings. Annmarie settled the affairs of her parent's estate and went about the business of building a life for herself and her son. It would be a life, she decided, that would best serve the boy with his father in it.

To his credit, Floyd tried to make it work. He wanted to be there for his son. It didn't hurt that Ann was still amazingly attractive, not to mention rich in her own right. Despite his six-figure earnings, Floyd managed to burn through money almost as fast as he made it. They married before their son turned ten.

At first, everyone seemed happy. The boy had his father and a man to follow. Ann had a popular and successful husband. Floyd had a trophy family and a McMansion in Westlake filled with all the toys that money and privilege could buy. Lawrence Rockport was happy too. Happy because it seemed his son had found his place. And for a few years, all was well in the Rockport universe.

When Floyd had left rehab, he was warned to stay away from other addictive behaviors. But as time passed and he settled into the comforts of predictable family life, Floyd became complacent. Soon he found himself taking frequent trips to the Indian casinos over the state line in Oklahoma. The more he lost in the poker room, the more he went, trying to win back money that would soon be missed by his wife.

The hole only got deeper, and that's when the fighting started. He'd lie to cover up what he was doing. She'd catch him. He'd call her names and blame her for his choices, changing the argument and deflecting it away from himself. She would kick him out. He'd stop coming home. And very soon after, the drinking and drugs re-entered his life. Then the affairs started.

This went on for two years until Floyd left his phone on the kitchen counter one Friday night before bed. Annmarie was cooking breakfast the next morning just as one of his friends texted a picture of Floyd doing a line of cocaine. If that wasn't bad enough, the line was positioned on the naked body of some young girl laying on the side of a hot tub. She loaded their son in the car and was gone before Floyd ever opened his eyes.

Floyd entered rehab for the second time in his life. Fortunately for Annmarie, Floyd's Uncle Lionel was more concerned about publicity than the personal failings of his nephew. Floyd fixated on avoiding a nasty, public divorce even more so than getting sober. Annmarie got everything, which amounted to just about three and a half million. This was considerably less than the five she had brought into the marriage, but then again, Floyd had had some pretty expensive habits those last few years.

Annmarie also got full custody of their son. But in exchange for limited visitation rights, Lawrence created a revocable trust for his grandchild worth one and a half million dollars. So long as the Rockport family was able to maintain a relationship with the boy, and so long as he stayed out of the press, he would receive ninety percent of the annual increase in the trust beginning at age sixteen.

Two years later, he received a birthday card from his grandfather with a check for one hundred eight thousand, three hundred seventy-nine dollars and forty-one cents. It didn't take long for Floyd's proclivities to surface in his son. He started down the road into manhood in a fast car with a different beautiful woman in the passenger seat every few weeks.

By this time, Annmarie had moved them back to North Carolina. They were living in Raleigh, and she was engaged to a nice, well-connected young lawyer with political aspirations.

CHAPTER 27

Chief Moffatt caught Meghan by surprise when he entered the squad room. "I'm glad you're here, Fowler. I was just about to call you. I need everything you got on the Stowe case. The FBI will be here within the hour."

"It's not much more than what I've already given you. I did, however, figure out why I followed that kid on the quad. I'm beginning to think he was our guy after all. Look at this video clip." She showed him the clip of the unsub putting the phone away and then checking his watch. "There, did you see? The phone is a prop."

Moffatt watched it again. "You're right. Why check the watch if he's looking at the phone? Good work, kid. Have you made an ID yet?"

"I just finished checking the class roster against the student photo database. I don't think he's enrolled in the class, but as I told you before, I didn't get a good look at him from the front."

"Pull all the footage from that day with him in it. The FBI has software that might be able to enhance the images. Did the city send the traffic cam footage?"

"Not yet. Maybe the FBI can get them to move faster."

Paul listened to the voicemail in the cab. "Hey buddy, it's Floyd. I know you don't carry this phone at home and it's the weekend, but I need you to call me as soon as you get this message. I think things are bad with the kid. He already has issues with the family. I don't want them to get worse. Oh, and don't say anything to my father or uncle. I want to keep this as quiet as possible. Just call me back."

"Idiots," Paul mumbled as he slid the phone back in his pocket.

"You say something?" The cab driver looked at Paul in the rearview mirror as he asked the question.

"To myself," Paul responded. "I was just listening to a message from an old friend. The guy's a fool, and his kid's following in his footprints. The family has more money and opportunity than 99% of the world, and they still can't manage themselves. A bunch of idiots that complicate my life."

Three years earlier, Floyd's son had gotten his picture taken rubbing tanning lotion on some supermodel while vacationing on the Island of Tortola. Not only did it cost him his trust fund income, but it also cost Floyd his job with IFIG. Uncle Lionel was serious about maintaining a low profile. He could tolerate all sorts of foolishness if it did not get into the press. But drawing attention to him personally, or any of the entities of Indiana-Fellows Holdings, was strictly taboo. Floyd was just collateral damage from Uncle Lionel's newsworthy grandnephew.

Floyd figured it was a miracle he'd lasted for as many years as he did. His forced departure was well overdue. Floyd's son, however, was furious. The boy already had a strained relationship with his father because of what had happened between him and his mother. The arrangement that Grandpa Lawrence brokered during the divorce went a long way toward keeping everyone in contact. Cutting off the money caused the rift to widen between the youngest and the older generations. Neither Lawrence nor Floyd had spoken with their descendent in over four years.

Of the roughly hundred people in Paul's organization, five were employed for the single purpose of monitoring the Rockport family. They evaluated the risk any of the member's activities posed to the reputation of the Indiana-Fellows brand. This team was segregated from the rest of the risk management staff. They reported directly to Paul, who now worked directly for Lionel as an executive for IFH. Paul was kept well informed about the status of both Floyd and his son.

The cab pulled to the curb in front of one of the more popular bars, about two blocks from the motel. Paul handed the driver a twenty and told him to keep the change. Walking the last two blocks would keep the motel address off the driver's log, in the event anyone inquired. And while he did not suspect he was the subject of any investigations, he certainly didn't want to give anyone leverage. He knew how the information game worked.

Entering the bar, Paul went directly to the restroom and relieved himself. While washing his hands, he checked his look in the mirror. He stuck a piece of gum in his mouth, plugged three quarters in the machine, and purchased a condom. When he exited the restroom, he left the building out the rear to the alley. It had been over twenty years since that night with Floyd, but every time Paul stepped into an alley, he got a sharp pain in his knee. He knew it was all mental. His mind's way of reminding him of the moment when he embarked down his current path in life.

There was no one in the alley as he walked the two blocks west. He periodically checked behind him to see if he was being followed. It was all clear. Paul entered the motel from the rear parking lot and climbed the stairs to the third floor. He paused at the top of the stairs for a minute. He needed to catch his breath and wanted to hear if someone was making the old wooden panels creak under their weight below him. Reasonably sure he was not being surveyed, he headed down the hall toward his place of escape.

———

Floyd was one of those people who, like a cat, always managed to land on his feet. He was left with nothing after the divorce except his clothes and job. He had to borrow money from his father to cover the deductible and coinsurance payments created by his stint in rehab. When he graduated from the program, determined to never again let addiction ruin his life, he poured his hours into his work.

His base salary had been two hundred and forty-three thousand dollars per year. The state of Texas had required him to relinquish seventy-five thousand annually to Annmarie as child support until their son graduated high school. Though it was not uncommon for him to get a bonus of another hundred thousand in an average year, a refocused Floyd had brought so many deals to a conclusion in his first year out of rehab that his bonus had amounted to almost double that amount.

He had gone to his meetings regularly and avoided the places that could get him into trouble. He stayed away from the people that knew and liked him in party mode. He bought a new, but modest, two-bedroom condo in a recently remodeled downtown high-rise three blocks from the office. He was rarely there except to sleep. When he wasn't at work or talking about his struggles with other addicts, Floyd had attempted to mend his body and the relationships he damaged with his past lifestyle choices.

He'd begun with his relationship with God. A friend from his meetings invited him to church one Sunday. For the first time in his life, Floyd had sincerely and earnestly sought more than an affiliation with his Creator, but a true bond to Him. There were now five places Floyd could be predictably found, including the Cross-Path Church. Not too long after getting right with God, Floyd had sought to fix things with his parents, more specifically Lawrence.

His mother had always been supportive to the point of being an enabler, or at least that's what his therapist said. She just wanted him to come around and avoided any topic that could cause conflict. His father, on the other hand, was a more complex entity. He'd always been there for Floyd, but his love and support came at a price. Sometimes it was just a lecture, but more often it was the unspoken disapproval that exacted the toll. Either way, guilt and shame were the currency by which Floyd bartered with his father when he needed help. Manipulation was Lawrence's tool of choice to get Floyd to conform to his wishes.

Floyd had finally realized he couldn't change Lawrence, but he could change the way he dealt with him. He desired his father's approval, but he no longer felt the need for it. He would appreciate his help and lay any guilt or disapproval that came with it on his Savior's Cross. He'd no longer avoid negativity or attempt to run away from it. Floyd was learning to take the bad with the good and properly deal with both.

Ultimately, his relationship with his parents did improve. Once during the week, Paul made a point to have dinner with them. Every Sunday afternoon, he went out to their mansion in Westover Hills for brunch and a round of golf at the club with Lawrence.

His relationship with Annmarie, however, was damaged beyond repair. The few overtures he'd made to mend the wounds were met with harsh tones and angry words. He took full responsibility for the failure of their relationship. He was also genuinely sorry for hurting her. Asking for her forgiveness was easy, and he understood why she was unable to give it.

On the other hand, the boy was more open to him but rightfully cautious. At first, it had been very hard and awkward for them both. Floyd was in Texas and the boy was in North Carolina. They'd spoken on the phone a few times a week in between visits. Once a month, Floyd would fly to Raleigh for a long weekend. Every third month, his son would fly to Texas. Annmarie had agreed to split the holidays. Floyd got him for spring break and three weeks in the summer. They'd gone skiing in Colorado, white water rafted the Grand Canyon, and went fishing in Alaska. Floyd had always felt the connection was forced, and the relationship was on shaky ground. Things had changed for the worse between them when the kid started getting the trust fund money.

Floyd had tried to warn him several times to be careful and keep a low profile. He told him the stories of his youth and tried to explain that the money was like a magnifying glass. It had the power to increase the magnitude of both his pleasure and his problems. The most profound thing Floyd ever said happened when he told his son that money had the power to turn a pleasure into a problem.

Over the Christmas break of his senior year, his son totaled his Corvette and put his passenger in the hospital. When Floyd tried to talk to him about it, the boy called him a hypocrite and canceled their spring break plans. Three months later, he was an international tabloid cover story.

Floyd had reached out to him every week since then, but not once did he answer. The message he left was always the same. "Hey Derick, it's your dad. I'm just calling to check on you and let you know I'm thinking about you. I'm here for you, Son. I love you."

CHAPTER 28

At five minutes to five, Jason Tuttle took the podium in the ballroom of the Willard Hotel. The occupants of the room, mostly press, had already been screened by the Secret Service but not for Parker's security. Some of the most powerful people in Washington would soon be on the stage, including the president. When Jason came out, the correspondents quickly settled down and found seats.

For the last three days, Stowe's election as an independent senator topped the national political headlines. The media built the story and fueled speculation as the country waited to hear which political party would control the United States Senate. It was all for show. The consensus among the most well-known and widely followed pundits was that Parker would, without question, side with the Republicans. Though unconventional, he was considered a conservative; few believed that he would grant any favor to the Democrats. The only open question was which committee Parker would be given as a gift for consummating the conservative wedding with the Republican Party. Almost to the last, they believed that upon being sworn into office in January, he would chair the Senate Committee on Health, Education, Labor, and Pensions.

But, as Parker and Jason suspected, shortly after noon, news of the morning breakfast had leaked to the media. Not too long after the leak, it was officially announced to the White House press corps that President Jenkins would be on stage with Senator-Elect Stowe later that day. This led to all sorts of wild speculation. So much controversy was generated that many of the famous weekday news personalities and commenters canceled their Saturday afternoon plans. They wanted to anchor the interruption of regularly scheduled broadcasting created by the Stowe press conference.

"Good afternoon. My name is Jason Tuttle, and I'm the campaign manager and chief of staff for Senator-Elect Parker Stowe. In a few minutes, the senator-elect will come out and deliver a statement regarding his caucusing and voting plans for control of the United States Senate. After his announcement, President Jenkins will make a statement, followed by remarks from the current minority leader, Jack Archer. Written copies of all three statements will be distributed at the conclusion of the prepared portion of the conference. Senator-Elect Stowe will field a limited number of questions following Senator Archer's remarks. If you are called upon for a question, you will be allowed one follow-up question. Neither President Jenkins nor Minority Leader Archer will comment beyond their prepared statements at this time. The senator-elect will take the podium in just a few moments. Thank you."

Parker was on the phone with Roni. "I just got word from the Secret Service. The FBI is going to investigate the incident at the university, and the USCP is going to assign us protection."

"We're fine, Parker." Roni was trying to get him focused on the speech. "It's almost five. Aren't you about to be on television?"

"Yes, dear." Parker took the cue that it was time to get off the phone. "I love you."

"I love you too. Now go inspire the nation. The kids are waiting to see Daddy on TV."

As he hung up the phone, Parker steadied himself and calmed his nerves. He closed his eyes and silently prayed, asking for His courage and strength, His wisdom and words. Opening his eyes, he felt Jason's hand on his shoulder.

"You're up, buddy." Jason applied pressure to the hand squeezing Parker's shoulder as if to give him a small hug. "Be yourself. You'll do fine."

"Thanks, Jay." Parker straightened his tie, buttoned the top button of his suit coat, raised his head, and squared his shoulders. "Pray for me."

"I always do."

Parker looked Jason in the eyes, smiled, and turned to walk to the podium. As he stepped out from behind the screen and walked across the dais to the podium, the room came to a quick silence. All that could be heard in the background was the clicking of cameras as the photojournalists sought to capture the perfect picture to memorialize the moment. He arrived at the lectern and began.

"Good evening and thank you. You honor me with your time, for which I am grateful and by which I am humbled.

"My name is Parker Stowe, and I carry many titles. I am a son to my parents, husband to my wife, and daddy to my three children. I am a teacher to my students, advisor to those who ask. I am an author to those who need help falling asleep." From this statement, a few chuckles were solicited and received. "I am a friend to many, but never enough, and an adversary to few, but far too many. To most of you, I am known as the senator-elect from North Carolina who will decide if the Democrats or the Republicans lead the United States Senate.

"But titles are only important if we have a common understanding of what they represent. If one person has an abusive father, then what the title 'father' represents to them is far different than what it means to the person who has a father who is loving, kind, and supportive. That's why titles are only as good as the values we commonly understand them to represent.

"When the founding fathers of this great nation put ink to paper and wrote the Constitution, the titles of president, congressman, and justice were commonly understood to represent service to others. They meant a sacrifice of personal self-interest for others. Political office was a diversion from the farms and mills, shops and ships, from which those who made up the assembly derived their livelihood. Being a politician was not a life-long career, but rather a temporary calling out from their professions to serve and represent the needs and interests of the people.

"Sadly, the title of politician no longer represents the values of service and sacrifice. Instead, the title has become synonymous with corruption, waste, deception, and division. Calls for greater transparency, humility, and empathy in our leaders go unanswered. The system continues to push forward people who, despite good intentions, either cannot or will not challenge the current state of mediocrity. They fear losing large donations from special interests or leadership positions within their party if they challenge the status quo. Rather than debating important issues and discussing proposals on their merits, far too often the discussion is reduced to personal attacks on the character of those who hold opposing views.

"I ran for office as an independent candidate, not to place blame on any person or party, but to restore by example the ideals of service and sacrifice to public office. There are many who claim that character is not important, only results. I believe they are wrong. Our founding fathers purposefully created a governmental system that requires us to work together to achieve.

"Trust, respect, and understanding are fundamental elements of teamwork. Without them, the results are poor and laced with accusation, contempt, and misdirection. I firmly believe that before this county can effectively move forward, we must reconcile our differences and reunite. We must remember how to move together.

"Though I always hoped to be a symbol of change and an example of how it could be done, I never imagined that a single vote, my vote, would carry so much weight. And though there has been much speculation and assumption regarding my ideology, I come before you tonight with a way that is true to my nature as an independent. My way is that of a regular citizen who has been called out of his profession to serve his countrymen, much as our founding fathers were called so many years ago. Abraham Lincoln once said that a house divided cannot stand. We are a house divided. We are Republicans and Democrats, conservatives and liberals, white and black, male and female, rich and poor. We have allowed ourselves to look at what separates us before we look at what we share, being defined by our titles and not by who we are.

"Instead of celebrating the core values that bind us together, such as liberty and justice, we have found it fashionable to promote our differences. Let us never forget that we are always stronger as one united people than we can ever be alone.

"Our system is not broken, but our sense of what it means to be a leader must be repaired. Leadership is not always being first. Being first is usually a byproduct of being a great leader. Being the wealthiest and the most powerful can be the result of good leadership, but not the cause of it. We need to stop following people because of the group to which they belong, because of how they look, or how successful they seem to be. We need to follow those whose actions and character best reflect the values we share, like fairness, generosity, and integrity.

America has fought against the institution of segregation, and yet we allow ourselves to be classified by our politics, religion, sex, income, and race. Good leadership is about putting the success of the team ahead of any special interest, especially one's own self-interest.

"I'm not on the conservative team. I'm not on the male team, the white team, or the rich team. Though all these terms could be used to describe me, I want to be known as being on America's team. Because without the blessings of this great nation, those titles have a much different context.

"While being white, rich, and male certainly grants advantage, there are few other places in the world where opportunity does not require one or more of these things to be successful. Only in America can you be of any race or ethnicity, male or female, hetero or homosexual, religious or atheist, rich or poor and have the freedom to live life, pursue happiness, and go as far as you prepare yourself to go. The United States is the very embodiment of opportunity, liberty, and justice for all. She only asks in return preparedness, responsibility, and accountability from all.

"Is there injustice? Yes. Is there oppression? Yes. But they will not be defeated in shouting matches on the floors of the Congress or the broadcast rooms of our favorite television station. Court rulings and legislation cannot put them out of existence. Injustice and oppression must be overcome in the hearts of those who cling to them by leaders whose very character set the example for us all to follow. Our leaders should first and foremost inspire us to be better today than we were yesterday.

"It is with the purpose and desire to have our governmental leaders be an example of the best leadership for others to follow that I have proposed a true sharing of legislative oversight and power, irrespective of party allegiance. There are over ninety

Senate committees and subcommittees. Under my proposal, each will be chaired by a different senator. Less than ten senators will be without a leadership position within the committee structure.

"As for leading the Senate itself, the current rules and structure grant the majority leader control of the flow of bills, which all too often allows the majority party the ability to either unduly promote or suppress the agenda of the presidency, a specific political party, or even the momentary desires of the citizenry. Proper debate is relegated to the media and only serves to deepen the segregationist format of the two-party system. I intend to disrupt the partisan monopoly of control by seeking leadership of the Senate either by creating a bi-partisan coalition that puts me in charge, by changing the rules of the Senate, or a combination of both.

"Under my leadership, both parties will equally share committee leadership positions and the control of legislation will neither be a rubber stamp nor an impediment to a partisan agenda.

"The House of Representatives will be controlled by the Republicans and the presidency by the Democrats. If they choose to conduct their business in a partisan way, that is their purview. But under my leadership, the Senate will conduct business without regard to party affiliation. Issues will be debated on their merits, and our shared American values and principles will guide us.

"We must work together to lead together. In the process of learning how to do this, I hope that we can finally tackle many of the challenges that face this great nation. I will know that this has been a successful venture when once again service and sacrifice are synonymous with the title of an elected official.

"President Jenkins and Minority Leader Jack Archer have graciously decided to stand with me this evening. They have prepared remarks for the nation. I will return to field a limited number of questions after they are finished. Please rise for the president of the United States."

Parker made every effort to demonstrate his respect for the president. Marcus Jenkins had achieved the highest elected office in the most powerful democracy the world had ever seen. Despite some significant differences in style and policy, Parker rightfully showed deference to both the office and the man who held it. He met the president halfway to the podium, warmly shook his hand, and left the dais to be occupied solely by the presence of Marcus Jenkins.

"Good evening, ladies and gentlemen." The president was open and familiar. His tone was friendly and pleasant. "I had the pleasure of hosting a breakfast this morning for Senator-Elect Stowe and the leaders in the Senate from both parties.

"At the beginning of the meeting, I had little hope that the senator-elect would leave my party, the Democratic Party, in the majority role. I humbly admit that I mistakenly believed that Senator Stowe requested the meeting to broker the best deal for himself. Like most, I assumed he simply wished to secure the committee chairmanship of his choice.

"Instead, I met a man who showed me a heart for others before himself. I met a man whose interests were about building relationships before brokering deals. I found myself wanting to work with him because he wants to work with all of us. Though we will undoubtedly have differences, I believe his focus on the commonalities that bind us together will help restore a sense of civility and decency many of us have not yet experienced from our government.

"I am not speaking as a lifelong Democrat. There are many in my party who will take offense to what I am doing this evening. But I have no more offices to seek, no more money to raise or promises to make. I have but a short time left in this office to guide this country to a better place. I believe I have a partner in Parker Stowe.

"Together with the other leaders in Congress, we can make significant bipartisan progress toward closing the income gap, overhauling the tax code, passing immigration reform, and a whole host of other important issues. The government, our government, will be more balanced. The Republicans control the House of Representatives. I'm still a Democrat and control the Executive. Under Senator-Elect Stowe's plan, the Senate will be shared by both parties, at least through the next election cycle two years from now.

"We have a historic opportunity to be something different, something more, something better. I am standing with Senator-Elect Stowe as a fellow citizen, as the president, and as a new friend. I share his desire to realize the promise of one unified nation that still stands indivisible and delivers liberty and justice to all who would embrace her.

"I offer my support for the newly elected senator from North Carolina. I am challenging the other ninety-nine members of the new Senate to get to know him. Listen to him. Explore his ideas and imagine the possibilities. I believe that working together in a new form of bipartisan cooperation can create a legacy for America, more so than any piece of legislation will ever do. Thank you, God bless you, and God bless America."

The room remained quiet as President Jenkins exited the stage and the minority leader prepared to take the podium. Jack Archer was well versed in custom and ceremony. He waited patiently until the chief executive had fully stepped from view before ascending the dais. As he walked across the raised platform to the microphone, the only audible noise came from a few people in the room adjusting themselves and the mechanical clicking of the camera shutters.

"My fellow Americans." Jack's voice was deep and his tone commanded attention. "This is a greeting that is often used by politicians when opening a speech. But tonight, in the context of the statements from Senator-Elect Stowe and President Jenkins, I hope it resonates differently in our ears.

"Differently, because a fellowship is more than an acquaintance. It is greater than an association and deeper than a friendship. The ties that bind it are inseparable, and the love its members share is sacrificial. Fellowships develop their members through activities and support them in their failures. Members contribute their strengths and draw on one another to compensate for their limitations. Fidelity is forged by faith in one another and respect for each other. And when under stress, the relationships grow stronger so that no challenge, no obstacle or foe can divide it.

"America's greatest moments have been achieved by fellowships of men and women who have shed their blood as soldiers, their sweat as builders, and their intellect as inventors. We have built a civilization and quality of life that has made us the envy of the world. We are a generous people and give more away to others than any nation.

"Have we made mistakes? Yes. We have made mistakes along the way. Grievous mistakes like almost wiping out Native Americans, holding people as property, and trading in human lives. But we learn from them and become better because of them. Perhaps what makes us exceptional is that we have created a system where people are free to fail, learn, and try again.

"We are failing now. We are in debt. We are divided. We are fighting short-term battles about how and what to do instead of first defining why we want to do them. It is time to learn from our mistakes. It is time to stop trying to do the right things and to start being the right thing.

"For the Republican party, that means that we support Senator-Elect Stowe's plan to share power in the United States Senate. For me personally, it means that I will focus my energy on being my caucus leader, so long as my colleagues will have me. And I will be endorsing Senator Stowe's bid to lead the Senate regardless of what his title may be.

"The senator-elect has made it abundantly clear he is an independent thinker, neutral in his allegiance, grounded in his values, and guided by his principles. He will not play partisan politics and has already gained my respect and friendship and that of President Jenkins. Like the president, I too would like to urge my esteemed colleagues from both parties to engage our newest member from North Carolina. It will be time well spent. Senator Stowe will return to take some questions in just a few moments. Thank you."

Jack turned and walked toward Parker, who began to climb the few stairs of the elevated platform. They met at the top of the steps, where the men shook hands and Parker whispered, "Thank you," to Jack. The cameras clicked away, and the energy level in the room increased tenfold as the journalists prepared to vie for Parker's bestowing of a question.

CHAPTER 29

Paul lay in the bed sipping his third Bud Light while Becky showered and prepared for work. It was a rare thing for people to captivate his attention. Parker Stowe did. His instincts told him that Stowe would succeed in ushering in a new political era. It would be a time where substance and character replaced money and title as the currency of influence. While he admired the freshman senator's vision for a better America, Paul made his living in a world fueled by greed and ambition. He needed to derail the Stowe Express before it left the station.

He muted the television as a still damp and very naked Becky paraded her comely curves in front of him. "Becky darling, how would you like to take a trip to North Carolina?"

"I'd love to." She was genuinely excited as she had never gone further from home than the beaches of Galveston. "But I probably can't." She sounded disheartened. "I need to make money, and vacation doesn't pay."

"I'm not talking about vacation. And what I have in mind will put you in a career that'll more than double what you make in a year."

She looked at him with confusion and doubt. "I don't need any trouble, Paul. What's the catch?"

"It won't be any trouble. I just need someone I trust to get close to another party. Can I trust you, Becky?"

"How close, Paul? I'm not doing anything that'll get me put in jail. Count me out."

"It pays two grand a week plus expenses. You won't be carrying drugs or anything illegal. I'm working a deal, and I need to develop a resource in Raleigh. The guy in whom I'm interested knows me, and we're not on good terms. If he suspects I'm connected to you, you'll be no good to me, and the job will end."

"What's this guy do that you have business with him?"

"He's a young guy about your age. Works at a distribution warehouse. That's all you need to know."

"And I'm supposed to do what, tail him like a detective?"

"I could hire a professional detective if that's what I needed. I'm looking for someone to get closer to him, more intimate."

Becky was insulted. "Screw you, Paul. I'm no whore!"

"I didn't say you had to sleep with him." Paul backed off, but he had planted the seed he intended to plant. "Make friends with him. Hang out. He's a nice guy, handsome, clean-cut, and educated. He's got financial and family troubles and is emotionally vulnerable. He needs friends. All I want you to do is make contact and see what develops. I don't care if you decide to sleep with him or not. Just get close to him and keep my people updated."

"I don't know, Paul. This is sketchy."

"You'll have access to a company car and a furnished company apartment for six months. The apartment is conveniently located in his complex. Your job will be in quality control with the Rygart Hotel brand."

"And all I have to do is make friends with this dude?"

"Well, that and perform your duties as a quality control specialist. You will be paid through Rygart and can keep the job after our business is concluded, but it will be on your own merit."

"When do you need an answer?"

"Soon. I'd need you to start this week."

"Jeez, Paul. No pressure or anything."

"Never forget that time is money."

"I'll let you know tomorrow." Becky had already decided she would do it but wanted to make Paul live with the uncertainty for the night.

Paul climbed out of the bed and walked to the chair where he had left his pants. He pulled out his wallet and removed a wad of bills. He counted out thirty hundred-dollar bills. Fanning them out in front of her on the table, he said, "Call it a bonus if you agree to do it now. I want you to catch the first flight out in the morning."

Becky looked at the cash on the table, and her eyes grew large. It was more than she would make working three weeks at her current job. "I'll call the bar and tell 'em I quit." She scooped up the money and put it in her purse.

"That's my girl." Paul was pleased with himself. "Get yourself home and pack. A car will come for you in the morning to take you to the airport."

"When will I hear from you?" Things were moving at a very fast pace. As the excitement driving her impulsiveness dissipated, it was rapidly being replaced by uncertainty and fear.

"There will be someone to assist you all along the way. You won't see or talk to me again. In the unlikely event that we do bump into each other, you are never to acknowledge you know me to anyone. Understood?" He put his hands on her bare shoulders and looked her in the eye. "I'm opening up an abundance of opportunity for you. A new life making good money in a great career. It's a chance to travel the world. Offerings like this come around but a few times in life and often extract a high price. This one comes at the expense of your life here and whatever this is that we have."

Becky's eyes betrayed her and glassed over with tears. "You're not in farm equipment, are you?" She smiled, her voice a little shaky with emotion.

"No," Paul whispered. "You need to forget about me and who I am. Focus on my gift, and in return, do what I ask."

She sniffled, and he kissed her forehead. She pushed into him, wrapping her arms around his body and laying her head against his chest. "I'll miss you."

———

Parker had already surveyed the crowd of reporters while the president was speaking. He found the one for whom he was looking. Trey Perkins was a blogger and podcaster from Raleigh-Durham, and one of Parker's biggest critics.

Trey was by no means a neutral reporter. He was an activist that promoted every special interest cause in the state. He gained a following during the gay marriage movement. When the opportunity to expose Crockett's affair presented itself, Trey positively reveled in it. He couldn't resist the opportunity to point out the hypocrisy of Crockett's affiliation with religious, conservative Republicans while engaging in an extra-marital homosexual affair. The irony of the situation was that Crockett never took a position against the legal recognition of homosexual unions.

But this did not matter to Trey. He didn't care that in the process of exposing the affair, he ruined not only the political ambitions of Steve Crockett but the lives of his wife and stepson too. He was fighting a war for legitimacy, and casualties would be necessary.

Trey was standing near the back of the room, close to the cluster of television cameras. He was far from the major news outlets' Washington correspondents seated at the front of the room. His dark hair was on the longish side, and his beard was defined but immature. No tie adorned his white shirt, which was unbuttoned at the collar. His look was somewhat professionalized by his khaki pants and suspenders.

He stood waving his notepad in the air, hoping, but not expecting Parker to call on him. Though he never outright named anyone associated with the Stowe for Senate campaign as his source, Trey had insinuated that he'd learned about the affair from someone on Parker's team. It was a lame attempt to discredit Parker and kill two conservative birds with one stone. In reality, he got the information from the jealous ex-lover of Crockett's campaign manager. The truth in these situations was rarely as useful as a well-positioned misdirection.

Parker stood at the podium. "Trey Perkins, your question, please."

Trey was caught off guard but recovered quickly. "Yes. Trey Perkins, *Raleigh-Durham Tonight*. Senator, you ran as a conservative alternative to Rodger Hall. How do you believe your supporters at home will react to your announcement?"

He was so predictable, thought Parker. Hype the conflict, ignore the substance. "I represent all the people of North Carolina, not just the conservatives. If I followed your line of thinking, I would only vote to confirm conservative Christians for cabinet positions and males for judicial nominations. It's a good thing that I don't follow your line of thinking.

"America is a diverse group of people. It isn't hard to find things that separate us from one another. I choose to focus on inclusion and the things we have in common. I can't do that if I'm trying to silence those with a different opinion or point of view."

Trey felt the sting of the rebuke, especially in such a public forum. Undaunted, he forged ahead with a follow-on question.

"You can't please everyone, Senator Stowe. To stand for some-thing, you must stand against its opponents. Take, for instance, gay marriage. Are you for or against giving gays and lesbians having the right to marry?"

"I am for allowing adult men and women the right to love whom they choose without the threat of discrimination. But before marriage was recognized by any form of government, it was established by God as the blessed spiritual, emotional, and physical binding of a man to a woman. If as a society we feel it necessary to recognize a same-sex union to protect it from being denied access to certain benefits, then that is a choice the citizens of each state should be able to make. However, I believe that calling such a union a 'marriage' is a mistake. Those unions, while representing the same feelings of love and commitment, are empirically not the same as the Biblical union between a man and a woman. People are smart, and you cannot tell them that two things are the same when they clearly are not.

"Just as denying equal protection under the law is an affront to homosexual couples, so is elevating a homosexual union to the same status as a heterosexual marriage an affront to many people of religious conviction. The key to resolving most issues lies in respecting the other person. We need to make an honest effort to understand what others are seeking to achieve even when we do not agree with their methods." Parker was done with Trey. "Next question."

A seasoned veteran of the Beltway press pool threw out a question before the others could inhale to shout theirs. "What legislation will be first on the agenda?"

"No piece of legislation can fix our problems. I'll focus on passing bills after the committees are organized and I visit with my peers. I want to better understand where we all can find common ground." Parker wanted to reinforce the message that working together was more important than writing laws. The culture of "doing" was putting up a fight.

"Are you abandoning income gap reform? Where does that fall in the list of priorities?"

"I'm not abandoning anything. But as I was so eloquently reminded at this morning's meeting, there are ninety-nine other men and women in the chamber. They are leaders with their own minds and agendas. They have earned the right to be heard. I intend to embrace them all. We'll figure out priorities together."

Referring to the morning meeting was a mistake. Now the press would be reminded of the gathering. More than one of them would be wondering why Senator Thach was conspicuously absent. He looked for a friendly face, hoping for a softball question.

However, it was not to be. The hounds had caught the scent of bad blood, and there would be no throwing them off the trail.

Julian Mossberg from a conservative-leaning cable network got a question off before Parker could pick a reporter. "Senator Stowe. What kind of reaction did you get from Majority Leader Thach this morning?"

The words hung in the air. Parker had anticipated the question, yet it still unsettled him. He disliked just about everything the current majority leader represented. Like it or not, Mike Thach was a powerful man, one with whom Parker knew he'd have to work. That meant he could not allow his personal feelings to creep into his answer.

"The majority leader has spent almost thirty years in Congress representing the people of Illinois. He's participated in the operation, strengthening and perpetuation of a system dominated by two political parties. Let's face it, this situation, my situation, is a freak of American election politics. It's the kind of stuff that makes good novels. No one places a bet on this kind of long shot.

"I could not have imagined or scripted that my vote would be decisive in determining the power structure of the Senate. For whatever reason, I have been given this opportunity in this place and at this time to be something more than I aspired to be.

"I could have taken the easy path. I could have done what was expected by the leadership of both parties. But when the landscape of the election was settled and I found myself alone with the choice, I could not do what was expected just because it is the way that things have always been done. I must stay true to my values and principles.

"I have a career I love. I didn't leave that life behind to run for office because I wanted to be part of something I believed was working well. I ran for office to be a voice for positive, constructive, and enduring change. Not just change in the sense of direction or ideology, but a change in the sense of restoration, revival, and renewal of what it means to be a united people.

"To his credit, Majority Leader Thach gave up some of his personal time and listened to me this morning. He currently has not embraced my vision, and that's okay. I respect his skepticism as it is born from his experience and wisdom. These are things that have served him well throughout his years.

"Nevertheless, I see a different way. I see new possibilities to solve our challenges. There will always be room for Senator Thach at the table should he choose to accept the invitation."

Parker was suddenly tired. Emotionally and physically tired. He wanted off the stage and to end the conference. There was still the *60 Minutes* interview to do. Looking at Jason Tuttle, he got the nod telling him it was okay to call it done.

"I have taken up enough of everyone's time this evening. I want to thank you for coming. Goodnight, and God bless."

CHAPTER 30

Miranda had watched the press conference in yoga pants and a tee-shirt as she assembled enchiladas in a casserole dish. She longed for home every time she made her abuelita's recipe. Miranda missed her dearly, even though she had passed nearly thirty years ago.

She was proud of Jack Archer and admired his courage. He wasn't sour or angry. He had helped Wade get it together after his tantrum in the car. The president's reception of Parker was remarkable too. Miranda found a respect for Marcus Jenkins that she would have never thought possible. She thought back to her conversation with Jason the night before. He had been remarkably accurate.

Parker did have a way with people. They wanted to be around him. She thought to herself that her job was about to become much more difficult if the new standard for being electable was Parker Stowe.

Now that the food was prepared and the kitchen clean, she needed to prepare herself. With a glass of wine in hand, she headed to the bathroom for a soak in a tub filled with the scents of cherry blossoms and vanilla.

Despite his drinking, Paul remained careful and focused as he left Becky. He wound his way through the alleys and back into one of the bars, where he ordered a final beer. Finding a dark corner of the room, he took stock of the people around him before exiting through the front door into the early evening twilight. Being November in Texas, the night was cool but not cold. Crowds of people would soon flock to the area to party away their Saturday night. Paul pulled out his phone.

"We need to meet. I have a job for you. Be at the usual place in an hour."

Paul disconnected the call, opened the back of the phone, and removed the battery and SIM card. He tossed the battery in a nearby trash bin, wiped the phone of fingerprints, and walked to Marine Creek. He found a suitable spot to dispose of it in a pool of muddy water. Hailing a cab, Paul returned to his office.

He made the rounds, checking on the few staff that were still there. After retrieving his personal items from his desk, Paul locked his office and then headed across the sky bridge to the parking garage. He climbed three flights of stairs and exited the stairwell on the floor just below the top level.

The garage was all but empty of cars. It was reserved parking for employees. He traversed the deck to its east corner, observing his surroundings for anyone who might remember seeing him later. As he approached the corner, a man dressed as a security guard rode up on a bike to meet him.

"Good evening, sir." The guy sounded official.

"Evening, Elton." Paul was polite. "Thanks for meeting on such short notice."

Elton climbed off the bike and rested it against the side of the garage. The two men stood next to each other and looked over the side of the structure. To the east of the city was the Trinity River.

"There's a girl named Becky Lang in Weatherford. I need her out of the area and near Derick. Is that fool still stalking Stowe?"

"As far as we can tell, yes." Elton headed the team assigned to Rockport family surveillance, but officially he was just director of security services. Most people thought he was a glorified rent-a-cop. "Who's the girl to you? What's the plan?"

Paul looked at Elton and smirked. "She's nobody. Just some bartender I've been tapping for a while. She's nice and all, but I need to get her out of the area. She ain't hard on the eyes, and she's the right age for Derick." Elton nodded. He had helped relocate several of Paul's affairs and understood the drill. The only difference this time was the angle with Derick. Two problems, one solution, he thought. Paul continued. "I want her on a flight to Raleigh tomorrow morning, first one out. Pick her up and settle her in the apartment you guys have been using to keep tabs on Derick and Annmarie. Give her the company car and all. Put her on the payroll at Rygart as a quality control specialist. One hundred and four thousand per year. Get her trained and official in her new job."

"How long before we cut her loose?" Elton inquired.

"She gets six months in the apartment, and use of the car as long as she stays close to the kid. She can keep the job, but that will be up to her supervisor after we're done with her. Make sure she understands after six months, she's standing on her own."

"What happens if it doesn't work out with the kid?"

Paul huffed. "When's the last time he got laid?" Elton shook his head and smiled.

"Junior reached out to me today. Wanted to know where we stood on Stowe. They see him as a big problem," Elton said. "He indicated the FBI is investigating a credible threat."

Paul reflected on this new information. His job was to protect the integrity of the organization and the privacy of the family.

Lawrence and Floyd wanted the kid in the family fold, if not in the family business. Becky was meant to pull him back from the edge. This obsession with Stowe could ruin everything.

The doorbell rang at seven minutes past ten, and Miranda glided down the hall to open it. The preparation of food sparked a nesting instinct in her. The bath oils had softened her skin and made it fragrant. She felt as femininely sexy as she looked.

Jason, on the other hand, felt completely unprepared for their date. Though he had showered and changed, it did nothing to relieve his exhaustion. There was no way for him to hide it despite his excitement to see Miranda again.

He had neglected to get flowers earlier in the day and had no luck finding any at this time of night. He did, however, see a liquor store and retrieved a rather nice bottle of Pinot Noir so he did not show up empty-handed. Jason was not a drinker but had taken notice of what she ordered the night before. He hoped it would be well received. It was.

"You didn't need to bring anything, Jay. I know it's been a long day." She leaned into him, and they kissed briefly. It was less awkward than the night before. His fatigue loosened his otherwise reserved manner, and he was less guarded in his ways.

Jason smiled, "And you don't have to fuss over me. Look at you! You look like a million bucks!"

Miranda felt the heat of her blush. She smiled and giggled like a schoolgirl on her first date. She put her chin on her chest and looked at him with doe eyes. Batting her eyelashes and in her most Texan accent, she said, "Oh Mr. Tuttle, I'm sure I don't know what you mean. This old thing is just something I threw on."

Her attempt at charming humor and disguise of her blush worked fabulously. They both had a good laugh at the unabashed flirtatious display. She took his coat and they walked down the hall to the kitchen, where she retrieved two glasses and a bottle opener.

"I'm not much of a drinker, Miranda."

"You sure you don't want a glass? This is an especially nice bottle."

"No thank you, but please go ahead. I'm sure it will put me to sleep, and I want to enjoy our time together."

She smiled and put one of the glasses back in its place. "Can I get you something else? I have tea, juice, some soda, maybe water?"

"You have tea? Impressive. Sweet or unsweet?"

"Now what self-respecting Southern girl doesn't have tea for their guests?" She laughed. "And since I'm from Texas, it's sweetened. May I pour you a glass?"

"By all means, do." Jason was smiling and he felt less tired, though he was moving slower than usual.

"How'd the interview go?"

"Long," he replied. "Parker didn't really need me, but I stayed because he asked me to be there."

"It went well, though?" Miranda was curious. She would watch it tomorrow night but liked to look behind the curtains.

"I think so. The energy around him is high right now. He's set the bar, and it seems like the whole world is trying to catch up. Did you watch the press conference?" Jason wanted her analysis.

"I did! I thought he did great. All of them did. It seems like he's brought out the best in Jack. I actually found Jenkins to be, well, presidential. He's going to need more coaching on how to handle the press. They kind of got away from him."

"You're right, and he knows it."

"It wasn't a disaster. I thought he handled the questions well. He just lost control of the pace and order of things."

"I was surprised how fast Jack and the RNC got on board. Wade seemed particularly ticked off when you left the White House."

"He was, Jay, trust me. But Jack is a very reasonable man, and he wants what's best for the country. There's no gain in fighting Parker. I think he admires him, even after the beating he took from him this morning. The thing about Jack is that he takes criticism well. The embarrassment stung, but the message was not lost in the delivery. He will be a strong ally for Parker."

"Parker felt bad about that."

The timer on the oven beeped, and Miranda checked on the enchiladas. They were done. "Ready to eat?"

"Yes, ma'am."

Miranda had a small table set for two towards the back of her house overlooking the greenway. It was complete with a candle and her best china and perfectly romantic. Jason's appetite swelled as the aromas of her cooking more potently filled the room when the oven opened. Though he offered to help, she insisted he sit and let her serve him.

"It's not a power thing, Jay. It's traditional and cultural. If it were expected or demanded, it would be different. In this context, it is a way of showing you honor and respect. Don't rob me of that. Just appreciate it for the gift of the heart it is."

Her statement was honest and open and an unintended level of self-disclosure. She felt vulnerable. She knew she had feelings for Jason, but they were undeveloped. It was not the right time to reveal them.

Jason was deeply moved by her candid expression and felt the weight of its meaning on him. "You see, it's only been a day, and I'm rubbing off on you." He smiled largely as she placed the plates on the table.

"What do you mean?"

"Your explanation just now. It was transparent and pure. You need not be ashamed or afraid. I am grateful for your gift. When people seek first to demonstrate honor and respect toward one another, it is seldom rebuked."

Miranda relaxed a bit. Jason stood as she took her seat and pushed her chair in for her. "Thank you," she said as he returned to his seat. "I must have hung out with the wrong people growing up. You and Parker are about the only people I know who are like this. I need to move to North Carolina."

"We are all programmed to be this way in our relationships. Watch young children. This is how they are with others. Open and real about how they feel and their intentions. We learn to be guarded and reserved as we grow up."

She thought about what Jason said for a moment. Reaching back in her memory, first to when her nieces and nephews were little and then to her own childhood, she exclaimed, "You're right! Where do you get these insights? It's amazing how simple this stuff is when you think about it."

"Lots of people think that way, but few put it into practice. Sometimes we have to unlearn bad ways rather than learn good ones. Haven't you had those moments when you look at a child and think to yourself, why can't I be that free, that open, and make it that simple? You can. You were created to be that way."

Once again, Miranda was both captivated and inspired by Jason. She was falling for him fast despite herself. She took another bite of her food in hopes of encouraging him to continue. Taking a sip of her wine, she said, "You still haven't told me how you came to know this stuff."

"It wasn't just one person or event. Most of the credit I give to my mother. She introduced me to Jesus and made sure I got to know Him. Everything else kind of fell into place from there. My Bible became my guidebook to life. When I found myself sideways with the world, I would go searching to see how God handled it."

Miranda had little affection for organized religion and was beginning to be sorry she had pushed Jason for his source of insight. "Not sure I'm following you, Jay."

"What makes the Bible great is how dysfunctional its characters are. Its chapters and verses are filled with very flawed people. Their stories show the best ways, God's intended way, to deal with any issue a person can face.

"For example, a few moments ago, you surprised yourself with your openness. Yesterday you admired me for mine. But you need only look to Genesis to see how God deals with concealment. What was the first thing Adam and Eve did when they realized they were naked after eating the apple? They covered or concealed themselves. God did not teach them to do that. And when He came looking for them, what did they do? They hid from Him. I've come to understand that the point is that hiding things is not how God intended us to relate to Him or each other. Concealment is a learned behavior."

Miranda was still not convinced. She was, however, more interested than she was a few moments earlier. "Okay, I get what you're saying. How can you be so sure you have interpreted its meaning correctly?"

"That's where observation and personal experience come into play. I have observed that my relationships work best and that the relationships between others who I admire work best when they are underpinned by openness, generosity, and respect. I have also observed that the worst relationships are riddled with deception, egotism, and contempt, which seem to be learned behaviors."

Her instincts were telling her that there was a simple truth to what he was saying. Something in her was still fighting against it. She found the struggle exhausting. Jason could tell he was losing her interest.

The time was moving quickly, even if he wasn't. His full belly and the long day had him yearning for sleep. He stood to clear the table and asked if he could refill Miranda's glass.

"Why Mr. Tuttle, are you trying to get me drunk?" She jested with him, trying to lighten the mood.

"Not quite my style, Miranda. But I'm getting tired and have just enough left in me to visit with you through one more glass of wine. It's my way of keeping track of time without checking my watch and being rude." He flashed her a smile, enjoying their banter.

"In that case, fill 'er up. I'll slow down to keep you longer. How's that openness working for you now?"

"Just fine, Ms. Cortez. You revealed you like me enough to want more time with me." He stood next to her with the bottle. She bit her bottom lip, closed her eyes, and eliminated the gap between her and Jason. The kiss lingered, and time was lost to them both.

"Hold that thought," she said. "Go sit on the couch. I'll be with you in a moment."

She excused herself, and Jason did as he was told. The couch was deep, and the brushed cotton was soft. The last thought Jason had as he fell asleep was to ask Miranda if the cushions were filled with real goose down.

When Miranda found Jason asleep, she smiled. "I guess I do get to keep you longer, Mr. Tuttle," she whispered. After she removed his shoes, she got a blanket and covered him up. Still smiling, she floated down the hall as she retired to her bed for the night.

CHAPTER 31

Sunday mornings were always the hardest part of the week for Derick. This one was no exception. When Annmarie was on an upswing, she wanted to keep it going and would party while he was at work. The place would be a disaster area upon his return. When she was down, she'd try to medicate away her sadness. This would leave the apartment in a different but equally intolerable state of disarray. It was usually better during the middle of the week when he was home and she was fresh from one type of therapy session or another.

Given her chipper mood the previous morning, he was sure he'd find the apartment looking like the common room of a college dormitory at the end of exam week. There'd be red Solo cups scattered about, some still holding the remnants of whatever beverage they held. There'd be bottles and cans too, some filled with cigarette butts because she can't bring herself to ask her friends to smoke outside.

Pizza boxes, chip bags, and open containers of dip that went funky from being left out overnight would complete the scene. Hopefully the only person in the apartment would be his mother. A few times he'd found people still partying or passed out on the couch. He was convinced that if he ever found someone in his bed again, he'd be facing a murder charge or two.

These people she called her friends were a far cry from the high-society crowd with whom she used to run. They were all damaged and broken, chewed up by life circumstances and bad choices. She met them at her various support groups. As the saying goes, birds of a feather. He didn't understand how groups of crazy, depressed people could possibly help one another when they were incapable of helping themselves. The last place he wanted to be was around other angry, broke, lonely people.

Without fail, as he opened the door to the apartment, it was there. The scattered remnants of the train wreck from the night before. Annmarie's bedroom door was shut. He was not about to go in there, not in his mood. If she was dead, there'd be nothing he could do about it anyway. And though it had never happened, if he found her in bed with someone, he'd have to be committed to an institution himself.

He started by opening all the doors and windows, hoping to air the place out. For good measure, he checked his hiding place under the cabinet by the sink. His items were still secure.

During the next two hours, Derick seethed in a fit of deep anger, made worse because every major television station was running interviews with Senator-Elect Parker Stowe. His step-father's campaign had fallen apart at the hands of that bastard. All his mother's assets were frozen until the bankruptcy was complete and her divorce from Steve Crockett was settled. When his grandfather had cut him off from the trust fund, he lost his ability to buy fancy toys and live life large, but his standard of living was not severely affected. His mother's money was more than enough to keep him well above his current state of existence. But now things were different, and he loathed being poor.

By ten-thirty, the apartment mostly resembled the place he'd left the night before. There were three large bags of trash in the breezeway outside the door that needed to make their way to the dumpster. All the surfaces had been wiped clean, the carpets and furniture vacuumed, and floors mopped. The dishwasher was loaded and ready to run after he finished his coffee and bagel. He was tired and should have been in bed long ago. He needed rest before returning for another twelve-hour shift.

The cell phone on the table began to bounce and dance with vibrations. It desperately asked to be calmed by his acknowledgment. He looked at the caller ID. It was Floyd.

"Hello." Derick was defeated in his tone.

"Hello, Son, I got your message. I'm glad you called." Floyd loved his boy deeply and didn't care why Derick had reached out to him. It only mattered that he did.

"Thanks for calling me back, Floyd." Derick's best memory of a father figure was of Annmarie's dad, his grandfather. Though he'd called Floyd "Dad" after he'd married Annmarie, post-divorce he chose to call him by his name. It was an overt attempt to remove the esteem of Floyd's role in his life.

"I know I haven't always been the best dad, but I'm here for you."

Derick felt the tug on his heart, but the bitterness surfaced first. "Well, you're getting an opportunity to prove that. Mom's in a bad way. We're struggling. All the assets are frozen with the campaign debts and divorce litigation. I had to drop out of school. My so-called friends ditched me when the money dried up. I got no one else but you. That's how bad it is."

Floyd felt the prick of his barb but didn't fight it. "What can I do to help? Would you like me to come out there or just send money? I'll do whatever you want."

"I need you to take care of Mom. I can take care of myself. I just can't take care of both of us. You owe her that."

"Owe me what?" Annmarie had risen and come down the hall just in time to catch his last words. "Who's on the phone?"

Derick cursed under his breath at being confronted by his mother. "It's Floyd, Mom. I'm talking with Floyd."

"Tell that asshole to go to hell!" Annmarie was obviously hungover and in no condition of reason. "Just hang up on him. He's done enough damage in our lives."

He pushed the button and hung up on his father. "I need help, and I've got no one else. I can't keep going like this. I should have been asleep an hour ago, but instead, I had to clean this place. I'm running on empty, Mom."

Annmarie looked at Derick. He was no longer her boy but a young man carrying a burden he was ill-prepared to shoulder. He was handsome like his father had been when they first met, and strong too. Much more capable, she thought. The manual labor he was doing in the distribution center had chiseled his physique. The few extra pounds he'd been carrying in their life of excess were long gone. He outwardly showed no weakness or flaw, but the desperateness in his voice was that of a person at his limit.

"I'm sorry," she said. "This is all my fault." Her tears were large. "I didn't want this for you. You should be finishing school, not taking care of your crazy mother."

"I shouldn't have called him. It was a mistake." He was trying to comfort her, knowing that her self-imposed guilt would likely lead to a harsh low on the bipolar roller coaster. "We're doing alright. I'll figure it out."

He walked out the door and grabbed two of the trash bags. As he turned around, he nearly bumped into a young woman who seemed a little lost. She was very attractive. Long, dark, shiny hair framed a symmetrical face holding two of the bluest eyes he'd ever seen. Her lips were full. Combined with her still tanned skin, they provided both texture and contrast that highlighted a bright, white smile.

"I'm sorry," he said. "Please excuse me."

"Well howdy, good look'n!" Her Texas drawl made her even more adorable. A few years working the Cow Town bars had taught her how to endear herself to just about anyone, especially men. "No harm, no foul. I'm your new neighbor, Becky Lang. Fresh off the plane from Texas."

"I'm Derick Harris from," he paused, "from across the hall." He was painfully aware of being dirty, sweaty, and carrying two rather large bags of trash that smelled like a barroom floor.

"Must have been one heck of a party. Sorry I missed it." She tossed her head back to move the hair out of her face and flashed that amazing smile at him again. "Maybe I can get an invite to the next one?"

If a girl like Becky had come on to him this strong six months earlier, he would have had her making wedding plans by sunset. This morning, however, he was stripped of his money and status, which in his mind, at least, changed everything. No way that a girl with her kind of potential would get involved with a guy in his situation.

"Trust me, it wasn't your kind of party. It wasn't even mine. I'm just dealing with the aftermath."

"Wow, sounds like quite a story. Maybe you can tell it to me sometime? I don't know anyone in this town and could use a friend. What do you say, buy a girl a drink later?"

Derick smiled a spontaneous, uncontrived smile. He shook his head in a nod and laughed. "Okay. I'm up for it, but it'll have to wait till tomorrow. I work a night shift tonight and won't be home till about eight-thirty in the morning."

"Tomorrow then. Not sure what time. My schedule is a little unsettled right now. Is it alright if I just knock when I have a few minutes?"

He wanted to tell her yes but did not want her stumbling unprepared into his mother's world. "It might be best if I just come to you. My sleep schedule is all messed up. I'll come by around six and try again later in the evening if you don't answer."

"Deal. Look forward to it, Derick."

"I will, Becky." There was a little more pep in his gait as he shuffled off to the dumpster.

During this exchange, Elton had been standing off to the side with her baggage. In the era of Uber cars, he came across as nothing more than a driver. Derick paid him no attention. As they entered her new home, Elton finally spoke. "You waste no time, do you?"

"A friend used to tell me time is money. The opportunity to connect presented itself, and I took it. He's better looking in person than the pictures you showed me. Did I do alright?"

"A trained professional couldn't have done better. You're a fast study and have natural talent." The two of them had been together since four in the morning when he drove up to her mother's modest home to get her. "Remember what I told you. You have six months, and then you're on your own. Save some money—get a car and then an apartment. I'll be in town for a while to help you get on your feet."

He walked to the table and picked up a cheap cell phone. "Carry this phone with you at all times. There is only one number programmed into the contact list. It belongs to me. Call if you need something, and don't call anyone else from this phone. I will pick you up at seven-thirty in the morning for orientation at your new job. You have two objectives, befriend Derick and establish yourself in your new career. Both are important and need to be your only focus. Questions?"

"Paul said something about a car?"

Elton picked up a set of keys. "Forget the name Paul. He's a figment of your imagination. Understand?" She nodded, and he continued. "There's a white Camry parked under the carport in the spot labeled 4606. It has a full tank of gas. I left some basic information on the table, including a map of the local area. There's some food in the fridge and pantry, but you'll need to hit the market soon. Go get freshened up. We have to get you a professional wardrobe for tomorrow. I'll be waiting in the car."

She nodded again and went into the bathroom.

As Elton stepped back into the breezeway, he dialed Paul. The voicemail was short and to the point. "She's settled and already made initial contact. You were right. There's chemistry. I'll be here a few days to keep an eye on things if you need me."

———

Hearing the tension between mother and son on the other end of the line, Floyd said nothing. When the call disconnected, he once again grieved the loss of his family. He'd failed at the one thing he'd most needed to get right. It gnawed at him.

Floyd didn't usually carry his failures on his conscience. There were too many of them. He'd learned early in life to pick himself up, dust himself off, and move on to the next thing. If he lost a friend, he'd make new ones. Pissed away money, no worries. He'd just make more. Floyd became good at the apology and sincerely tried to make amends for his mistakes, but he did not beat himself up when they weren't enough. Derick and Annmarie were the only two relationships he truly wished he could fix.

The car came to a stop at the crest of the drive, where he placed it in park. Floyd climbed the steps to the house for Sunday brunch with his parents. He decided to fly to North Carolina in the morning.

CHAPTER 32

Jason had awoken in the middle of the night and realized what had happened. He'd been embarrassed, but he couldn't just up and leave. He'd found his phone and texted Parker, reassuring him he'd be at the hotel in the morning to get him to the studio. He'd set his alarm for six, which was late for him, but he did not want to disturb Miranda's sleep prematurely. Finding his place on the couch once again, he secured another two hours of rest.

Miranda stirred at her usual time, ready to start her day. She quickly arranged herself, not wanting Jason to see her in any state of imperfection. She exited her bedroom dressed, makeup done, and not entirely surprised to find Jason already preparing to go.

"I'm sorry I fell asleep. I didn't mean to cut our evening short like that." He was endearingly sheepish.

"It's quite alright. You obviously needed the rest. I feel bad you slept on the couch when I have a perfectly good guest room. What time do you need to get Parker?"

"We need to be at the studio by eight-thirty."

"Good, you have time to eat."

"But I need to shower and change. It's probably best for me to get going."

"Nonsense." She walked down the hall and returned with a towel and robe. "Go shower and get ready for your day. Everything you'll need in the bathroom is under the sink. Give me your clothes and I'll wash them while you freshen up. Are you an eggs and bacon kind of guy or oatmeal and fruit?"

Jason knew he was being managed but did not fight it. "Whatever you're doing for yourself will be fine. You don't..."

She cut him off. "Jason, please. We're adults with crazy lives. This will make it easier for you, and I don't mind. I want to help. Do you like your coffee black or with cream and sugar?"

"Black, please," he relented.

"Flavored or just plain?"

"It's five o'clock in the morning, woman. You're giving me too many decisions to make. I'm not used to all this fussing. Whatever you do will be fine, trust me. I'm sure it will be more than I'd do for myself. You are gracious to do anything, and I appreciate your hospitality."

"Know that I don't fuss over just anyone, Jason Tuttle. Now do as you're told and give me those clothes so I can put them in the wash." Her look was coy, as if she were unsure if she'd taken it too far.

Jason was an easy target and did as he was told. Lilly had trained him well, and he knew when he was bested in a test of wills with a woman. The attention made him self-conscious, not unhappy. He secretly liked it. It had been a long time since someone had doted over him, let alone asked him what he would like for breakfast.

"I like you too, Miranda. I just don't know how to do this. Thank you for your hospitality."

Miranda exhaled. She hadn't realized she had been holding her breath. "Well now that we've settled that, get moving before you're late."

He went down the hall to the bathroom, where he undressed and put on the robe. By the time he delivered the clothing to her, she already had sausage in the frying pan and eggs scrambled in a bowl waiting to be cooked. The robe was white and not feminine in the least, but she couldn't help smirking at the image of him wearing it.

"Please Miranda, this is hard enough for me."

"But you're soooo cute!"

He scurried back to the bathroom as quickly as possible to groom, torn between the thoughts of wanting to spend more time with her and having spent too much time with her.

By six-thirty, they had finished breakfast, and Jason had restored his dignity by donning his clothes. He found himself thinking how simply wonderful it was to have a hot breakfast in a home with another person instead of a cat. He could get used to it.

They visited for a while longer over a final cup of coffee. As the clock approached seven, Jason started to get antsy. "Are you going to Texas for Thanksgiving?"

"Maybe. I haven't decided yet. I usually go for either Thanksgiving or Christmas, but not both. I prefer Christmas." The implications of the question intrigued her, and she found herself hoping for an invitation. "Why do you ask? What do you have planned?"

"My kids usually come home from school for the week, and we have family time, but they are getting older and living lives of their own. My daughter is in a fairly serious relationship, and she is going to meet his family for the first time. My son wants to go with a friend down to the Caribbean where he has family. If you don't have plans, maybe we can spend some time together?"

"That sounds like a great idea. Let's do that. Maybe I can come down to North Carolina and see you this time."

With their next meeting solidified, both felt better about parting. She walked him to the door, where their lips shared a few intimate moments. By seven-thirty, Jason was pulling up to the hotel and arrived back in the suite just in time for his third cup of coffee.

Parker looked at him inquisitively. "I guess you had a good date." It was a statement that felt like a question.

"It was a nice night. I fell asleep on the couch after dinner."

"Way to make a girl feel special."

"It wasn't like that."

"I'm sure it wasn't. I'm just giving you a hard time. I do think she's good for you. It's nice to see someone can shake you up and push you out of your comfort zone." Parker was sensitive to the fact that it had been the four of them before Lilly had died. Jason needed to know he and Roni were supportive of any effort to fill that void in his life.

"Don't you have better things to think about than my love life?" Jason was still processing through all his feelings for Miranda. The scrutiny he was getting from Parker kept it in the forefront of his thoughts. "Where are we with security?" Two uniforms had already been posted outside the door to the suite when he arrived back this morning.

"We're still watching the family," Bull chimed in. "The Capital Police won't put a detail on the dependents. That may change. The FBI is in Raleigh working with the locals to see if they can identify the threat."

Jason frowned and looked at Parker. He knew his friend was worried about his family. "Let's get packed and checked out. The sooner these appearances are over, the sooner we can get home."

To Parker's surprise, the studio was quite comfortable and offered technology that made him feel like he was in the room with the hosts. The interviewer with Fox spent considerable time talking about which senators he saw chairing which committees. Parker simply stated, "Each party will offer up a slate of candidates for each committee. I've given them guidelines. So long as they stick to them, the process should be fairly smooth."

This drew a flurry of other questions attempting to draw out the details. It would give the pundits something to speculate about until January. "What guidelines did you give them?"

He answered as vaguely as possible. "Very general stuff. No senator can chair more than one committee. No current chairperson or ranking member in their respective committees will be considered. I intend to shuffle the deck. Gain some fresh perspective. New blood, so to speak."

"And committee membership will look like what? Usually the majority party has majority seats on each committee."

Parker had foreseen this question as inevitable. "Majority membership will go to the opposite party chairing the committee. The whole point of this is to force the leaders to lead and not simply promote an agenda."

"Aren't you afraid nothing will get done?"

"How much is getting done now and for whom? Let's just agree Washington isn't working for most Americans regardless of party. If it comes to gridlock, I might take some heat, but I'm not in this alone. There are one hundred leaders in the Senate. We will succeed together or fail together. Either way, we will do it together."

The interviews at CBS and ABC went much the same but focused a little more on trying to nail down a legislative agenda. Would it be legislation focusing on regulating the income gap, immigration, tax reform, health care, gun control, or something else?

Parker was well prepared for these questions too. "What we do and when we do it will be a joint effort of the Senate, House of Representatives, and the president. I look forward to working with the leaders in the Senate as well as the other bodies to put an agenda together."

There was only one interview where Parker found himself aggravated by the process. While the host and producers thought it was a great idea, much to Parker's surprise, Mike Thach appeared in the same segment. The current majority leader came loaded for bear and he had no intention of being schooled by the freshman politician.

For a man in his seventies, Mike Thach had considerable stature and presence. The smile on his face was warm and inviting. His hands were visible and open on the desk before him. The tone of his voice was soothing and kind. The cameras loved him.

The host began with a question to Senator Thach. "Mr. Majority Leader, you were noticeably absent from the press conference last night. Senator-Elect Stowe indicated that you are not on board with his proposal to share control of the Senate committee structure. Is this true? If so, why are you opposed to it?"

"Well, I don't know that I'm exactly opposed to it as much as I have my doubts about how effective it can be." The majority leader was also well prepared. "At least when there is a clear majority in power, important legislation can be pushed through the Senate by force if necessary to get things done."

"Except for the filibuster," added the host. "With limited exception, sixty votes are required to break one, right?"

"Yes, and that's another good reason the current structure works. There are already checks and balances in place. This idea of the senator-elect is novel but unnecessary. Quite frankly, I believe it's disruptive."

"Senator-Elect Stowe, your response?"

"While I understand the majority leader's point of view, I believe I have a stronger case. I respect the senator's wisdom and experience, but I will also reject the notion that we must be divided and separated into groups by our differences to get things done. It is a recipe for disaster. We are increasingly segregating ourselves into opposing sides. What will be the flashpoint? The Senate was designed to temper mob rule but is increasingly demonstrating how close to it we are getting. Leadership has been determined by slim majorities for years and yet the party in power acts like they have a mandate to either wholesale block or support a president's agenda. It's no longer working as it was intended."

Thach jumped into the conversation without being prompted. "Senator Stowe chooses to see our long-established two-party system as divisive. I see them as groups of people with common interests and philosophies. It's the senator-elect who's choosing to segregate us." The majority leader was excellent at turning the tables. While it appeared he was attacking the idea, he was in reality attacking the character of the person.

Parker didn't bite. "There is nothing wrong with choosing to associate with like-minded people. This great nation was founded in part on the premise of free association. So much so that it made it into the Bill of Rights. However, our connections to all our countrymen should come before our connections to party special interests. I have a duty to represent all the citizens of North Carolina, not just the ones who voted for me, or with whom I associate, or especially that funded my campaign. And what I do affects all Americans, so I'm mindful that my obligation extends beyond the borders of North Carolina."

In Thach's mind, he'd scored a point. The population of North Carolina was about ten million. He figured most of them were now wondering who represented them specifically if

Parker was representing all Americans generally. He could hardly contain himself but refrained from speaking. He preferred in this case to let the host make his point.

"So, Senator Stowe, are you saying that if it made sense to close a military base and there were two to choose from, you would vote for the one in North Carolina if it saved the federal government more money than closing the other? Wouldn't that cost jobs belonging to people who may have voted for you?"

Thach was thinking it was like watching one of his paid thugs beat that jock in the alley all over again. *Always get someone else to do your dirty work is lesson number two, Senator Stowe,* he repeated to himself.

No flinch from Parker. "Everything else being equal, yes, I would. Service and sacrifice to one another come in many forms. Sometimes we think of them only in terms of risking our lives like our first responders and our military do. But we are all called upon at one point or another to contribute to the welfare and betterment of our society. Sometimes it's in the form of jury duty or even just paying our taxes. During World War Two, our grandparents who stayed at home sacrificed many comforts in the form of rationing. They grew victory gardens in support of the war effort. Citizens have been asked to sell ancestral homes and businesses to make way for highways and railroads. Teachers and civil servants often sacrifice higher-paying jobs in the private sector to educate our children, provide sanitation and transportation, and keep us safe. If it is the right thing to do, then yes, I would vote for it, even if it is locally unpopular."

The host decided to shift the line of questioning. "Say you are successful in pulling all this together. What happens in two years when the next election cycle comes around and one party takes a clear majority? Do things go back to the way they are now?"

"I don't know. I hope not. I have faith that enough senators will like the new spirit of cooperation to resist coming back to this state of being. I believe the American public wants it because, in their everyday lives, they see teams that work and play more effectively together than they do as fragmented groups. It happens in our families, on our sports teams, and in our boardrooms. Teamwork and team play are critical elements to success. It's why our country is struggling right now, and other countries like China are gaining ground on us. They are working together better as a people than we are."

"Surely you're not comparing us to a communist regime. They play together because dissent is not tolerated. They kill or jail those opposed to the power structure." Thach saw an opening and couldn't help but insert himself.

"Their methods are deplorable, no doubt. Human history has proven them unsustainable. The Chinese are expanding their territory unchecked and their economy has been flourishing. It's not because they have better methods, it's because they are more united in their approach. A less mature team can beat a more advanced opponent if they are more cohesive in their play. We see it happen all the time. It is why leadership is more important to consistent success than our knowledge and skills."

Parker was talking from the heart, but unsure if he was making any ground. The majority leader was feeling in control and confident. He decided to press Stowe and see if he could extract a little blood. "The Senate of the United States is not a university lab where social experiments should take place, Professor Stowe."

"There are many ways to lead, Majority Leader Thach," Parker responded. "Lions, for example, choose their leader from amongst the strongest of the pride. If one of the younger lions decides he can do better than the established leader, all he must do is challenge him for control. It's a battle of physical strength and will. It's a hard way to live because the lead lion spends as much time defending his position as he does defining a path forward for the pride.

"A flock of geese leads itself differently. Geese know they can travel a longer distance as a team than they ever could as individual birds. They accomplish this because of the aerodynamic benefits of flying in that 'V' formation. It's like the concept of drafting when racing stock cars.

"The only problem is that the lead goose must work harder than all the others, just as the forward car expends more energy to maintain speed in a drafting scenario. For the flock to succeed, every individual goose must take a turn leading at the point of the 'V.' Otherwise, the entire gaggle is limited by the distance a single goose can fly by itself. Together, they are more effective than they are alone. This concept is so strongly part of who they are that if one bird is incapable of going on with the group, two others stay behind with it. No bird in the flock is ever left alone to fend for itself. They are all leaders, they all work together, and they all thrive.

"Our system allows us to choose our leaders without a physical contest. But nonetheless, we have this constant power struggle that distracts our leaders and consumes time, effort, and focus. We have of late been doing it more like lions than geese. Which way do you prefer, Mike?"

The majority leader was suddenly less sure of his standing in the debate. Stowe's ability to appeal to the instinct of a person and have them draw on empirical knowledge derived from their own experience was more powerful, he feared, than his rhetoric. He saw himself as a lion, but after hearing Parker's comparison knew it was better to live as a goose. He surmised that most watching the broadcast would be coming to the same conclusion.

Thach's pride could not accept the idea of conceding to the likes of Parker Stowe. He could not yield to his own better nature. From somewhere deep inside, a fiery desire to continue the fight burned. He slammed his hand down on the counter and said, "This is not a zoo, Mr. Stowe! We were sent here to solve problems."

Parker smiled. He had him. "This is where we fundamentally disagree, sir. A solution to a problem is a result. I believe we are sent to Washington to lead. It is our purpose. If we lead poorly, our results are poor. Maybe if we lead better, the approval ratings of Congress will increase."

Thach was losing the argument. Time to attack Stowe's character head on and expose him as a hypocrite. "If leading by example is so important, then what kind of example did you provide running your campaign? You won because your campaign or someone who supported it outed your opponent. You appealed to homophobia and self-righteousness to get elected. You couldn't win on the issues and so your inner lion bit the head off your opponent."

Now Parker was the one feeling the fire. He could feel the anger rising in a wave of heat from his gut to the tips of his ears. Focus. Breath. Love. "My campaign had nothing to do with outing Steve. I am neither homophobic nor self-righteous. Steve Crockett has a record of outstanding public service. He would have been a fine senator. His transgressions were against his wife. They are his to resolve with her and his God."

Parker was calm and measured. "Accusing me of tactics you use all the time says more about you than me. It's what's wrong with this town. It's why things must change."

The host thanked Parker and Thach, and the show cut to commercial break. Parker thanked the host and made a hasty exit out of the lion's den.

CHAPTER 33

Officer Fowler was irritated when she went to bed Saturday night. She had a fitful night's sleep, which did not improve her mood Sunday morning. Her afternoon with the FBI had been unproductive, and she was unsure how she would fit into the investigation going forward, if at all.

They secured all her work, thanked her, and after a brief interview that lasted about an hour, patted her on the back. They dismissed her, and that was that. The video from the various security cameras was sent to the FBI lab in Quantico, Virginia for analysis. Hopefully, they could piece together enough of the footage and angles to get a picture of the suspect. They were also able to secure the traffic camera video from the city but did not share it with her department. Apparently, information sharing would be a one-way street.

Meghan was a creature of habit and predictably had just finished her morning jog when her phone rang. She didn't recognize the number and almost let it go to voicemail. She thought better of it and answered the call.

"Officer Fowler?" The voice on the other end was male, pleasant, and professional.

"Who's calling, please?" Meghan was sure it was a telemarketer but was careful not to be rude.

"This is Special Agent Oscar French with the FBI. Is Officer Fowler available?"

Meghan was suddenly much more interested in the call but a little embarrassed for being elusive. "Yes, this is Meghan Fowler. I'm sorry for the twenty questions, but it keeps me from having to speak with a lot of solicitors. How can I help you, Special Agent?" She always thought the title of special agent was a little pretentious but probably because she envied it.

"I'm involved with the Stowe investigation. The lab in Quantico came back with a rendition of sorts from the various video sources collected. The problem is that it's not that great, and the facial recognition software hasn't matched it to anyone in the university or the North Carolina Department of Transportation databases. We're expanding the number of database searches but believe in employing multiple methodologies. Our experience tells us in situations like this, our guy is likely local. The picture just isn't good enough for the technology to give us a positive match."

"I guess the shows on TV make the tech seem better than it is." Even Meghan had thought that the lab would craft a good rendition from all the clips. She was a little surprised. "And I can help, how?"

"We'd like for you to start reviewing the matches the computer finds to be above ninety percent in probability. The computer takes the best facial matches and then factors in other known parameters like approximate height, weight, age, race, and location to prioritize potential persons of interest. Historically, we usually have our unsub on the list. It just takes some old-school investigating by human beings and a little luck to pull the needle from the haystack. Since you got closest to him, we think you should be involved. Your instincts got us this far."

It didn't take much flattery of her law enforcement skills to endear himself to her. She loved the chase, and the university force was just an early steppingstone in her career. She hoped to eventually make it to the State Police or FBI as an investigator one day. "When do you want me and where?"

"Can you be ready in an hour? I'll pick you up and bring you to our office in the federal building in downtown Raleigh. It'll be easier getting you in and out on a Sunday if you're with me." Oscar was well versed in the security of the building. Someone would have to escort Meghan everywhere. What he didn't disclose was that he was the special agent in charge, or SAC, of the Charlotte Field Office. Ultimately, he was responsible for the whole investigation. Meghan's work on the case had already impressed him, and the hour plus car ride would afford him the opportunity to get to know her better.

"I'll be ready. Do you need my address?"

"We're the FBI. I know where you live. See you shortly."

Back in the game, her dejected feelings were gone. Meghan raced to the shower to clean up from her jog.

At the beginning of the twentieth century, a person almost had to be caught in the act of committing a crime. Thirty-five years ago, the science of forensics had made it necessary for a criminal to clean up, so as not to leave DNA or other identifying evidence behind. In the technology-driven world of today, it was equally important to not leave electronic evidence. With the ever-growing networks of surveillance cameras and use of handheld devices, Paul knew it was almost impossible not to leave a digital footprint.

It was just a matter of time before Derick would be identified as a person of interest stalking Stowe. Paul couldn't let Derick go forward with his plan. He'd be caught. Big embarrassment to the family and the company brand. Paul would surely lose his job.

Killing Stowe would end the threat Derick's fixation posed to the family and business. Yet Paul had a more personal, and so for him more important, reason for wanting Parker Stowe out of the way at all costs. His income and power were derived in large part from the ability to navigate and influence the massive bureaucracy of government. Parker Stowe was threatening to dismantle the complexities of the laws, rules, and regulations that were the foundation of his success.

If Paul thought Stowe would simply stop with income gap reform, then plotting to have him assassinated would never be an option. Paul saw the future and knew there was a growing cry from grassroots efforts to make government simpler, less corrupt, and more accountable. Parker Stowe was just the kind of principled leader who could make that happen. He needed to be stopped before he could ever really get started.

Risk and opportunity were two sides of the same coin. The greater the risk, the greater the opportunity. If he could pull Thach into the plan, he would have leverage over one of the most powerful men in Washington. He'd own him. Failure would mean prison.

The three elements he needed to pull off an assassination were to first make the story believable, second corroborate it with the testimony of others, and third support it with the evidence. Credibility was the easiest. Like any good mystery story, he just needed the suspect to have motive, means, and opportunity.

Derick had all of them but opportunity. Becky Lang would be the vehicle to keep Derick away from Parker. Now he had to find someone else with all three. Someone he could nudge into murdering Stowe.

Lionel had made his billions by staying ahead of the needs of people, not by trying to shape them. In the same way that Cornelius Vanderbilt constructed a railroad empire and J.D. Rockefeller built an oil monopoly, Rockport was simply good at anticipating the need before it became one. Income gap reform was coming. Raising the minimum wage was not the answer and everyone knew it. It didn't solve the problem and it was laughable considering how wide the gap truly was. Raising taxes on the wealthy wasn't going to work either.

The ugly truth was that both of those measures hit the middle class far worse than the ultra-rich. They were unsustainable propositions. Lionel was not going to fight the inevitable. He would just use it to produce the next generation of businesses to service the needs created by it.

He asked Paul to have his team gather data on where the various holdings were vulnerable. How large were the gaps between the top and bottom of each entity? He also asked for research on staffing firms and outsourcing boutiques.

Perhaps the loophole would be to outsource the lowest-earning jobs to independent companies. Maybe he should be ready to invest in a few of these firms, or build his own? There were so many possibilities, but he needed to meet with Stowe. If done right, he might even be able to influence the actual legislation. He was in no hurry to make a move. It was early in the game, and time always favored those with the deepest pockets. Right now, he just wanted knowledge. The opportunity would reveal itself.

Derick fell into bed exhausted. If he was lucky, he'd get six hours of sleep before his alarm went off. He settled things with his mother as best he could and found himself thinking about Becky. She was amazingly attractive, but not in the artificially accentuated way. Those sapphire blue eyes against that deep, coffee-brown hair was a stunning combination, comfortingly familiar and dramatically distinctive at the same time. It was like finding large, cerulean crystals framed in rich, fertile earth. He found her accent sexy, not dumb sounding like some country drawls conjured. His mind began to reconstruct every detail of their encounter. For the first time in months, his last thoughts before he drifted off to sleep were not focused on ways to kill Parker Stowe.

CHAPTER 34

With their business in Washington concluded, Parker, Jason, Bull, and their new protective detachment sought their way south out of the District of Columbia. They hoped to be back home in time to catch the airing of *60 Minutes*, but still chose a slightly longer route on the return trip. Instead of taking Interstate 95, they opted to travel through the Shenandoah Valley down Interstate 81. It added about fifteen minutes of travel time, but it was both more scenic as well as advised by the USCP. If all went according to schedule, they'd make it home just in time. Roni, despite her desire to have family time with her husband and children around the table, had already given them the green light to eat dinner in front of the television.

———————

Oscar French was a big, burly man with thick hands that made him seem more like the stereotypical mob enforcer than a G-man with roots in New Orleans. His accent was not exactly Cajun, more like something from Chicago or New York. It only added to his Cosa Nostra image. He purposely told Meghan he'd be there in an hour and showed up twenty minutes early, just to see how easily she could be pressured. She was already ready to go. Her hair was in a ponytail. Though she wore a black shirt to hide it, he could tell that the tight weave was still damp by the dark area on the fabric where it lay. She had put some powder on her face, but no eyeliner or heavy makeup. Her lips were shiny with lip wax or gloss, but not colored, and so they were a natural shade of pinkish-red.

"Hello, Meghan. I'm Oscar French." He had a deep voice, and Meghan thought in another life he could have given Al Green a run for his money.

"You're early, Agent French." Meghan was still unaware of Oscar's title as SAC. She didn't see him as her superior but more like a sibling in the family of law enforcement.

"Do you need more time to get ready?" Oscar knew how to play the game.

"Nope. I'm ready to go. Lead on."

"Well, then I wasn't early. I am right on time. That's me in the black Yukon."

"Really? An FBI agent driving a black, American-made SUV isn't too obvious for you? You do watch TV, right?"

This evoked a smile from Oscar. He was glad to see her sense of humor and observation were both well intact. "I don't order 'em. I just drive what they give me."

"Me too, only mine is a five-year-old Chevy Impala, and I can't take it home with me. Don't get me wrong, it does the job, but it's nothing compared to this. I need to come work for the FBI."

"You are today." Oscar was pleased. "Let's see if we can nab us a bad guy. Then you can start dreaming of your own government-issued SUV, complete with lights and siren."

They continued their banter back and forth all the way to the Federal Building in Raleigh. The vehicle entered a barricaded lot through a gate manned by a guard at its entrance. They proceeded to an underground garage secured by a door that could only be opened by sliding an ID card and punching in a code.

As the door raised, Meghan commented, "You weren't kidding about it just being easier to come get me. This place is locked up tighter than Fort Knox."

"Every federal building is since Oklahoma City. The attacks on September eleventh only reinforced the need. Governments and the people who work in them have always been targets of malcontents. Technological advances require that we adjust our defenses from time to time. The trick is to still be able to conduct business with the public and keep the environment secure."

They entered the building through a locked door that required Agent French to once again swipe his card and enter a code. This time he looked into a camera and had to wait for an unseen person to manually release the magnetic lock securing the door. They went through another door and up an elevator, both requiring the badge and code. Every area was indiscreetly surveyed by cameras. As they exited the elevator into a small hallway, Oscar had to repeat the process one more time just as he did in the basement. He waited for the faceless person behind the camera to release the steel security door.

The work area was small, about the size of the squad room back at the university. It contained about a half-dozen cubicles, one office and a large conference room. There were at least two other doors for which Meghan could not conclusively identify a function. There were four people in the conference room, three men and a woman. Oscar and Meghan joined the others in the conference room. The occupants became a little stiffer and less relaxed. Meghan got the feeling all was not as it appeared.

"I thought an FBI field office would be bigger," Meghan probed.

"This is a resident agency office. The division field office is in Charlotte." Oscar answered the question as though he was prepared for it. That unsettled Meghan even more. All four inhabitants stood as she and Oscar approached the threshold.

"Relax, everyone," said Oscar. "This is Officer Meghan Fowler with the Wake Forest University Police Department. She's the one responsible for getting us most of what we've got." He then went on to introduce the others. All were special agents except Neil Anderson, who was introduced as the supervisory special agent.

"And who exactly are you, Oscar?" Meghan wasn't shy. "I'm guessing you've been holding out on me."

"I'm the special agent in charge. I work in the field office in Charlotte. This resident office, as well as about a half-a-dozen others like it, make up the division I'm responsible for leading. Neil runs this office."

"And what brings you all the way from Charlotte to personally pick me up at my apartment on a Sunday morning?" She was flattered by the gesture and intrigued by what it meant.

"For one thing, I wanted to meet you personally, Meghan. Your work on this case thus far has been quite good. Especially for someone with limited experience and training. Your Chief Moffatt speaks very well of you and your instincts."

Meghan blushed. Moffatt was a true mentor and friend. She'd have to thank him later. "I appreciate the compliment, Agent French, but I could have come to Charlotte to be interviewed. I'm sure you're a very busy man. Too busy, in fact, to justify coming out here only to meet me in person."

"Very discerning of you, Meghan," he took a breath.

"Threats on United States senators tend to end careers if they're successful. I'm near the end of my career, but these four agents have a lot of runway ahead of them. I owe it to them to make sure they have all the support they need to bring this thing to an uneventful conclusion."

His answer was good enough to satisfy her. "Where would you like me to begin?"

Neil brought up a computer-generated rendering of their subject. It was a good likeness of a young man, but she could see why there wasn't enough detail for the facial recognition software to make a match. No eye color, no real cheek, forehead, or mouth structure. It was just too generic to eliminate all the combinations.

Neil pushed a button and the monitor moved to the next screen. "We gave the computer some additional parameters to narrow the search, and we have approximately twelve hundred subjects in the pool. If we made good assumptions, statistically speaking, our guy should be in this group. Better than a ninety percent probability."

"If your assumptions are good." Meghan exhaled loudly. "Twelve hundred is a lot of people to research on assumption. Can you share that list of additional parameters with me?"

Oscar was watching and listening. It was Neil's show to run, and he'd let him work it. He hoped Neil would say yes to Meghan's request. She took nothing for granted.

"Absolutely." Neil looked at Special Agent Lynn Drake, who tapped a few keys on her laptop and read off the list of assumptions. "He's white or Hispanic, five foot eleven to six foot one, one hundred and eighty-five to one hundred and ninety-five pounds, eighteen to twenty-eight years old. The car was stolen in Raleigh and abandoned in Winston-Salem, so we limited residency to within fifty miles of the center of both areas. We excluded anyone whose whereabouts we could confirm."

"Wait. What?" Meghan was taken aback by Neil's last comment. "You had subjects in the pool that were eliminated because you knew where they were? How?"

"I can't reveal all of our sources, but suffice to say that anyone who was in law enforcement custody, a county morgue, or another database which could conclusively place them elsewhere at the time was pulled from the list."

Meghan grimaced at the realization of just how far the intrusive hand of government surveillance might be. Yet she was immensely impressed at how efficiently it could be employed to narrow a pool of suspects. "What about cell phones? Did you ping the locations of subjects in the pool?"

Neil looked at Oscar as if unsure how to answer the question. Oscar gave no indication about how to proceed. "If we could eliminate someone that way, we would have. It's rather unreliable since the phone could be off or purposefully left somewhere to create an alibi. It's more useful to look for phones that pinged a tower in the vicinity of interest during the time of the incident to see if we got a match to our list. Even that methodology is dubious since the absence of a phone's location does not mean a person of interest wasn't there. It's one of the reasons we believe your conclusion regarding the phone being a prop is correct."

Meghan suspected that they had already attempted to use the phone data but were unsuccessful. It didn't matter; nobody in the room was about to affirm her suspicions. "Where does that leave us?"

"With about two hundred and fifty people for each of us to research," concluded Agent Drake.

CHAPTER 35

Brett Greene was the newest and youngest member of the *60 Minutes* reporting team. In his mid-forties, he was chosen to interview Parker because the producers felt like he would connect with the new senator-elect. Both men held advanced degrees, were married with children, and were from the South.

The opening sequence highlighted Parker's path to the Senate and the historic nature of his deciding vote. Woven into the fabric of the account were details of his family life with Roni and the kids, his professional life with the Federal Reserve, and as a professor at Wake Forest. His lack of military service was mentioned, but his contributions to the intelligence community were also noted, which gave the piece equity. It touched upon his religious affiliations but was not critical of them. Parker felt as though it was a fair and accurate biography of his life to date. The interview portion of the video was shot in the suite.

"Why did you run for office? You have a nice life. Both you and your wife are successful and respected in your fields. Why take on the complications of public life?" Brett was good at his trade. The first question usually sets the tone for the whole interview. Come on too strong, and the subject would be defensive and reserved in his answers. Too soft, and the audience would lose interest and call it a fluff piece.

Parker smiled. "There are moments, way stations in the life of every person, where ability and accomplishment should be measured against the goals and objectives they set for themselves. I was in one of those moments and found myself satisfied. Roni and I have a relationship that exceeds every hope that I have had for a partner and helpmate. My children are capable, healthy, and God-loving people whose hearts are filled with kindness, modesty, and integrity. As a family, we have been blessed with abundance.

"I wasn't looking for the challenges of public office. I certainly never expected that winning would put me in the position I'm in now. But we are all purposed for something in this life. I believe mine is to serve the developmental needs of others. And so, I found myself running for Senate."

"That's kind of odd, isn't it?" Brett was a little confused and figured the viewing audience would be too. "I get how being an educator fills this purpose. I'm just not sure I see how becoming a senator does."

"For me, it's big picture stuff. It's less about what I do and more about how I think. Call it my sense of maturity. First, I learned how to lead myself in a way to be a good example to others. This led to opportunities to expand my knowledge and opened doors for me to take on professional duties. At some point, I was encouraged to teach others for a living. And then last year, a group of my students challenged me to go to Washington and try to teach here."

Brett kept him on the issue a little longer. "That's a big statement, considering the accomplishments of the people in this city. A little arrogant, maybe?"

"It would be very arrogant, except it's not what I wanted. It's what others wanted of me. I was perfectly happy with what I had. At first, I said no, but they persisted. They really got me when they said, 'We need leaders like you in Washington. What hope do we have if our best won't serve?' I didn't see myself as the best but realized that's how others see me."

"Hence the theme of service to others?"

"Yes and no. The purpose has always been service to others in my life. It's just forayed into politics. My time in the Senate is just the current vehicle through which that purpose will be filled. The same as being a husband, father, and professor have been vehicles through which I live that purpose."

"And where does this sense of purpose come from?"

Parker paused and smiled. "For me, it comes from God. I believe we were all created with a purpose. This country was created for a purpose. It's what gives meaning to life."

"You're not suggesting one has to believe in God to have a purpose, are you?" Brett caught a whiff of controversy.

"No, Brett, I'm not suggesting that at all. But a purpose is derived from a set of values. Values are woven into the fabric of everyone's life. They are the cornerstones of our purpose. For me, the example of Jesus's life as one of love, service, and sacrifice helped to solidify how I see my purpose. If you want to better understand how people will lead, see what values are reflected in their purpose. See how that purpose has been lived out in their own lives and the decisions they've made."

"What does this look like in reality, in your life?" Peel the layer back a little further, thought Brett.

"The founding fathers in the Declaration of Independence stated that life, liberty, and the pursuit of happiness are inalienable rights bestowed to all humanity by the Creator. These concepts are woven into the belief system of every American, so much so that values like liberty and freedom are touted by every man and woman running for office. But is that really so? How can you espouse to stand for liberty and freedom and want to restrict the ability of a woman to get an abortion or likewise restrict the right for someone to own a gun? The audio and video don't align. It seems like most politicians selectively apply their values when it suits their agenda. I support the strengthening of institutions that teach us how to value life so that we don't have to sacrifice liberty. We don't need to legislate restrictions on abortion or guns if valuing life is at the top of our hierarchy of values as both individuals and as a society."

"When you say institutions, you mean churches?"

"Churches, the family, our schools, the Scouts, and any number of other community-based programs. The institution is less important than the values taught through them. We have to agree that not all values are equal, decide what our common values are, and then how we will reflect them in the lives we lead."

Brett didn't miss a beat. "Many would say that America and Americans thrive because of a competitive open market system. Does that mean we promote greed as a value?"

"The value represented in the concept of an open market is liberty. Greed is not a value. It is a result, driven by the emotion of fear, specifically the fear of scarcity, not getting what you deserve. Or feel you deserve. Greed drives people to abuses of liberty for personal gain."

"So how do you prevent those abuses from happening?" Brett hoped Parker's next answer would provide a conclusion so they could move on.

"First, instead of trying to take values out of society, integrate them into our common way. Second, incentivize people to act in ways that are compatible with those values. Third, write common sense legislation. Laws need to be easy to understand and equitably punish those who willfully transgress the principles that support those values."

"Give me an example?"

"The tax code is a great place to start." Parker was at ease with the transition. "The Pledge of Allegiance ends with the statement that America is: 'one nation under God with liberty and justice for all.' The stated values are liberty and justice. Where is the justice that some should pay thirty-eight percent tax and others pay no tax? The only just tax is a flat tax."

Brett smiled. He'd hooked Parker and was ready to reel him in. "So is it just that the guy who makes twenty-five thousand per year pays the same percentage as the guy that makes one million?"

"It's the same percentage of each dollar, so yes. Only people who believe that it is fundamentally unfair that the man made a million dollars in the first place can say otherwise. And if they do, then they are in contradiction with the stated value of liberty."

"You're in favor of a flat tax? "

"I am so long as we state that both liberty and justice are two of our core values. It is the only way to be consistent."

"But won't that benefit the rich who have accumulated wealth already? Wouldn't they end up paying less, while people who make barely enough to pay any taxes would see their rates rise?"

"Under the current tax code, it would unfairly benefit the wealthy, which is why instituting a flat tax would require starting over from scratch. If I were to write the code, it would be a flat fifteen percent tax with deductions only for charitable contributions and mortgage interest. Those deductions would be reduced as income levels rise. For example, someone making less than sixty thousand per year could deduct one percent for each half percent made in charitable contributions or paid in mortgage interest up to ten percent of their total tax burden. A person making sixty thousand up to two hundred and fifty thousand could deduct one percent for each one percent made in charitable contributions or paid in mortgage interest up to seven-and-a-half percent of their total tax burden. The reduction in deductibility would progress with increased income until the deduction is not available at all. It is a system that is easy to understand, promotes investment in homes and charitable giving, and offers no shelter for the super-wealthy to hide from their tax burden. Best of all, it upholds both values of liberty and justice."

"What about the people who rent and can't afford to donate?" Brett let a little sarcasm slip into his tone. "You make it all sound so easy."

"No, it's not easy at all. Far from it. There are too many special interests who benefit from all the deductions that are allowed in the current code. It's why our tax code is over seventy thousand pages long. It's a perfect example of what happens when the legislative process becomes detached from our common values and the guiding principles that support them."

"Okay, Senator. Earlier in the show, we previewed your stance on the income gap and minimum wage debate. Isn't imposing an artificial limit on the earning gap between the highest-paid executive and the lowest-paid employee an infringement on the value of liberty too? What's the difference between that and your justification for a flat tax?"

"That's an astute observation, Brett." Parker was sincere. "The difference is subtle, but there is a difference. A progressive tax structure, in effect, penalizes success. By taking a greater percentage of every dollar earned at certain thresholds, it encourages the rich to invest in lobbying efforts to create loopholes. It's how we end up with a seventy-thousand-page tax code that still favors the super rich.

"However, my ideas about income gap reform do not penalize someone for being successful or rich. It simply requires organizations to justly recognize the contributions of all employees and not just those at the very top."

Time to switch topics, thought Brett. "What was the worst part of running for office?"

Parker inhaled deeply, sat back in his chair, and looked directly at his guest. The camera began to zoom in on Parker's face in anticipation of his answer. His look was tortured as he reached into his experience as a candidate.

"When I began my candidacy, I never believed I could win. I entered the race to simply influence the dialogue. I didn't have a lot of money or a political party behind me. I gravely underestimated the hope and faith my loyal supporters placed in me. I assumed that at some point, I would have to drop out of the race and was preparing to endorse Steve Crockett when he withdrew."

"So you categorically deny that your team had anything to do with the revelation of Crockett's affair?"

"Yes. I wouldn't wish what happened to him on anyone. I don't know who leaked the information to the press, but it did not come from me or my people."

"But you benefited from it, didn't you? After all, Senator Hall was sure to keep his seat so long as you and Crockett were splitting the conservative vote. He had no incentive to boot one of you out of the race."

"True, but if he knew I was about to drop out, he might have decided getting rid of Crockett would be preferable to me withdrawing." Parker wished he could take the statement back. It sounded defensive and petty. He had no evidence to support the allegation that Hall's campaign was the source.

"Are you implying that Hall's campaign may have leaked the story in hopes of keeping you in the race as the weaker candidate?" Brett had his teeth in Parker and was not about to let go.

"I am not accusing anyone of being the source but merely pointing out that there are plenty of others who could have anticipated benefit from the situation," Parker backtracked as quickly as he could. "All I'm saying is that my organization had nothing to do with leaking the story about Steve Crockett's affair. He made some mistakes, but I wouldn't wish the shame and humiliation of such a public revelation on anyone."

"Do you think Crockett got what he deserved?" Brett was going in for the kill.

"As an evangelical Christian, I believe we all, myself included, deserve to get a whole lot worse. I thank God every day for His mercy and grace. The subjects of my sin are different from Steve's but no less severe in the eyes of God. To God, it's all dirt, and we're all filthy." There was a sadness in Parker's eyes, which the camera picked up, a sincere pain for what Steve and his family endured.

Brett decided to double down. "What are Parker Stowe's sins?"

Parker smiled. "The same ones as you. The same ones as everyone. Pride. Anger. Selfishness. Desire. Laziness. Excess. Jealousy. They just manifest in different ways and at different times. We all carry them."

Brett decided to approach the subject from a different angle. "You're not traditionally conservative nor traditionally Christian, are you? Yet you are comfortable with both titles. Why?"

"Because I am." Parker liked where this line of questioning was going. "Traditional conservatives and Christians too often get caught up in apologizing for who they are or profess to be. I am what I am. Funny thing is that I think this attracts people to my brand of leadership. Too many politicians calculate their positions on gaining support from a political base and then move to the center to get the popular vote. It makes them look hypocritical and phony.

"I believe that the American voter is tired of backing people who can't be trusted to govern from a known set of principles. Candidates who promise something when running for office but never deliver when elected. I said from the get-go that I would be who I am regardless of the circumstance. It appealed to the voters. I don't want to label myself in generalities. Christian and conservative both mean different things to different people. I just want to be known as consistently trustworthy, thoughtful, and extraordinarily ordinary."

Brett laughed and found himself liking Parker. Not that he hadn't liked him when they started, but suddenly he was drawn into the signature sincerity of Parker Stowe.

"Tell me more about the concept of being extraordinarily ordinary. It's an odd phrase."

Parker became somewhat sheepish. "It means I don't ever want to project that I am better than anyone else or that I am above them because of my education, title, or background. Being extraordinarily ordinary is a desire to connect with people through our commonalities. We all love. We all want to be valued. We all struggle to manage our resources. We all want a better future for our children. We all seek to identify with something greater than ourselves. These are the 'ordinary' things that link us. The ones which matter most.

"Jesus did not lead by the tip of a spear or with a carrot on a stick. He did not lead by His position or with His power. He led with a love for people, not condemnation for their failures. He led with honesty and openness about His purpose, vision, and mission for being. He humbled Himself by living the ultimate life of sacrifice. Jesus is my best example of what it means to be a leader. I would consider my life well lived if

I could have but a drop of the influence His ocean has had on the world."

Brett saw an opportunity to press further, possibly against his journalistic training. "Surely you can't say that all of His impacts were good. Wars have been fought in the name of Jesus."

It was hard to tell if the frown on Parker's face was prompted by what Brett said or by the fact that he chose to say it at all. "Many of God's given gifts are used in Godforsaken ways. If humanity were capable of perfection, there would be no need for a Savior, and Jesus would never have had to come. Being a Christian does not mean being absent of sin or incapable of committing horrible acts. Just because the Crusades were prosecuted in the name of Christ doesn't mean that Christ would have approved of them. Believing what I believe about who He is and what He stands for, I'm quite convinced that he would not have approved."

No matter how hard Brett tried to get Parker to say something extremist, it didn't work. There was no backpedaling, no inconsistency, and no apology from Parker for his faith. As the program ended, Brett couldn't help but think that one day he'd be able to say that he interviewed the future president of the United States.

CHAPTER 36

Derick knocked on Becky's door shortly after six-thirty. He'd heard her arrive about an hour earlier, but he didn't want to seem too interested by showing up early, or even on time.

"I was beginning to think you forgot about my invitation." Her tone was playful, not accusatory. She flashed him that amazing smile to let him know she wasn't offended.

"Forget about an invitation from a pretty girl like you? Never." His confidence was building.

Becky was used to being hit on from working at the bars, but coming from Derick, it seemed more genuine, more mature. Acquainting herself with Derick was part of the plan, but now she wanted to get to know him. Maybe it was all the uncertainty of her whirlwind life change that left her longing for a connection. The reasons didn't matter to her now. She just knew she liked the idea.

"Are you hungry? What kind of place interests you?" Derick had some places in mind but wanted to see if she had any preferences.

"Actually, how do you feel about just hanging out here? I kind of had a long first day and don't feel like going out. I have some beer in the fridge. We can order pizza. Is that okay?"

"Fine by me. I used to go out a lot. I know a bunch of great places, but lately I've been much more of a homebody." He wasn't lying. Between the press coverage of his stepfather, his mother's mental health, and funds being tight, he'd been living a low-profile existence. Becky's allure was the first thing to overcome his instincts to withdraw in quite some time.

"Great!" She was so perky. A quality which only endeared her more to him. "How do you feel about bacon and banana peppers?"

"Tasty." Derick was too busy trying to sort through his new surroundings and didn't realize his answer sounded distracted. Her place smelled faintly floral, like clean laundry. Though the apartment was furnished and neat, no personal effects were garnishing any of the surfaces. It was more reminiscent of a hotel room than a personal apartment.

Becky began to second guess staying home and became afraid she couldn't hold his attention. "Will you order the pizza while I go and change? Since we're not going out, I'm going to get a little more comfortable."

Derick nodded, and Becky went into the bedroom to change. She'd been wearing jeans and a form-fitting sweater. She looked phenomenal, but he decided not to overthink the situation. Order the pizza.

As he hung up, Becky reentered the room and grabbed two Bud Lights from the kitchen. While Derick had admired her figure in her jeans and sweater, he was positively entranced by her display of sweatpants with the word PINK printed across the well-defined curves of her bottom. The tee-shirt seemed too small for a woman of her development to be wearing as it accentuated the ampleness of her chest. He was no longer concerned about life outside the confines of her apartment. He shifted completely back into the mindset of his former playboy self.

It was close to midnight when he returned to his apartment. Annmarie was asleep, and all was in order except for the odor of stale cigarette smoke. The mustiness of the room was in stark contrast to the sweetness of the place he'd just left.

He opened the patio doors and stepped back into the earthiness of the cool, autumn night air. There was a small bench on the patio, and he sat down. A set of chimes softly tingled in the shallow breeze. They made the only sound he noticed over the humming of the fluorescent security lights illuminating the parking lot.

Taking a deep breath, Derick could still smell Becky on his clothes. He'd wanted to stay longer, but she had to go to work in the morning. They had connected. He knew it. It was in the way she had looked at him as they shared their stories. He hadn't lied, but he hadn't told her everything either. They'd talked mostly about their mothers. She felt guilty about leaving her mom in Texas. He felt guilty about wanting to leave Annmarie in her current state of dysfunction.

He replayed the moment Becky had cuddled up next to him on the couch as they watched the movie. Her body was so warm. She smelled so good. Her hair was like perfumed silk of the finest grade. And those eyes, those deep pools of blue that drew him in with their mystery and promise. They were like beacons calling to him, luring him like the songs of the sirens. What secrets did they hide, and what wonders had they seen? The possibilities were endless.

Derick was high. Not from a drug or alcohol, but from his natural endorphins. Becky was his ticket to feeling good, feeling normal. She was making everything else in his life tolerable. Becky was simply intoxicating, and he'd consume as much of her as he could get.

As Becky's head hit her pillow, she was tortured. Seventy-two hours ago, she was with Paul. Despite her best efforts, she had indeed developed feelings for him. Sure, he set her up on this amazing career path, but the idea that she had been bought kept gnawing at her. Now that she was alone with the reality of her situation, she was looking back on the whole affair as transactional. She decided she was a whore after all. She was angry at Paul and herself.

Her thoughts drifted to Derick, whom she already liked. He was handsome, well spoken, and well mannered. She certainly could use a friend. But doing Paul's dirty work, especially under the weight of her current contempt for him, made her question her motives. Her conscience wrestled with her feelings for almost an hour before she finally succumbed to sleep.

CHAPTER 37

Floyd didn't confirm with Derick how he could help him. He toyed with the idea of calling him back. Things seemed especially bad, and he didn't want to make them worse. Floyd decided he needed to see his son.

The flight landed early Monday evening. By the time Floyd arrived at the apartment, Derick was already with Becky next door. With no desire to get into a confrontation with Annmarie, Floyd chose to observe the apartment and approach when she was not around. He watched her leave and decided to knock on the door. When Derick didn't answer, he sat in the parking lot and waited.

Three hours later, he watched as Annmarie unlocked the apartment and then stepped onto the patio to smoke before heading to bed. She still had an attractive figure, but he could tell she wasn't well. The way she carried herself was defeated, almost crushed under the weight of an invisible burden. His guilt welled up in him as he watched her stare off into the darkness. She'd fallen a long way from the girl he'd known her to be. He bore much of the responsibility for it.

There was still no sign of Derick. The clock in the dashboard of his rental passed midnight. He assumed his boy had grabbed an extra shift at the distribution center. He was about to leave when he saw Derick exit the apartment across the hall. It caught him off guard and left him no time to intercept his son before he entered his own apartment. Floyd cursed. But then as fortune would have it, Derick stepped out on the patio. Floyd decided he'd been given the chance for which he'd been waiting.

Derick was sitting on the bench with his eyes closed and head tilted back when Floyd approached. He was at peace with the world. There was no tortured look on his face. Floyd paused for a few moments just to look at his son. Derick was now truly a young man. He thought better of disturbing him and turned to leave when the silence was broken.

"Where're you going, Floyd?" Derick's voice was calm, not accusatory.

Floyd turned back around and looked at Derick. "Hello, Son. It's good to see you. I thought you were sleeping, so I was going to come back another time."

"I work nights, and Mom's asleep. Now's as good a time as any."

"Are you hungry? Can we go somewhere? I don't want to disturb your mother." Floyd was genuinely afraid to see Annmarie and take another dose of her wrath. He knew he deserved every bitter and harsh word she had for him. However, upsetting her and creating a scene would simply be another bad moment created between them. There were enough of those already.

"Yeah, why not? There's a twenty-four-hour diner down the street." Derick was in a good mood and capable, at least on the surface, of sharing a meal with his father. "Let me lock up. I'll be out in a minute."

Floyd returned to the car while Derick checked on Annmarie and secured the apartment. The ride to the restaurant was uncomfortable and tense for them both. Derick was strangely relieved to see his father and rather impressed that he came. At the same time, he was also having difficulty reconciling those positive feelings with his general attitude toward him. The conflict of emotions was utterly maddening, considering the daily emotional ride he was on.

Floyd was overjoyed just to share the same space with Derick. He was acutely aware of the fragility of their relationship. One misplaced word or phrase, one defensive posture, one insinuation of blame or judgment could seal him off from him for good. Floyd needed to be humble, more conciliatory, and more loving than he'd ever been with anyone in his life. The pressure he felt was immense.

They sat in a booth in the middle of the near-empty restaurant.

"Why did you come? How'd you know I'd even see you?" Derick's tone told Floyd a lot.

Floyd paused, contemplating his choice of words. "Because I love you, and I want to help. I didn't know if you'd see me, but I had to try. I've done a lot of things I'm ashamed of having done. Chief among them is not having been there for you. I can't change the past, but I don't want any more regrets. If there's something I can do for you now, I will."

The words resonated with Derick. There was no basis to trust his father, but he wanted to believe him. Floyd had been largely absent from his life, and all the difficulties of his current circumstances were woven with threads tied to him.

Floyd had been consistently reaching out to him week after week for years. He was here now. It wasn't like there was a crowd of people in his corner.

"Mom should be in a facility. All her regular doctors are doing is just drugging her, and I think it's doing more harm than good. She has high-highs and low-lows. The doctors call it bipolar disorder, but I think she just had a breakdown when

Steve's campaign imploded. She lost her husband and her money in a very public way. That made her look foolish. I can't afford what she really needs."

The experience Floyd had with private facilities was good. He came out each time clean, sober, and better equipped to deal with life's challenges. "If you can get her to go, I'll pay for it. How about you? What are you doing about school?"

"I dropped out. I had to take care of Mom and clean up the mess you and Steve made." The anger in Derick's voice was palpable.

"Where's Steve now? Are you in touch with him?"

"Don't know, don't care. He called me at school right after the story broke. Said he was sorry. Told me I'd better get home to help Mom. We had less than twenty-four hours to get our stuff together before the injunctions started being served and assets started to be frozen. It wasn't even an hour before the media camped out on the front lawn. The circus was in town, and we were the main attraction. The last time I saw Steve was the next day when he withdrew from the race."

Floyd frowned. "It must have been awful. I'm sorry I wasn't there to help."

"Your presence would have made things worse. Mom deteriorated quickly and spent a few days in the hospital. Your being here might have killed her. Could have pushed me over the edge too." Derick surprised himself with his self-awareness. He thought about the gun he'd acquired while his mom was in the hospital.

"Re-enroll for the spring semester. I'll pay for it."

"Won't that put you sideways with Lawrence and Lionel? After all, I've been excommunicated from the family church. Voted off the island. The Big Brothers kicked me out of the house." Derick's voice was laced with sarcasm. His loathing of the Rockport name was purposefully punctuated by his references to reality TV. He bet old Lionel woke up in a cold sweat when he made them. Derick smiled at the thought.

Ever the salesman, Floyd took the opportunity to align himself with his son. "I've got my own money, and it's no business of theirs what I do with it. I don't work for either of them. They hold no strings on my wallet or my life. Besides, I'm not happy with your grandfather right now for reasons I'll discuss with you at another time. Let's just focus on getting you and your mom into a better situation."

CHAPTER 38

The call with his boss went smoothly. As promised, Paul had delivered a stack of research outlining the potential exposure IFH had to income gap reform as laid out in Parker's book and speeches. Even with the minimum wage set at seven dollars and twenty-five cents per hour, there were few executives in the organization with base salaries exceeding six hundred thousand dollars. The executive compensation packages, which include bonuses, real estate, vehicles, and stock options, posed the greatest exposure. Lionel only drew a base salary of one dollar. Over the previous ten years, his non-cash compensation had exceeded two hundred million dollars.

Paul did not like what he was reviewing at all. He was one of the few whose salary did exceed the six hundred thousand mark. That was before the implications of his other perks. He stood to lose more than most, including even Lionel. The bulk of his boss's compensation was stock options. Paul had a lot of time left in his career and feared its earning potential was about to be severely stunted.

Lionel Rockport simply listened and absorbed the information. If he had any emotional response to the data, he didn't show it.

"Solid work, Paul. Thank your team. What else do you have for me?" Lionel was no longer on the yacht but at his estate in Florida.

"I got you a meeting with the senator-elect. It's the first Thursday in December at the Grand Banks in Raleigh. I sent your assistant the details." Paul held his breath as he waited for Lionel's response. Getting the meeting was difficult and changing it might prove impossible.

"Good," was all Lionel said, but Paul was sure he detected a hint of enthusiasm from his chief.

Officer Fowler was now firmly ensconced in the FBI's investigation. SAC French had worked it out with Chief Moffatt, who saw no downside to having one of his officers on loan to the agency. It would be good for Meghan's development. If she did not seek a career with the feds, she'd come back to the department with knowledge and experience he couldn't pay for her to get somewhere else.

The small task force divided the people of interest into four groups. The first group consisted of young men with known affiliations to fundamentalist groups. It then sub-divided them into radical left-wing and radical right-wing groups. While it was often assumed that violent groups tend to support conservative causes, the liberal left had its particular breed of nut jobs that chose violence to their end; the right did not have exclusive ownership of gun-toting crazy people with social-political agendas. According to what Meghan was seeing, the lunatic fringe existed about equally on both ends of the spectrum.

Since Stowe was more conservative than liberal, it was more plausible that should their unsub be politically motivated, he would be more akin to the left-leaning, Unabomber, Ted Kaczynski type than the conservative-leaning, Oklahoma City bomber, Timothy McVeigh persona. The task force didn't really care. They were all violent radicals and needed to be vetted. The agents desired a way to prioritize where to start working through the stack of suspects. In this case, the left-leaning wackos got to go first.

The second major group was comprised of individuals who could gain economically from the demise of Parker Stowe. This was a relatively short list. But considering the implications of the newly elected senator's widely publicized proposal to balance the income gap, it needed to be considered a strong motivating factor.

The next group consisted of people who could be connected to the senator-elect and have a personal motive to want him dead. This group was made up of people associated with his political opponents, his work at the university, and his family.

The final group consisted of people who had no apparent motive and could not be logically placed in any of the three previous groups. This group was the largest, but also posed the lowest chance of harboring their suspect. It consisted of young men with no obvious connection to the senator. These subjects fit the demographics of the unsub and met at least one other criteria, such as a record involving violent crime or threatening social media posts. Meghan saw the logic of creating such a group, especially in light of the increasing incidence of high publicity, random public shooting sprees. She cringed at the ability the government had to collect such data and attach it to individuals. Of course, she knew better than to ask how the FBI had obtained it.

On Wednesday afternoon, the name Derick Harris crossed Meghan's desk and piqued her interest. She was working on a stack of files from the third group when she realized this was the stepson of Steve Crockett. He was on the younger side of the age range. As a college student himself, he would have known how to perfectly blend into the background of a university campus.

Derick had dropped out of school shortly after the affair went public. The family's financial woes were public record due to the pending legal actions against Steve's campaign. There was also the sensational tabloid scandal involving Derick, the supermodel, and his link to his estranged father, a member of the very wealthy Rockport family.

The more Meghan dug into the life of Derick Harris, the more she became convinced she was onto the right guy. She located the apartment where he was living with his mother and the distribution center where he worked. They were both in proximity to the club from which the car was stolen.

She checked with his employer and found that Derick could not use work as an alibi for either the time of the car theft or the time at the university. His cell records could not be used to confirm his location either. It appeared to have been off for the periods in question. The search she ran of his credit cards, hoping to catch a transaction that might confirm or even eliminate him from the suspect pool, provided no insight. In her mind, the complete lack of any evidence of his location was almost as damning as if everything had led to him. It was just not possible to go twenty-four hours without leaving a footprint.

They had spent the day together interviewing doctors and touring several exclusive and very private facilities for Annmarie. Despite the circumstances that brought them together, Floyd was enjoying the time with Derick. They settled on a place north of the city overlooking Falls Lake. The staff there had reviewed Ann's case. They agreed with Derick that his mother was overmedicated and underserved in her current setting.

Derick was ecstatic to find a program that would treat her with minimal drug therapy. Floyd just wanted to make Derick happy.

"Thanksgiving is next week," Floyd tested the water. "Got any plans?"

"I hadn't thought about it. I suppose Mom will want me to come out. I didn't think to ask them at the center, but I assume that they do holidays with family. They said we're welcome anytime."

"You're welcome anytime. Your mother wants nothing to do with me." Floyd's tone was sad but laced with a harsh undertone, as if Annmarie's grudge was unwarranted.

"Do you blame her?" Derick felt the surge of anger well up in his body. "She says the only good thing that came out of crossing paths with you was me. Everything else was heartache."

"I blame only myself. I messed it up, not her. She is right though. You are the best thing that came from us. I wouldn't change one event if it meant not having you. I just wish I could fix all the stuff I did wrong. I wish I could do it again and be better for you and her."

Derick softened a bit. "Well, you're here now. It counts for something."

"I'm glad to hear that." Floyd smiled. "What about that girl across the hall you've been seeing? Does she have family here?"

"No. She's from Texas. Weatherford, I think." Derick's whole demeanor changed as he fell into thoughts of Becky. They'd gotten together again the night before, and he was completely smitten.

"Really?" Floyd's paranoia radar began to ping his gut. "What brought her out here?"

"Some job she got with an upscale hotel chain. Rygart's the name. She's in training as a corporate quality control specialist."

Floyd was well versed in everything Rygart. He'd brokered the acquisition for IFH when the patriarch and founder of the brand had suddenly and unexpectedly expired without adequate life insurance. It had been one of his first major deals. His radar had now locked onto a firm target, and his name was Paul Harper.

"How long has she been here?"

"This is her first week. It was just dumb luck that I happened to be outside when she arrived on Sunday morning. She's the whole package, Dad." The endorphins were saturating his brain. Derick forgot himself, but Floyd didn't miss a beat.

"She must truly be something for you to call me Dad!" He added a chuckle to lighten the observation and hide his growing concern.

Derick laughed too. "She is."

"Try to take it slow, Son. Remember you just met her. Things rarely turn out to be the way they first seem."

"Spoken like a true Rockport, Floyd." Derick snorted, and that was the end of the conversation.

CHAPTER 39

The conference room in the Federal Building had been set up as a command center since Thursday morning. SAC French had decided to office out of Raleigh for the time being. Everyone agreed that Derick Harris was the person of the highest interest in the case. French had returned from Charlotte with more agents to assist the local team. There were too few resources to surveil him and continue vetting the other suspect files. On Friday morning, everyone was in the office for a briefing except the two agents who were assigned to tail the only active subject of interest.

Neil Anderson started the briefing. "Derick Harris is the son of Floyd Rockport, who is the nephew of Lionel Rockport, one of America's wealthiest citizens. Floyd was married to Annmarie Crockett, the mother of Derick Harris. She is the estranged wife of Steve Crockett, whom you all know as the recently disgraced Republican candidate for United States senator. Crockett's opponents in the race were Democratic incumbent Rodger Hall and the independent candidate Parker Stowe. This is our connection between Harris and Stowe." Neil then yielded the floor to Agent Lynn Drake.

"We believe his motive is revenge. Harris was cut off from the Rockport fortune a few years back after a tabloid featured him with Katrina Brooks. He was able to maintain a semblance of his lifestyle because Annmarie is wealthy in her own right. However, her assets were frozen by the creditors of her husband's campaign after Steve Crockett withdrew from the race. Annmarie Crockett suffered a mental breakdown, and Derick was forced to drop out of college to look after his mother.

"From what we have gathered, Derick was primarily raised by his mother and is very loyal to her. We believe Derick is under a lot of stress. His targeting of the senator-elect is likely linked to a belief that the Stowe campaign is responsible for the leak about his stepfather's homosexual affair. He probably blames Stowe for his current circumstances."

Officer Meghan Fowler stood up and took over as Agent Drake concluded her portion of the briefing. She was too excited to be nervous. She jumped right in as though she'd briefed a room full of agents a million times before.

"We can't alibi Harris at the time of the car theft or for most of the day when the incident at the University Club took place. There is no record of a federal firearm background check, nor of his obtaining a pistol purchase permit as required by North Carolina state law. That said, we can't rule out his possession of a weapon. The most recent intelligence on him shows that his biological father, Floyd Rockport, arrived Monday from Texas. It appears that they are looking to get Annmarie into a private program to help with her illness.

"Floyd has also retained the Rosen law firm to represent Derick's interest in the pending bankruptcy litigation sparked by Crockett's campaign debacle. Derick appears to have a new love interest, one Rebecca Lang, who until recently resided in Weatherford, Texas. The suspect's movements this week have been focused on Lang and Floyd. No suspicious activity or interest in Senator Stowe has been noted."

Oscar French stood and shook Meghan's hand. He thanked everyone for their hard work and reminded them to stay vigilant. He concluded with two cautionary statements. The first was about the ramifications of a successful attack on a U.S. senator, especially this U.S. senator. The second was a cautionary statement regarding the Rockport family.

"The Rockport family is well funded and well connected. We have no direct evidence that Derick is the perpetrator. The only reason we are looking at him is that he fits the profile, and he has a motive. If Derick is our guy, you can be sure he will have the best lawyers in the country. Everything must be done by the book. We will not just strive to exceed the minimum standards required of us, but we will operate as though excellence is the standard. To that end, it is in the best interest of justice and the investigation that operational secrecy is maintained.

"If Harris or his Rockport relatives get a hint that he is a suspect, you can be sure of three things. The investigation will be shut down. Derick Harris will disappear. The FBI will deal with a mountain of legal filings and maneuvers to keep him from us. The AG himself has cautioned me about the career-altering implications of even the smallest divergence from policy, misstep in procedure, or mishap of action. I assured both him and the director that you were among the finest agents the Bureau has ever produced. You are up to the task. I have your back. Be safe."

Meghan suddenly felt the enormity of the situation, and it occurred to her that she was on the team for a less obvious reason. A reason she didn't anticipate. It was no coincidence that Derick Harris had ended up in her stack. If something went awry, she was to be the scapegoat.

Floyd's suspicions were confirmed Friday morning when by happenstance he and Elton were on the same flight back to Texas. Floyd made no overture to indicate he recognized the director of security services at IFH, but there was no doubt in his mind he was one of Paul's men. At a time when he and Paul were closer, Paul had warned him to be careful. Uncle Lionel had eyes everywhere.

Over the years, Floyd had successfully identified a handful of the people employed to watch the family. Elton had surfaced off and on throughout the highest-profile times of his life. He didn't actually know the guy's name or position, but he sure knew his face. This time, there were more wrinkles and less hair that had silvered over the years, but he was for sure one of Uncle Lionel's minions.

Given what Lawrence had told him before he'd left, Floyd was not surprised by his presence. He was now convinced that Becky was a plant. It might be time to pay Paul a visit since he couldn't be bothered to return his call.

CHAPTER 40

"I warned you about your father and uncle. They don't mess around when it comes to family and reputation." Paul and Floyd were sitting outside a bookstore on Sundance Square in downtown Fort Worth.

"So, the girl with Derick is one of your people." Floyd was purposely presumptive with his statements and direct with his questions. He wanted Paul to believe he knew more than he did.

"Yes, Floyd, she is. After I got your call, I sent her to distract the kid. I gave him something positive on which to focus his attention. What's the matter, you don't approve? She's like an eleven on a scale from one to ten."

"That's not the point. He's falling hard for her. What's your endgame, Paul? I don't think he can handle it falling apart. Which, by the way, it is likely to do, since it's all contrived. He's so desperate that he reached out to me for the first time in nearly five years."

"Then your father's plan worked, sort of, anyway. It's why he had us leak the Crockett story to the press in the first place. He wanted Derick to see he needed you. The supermodel thing was a flash in the pan. Lawrence used it to prove a point. He wanted to get Derick off the path you followed.

"Once he separated him from Annmarie's money, it wouldn't take long to appreciate and respect what being a Rockport means. Steve Crockett was just the poor bastard who gave us the opportunity by which to bring the boy back into the fold. By this time next year, this will all be a bad few months fading in the rearview mirror of life."

"What about Annmarie? She didn't deserve any of this!" Floyd was just barely capable of hiding his utter disgust with the whole affair.

"A casualty of war. A sacrifice for your son's future. Her lot was cast twenty years ago when she went to bed with you. You're helping her get excellent care. What else is there to do? Relax, buddy, you might even get her back when this is all said and done."

The smirk on Paul's face was nauseatingly disingenuous. Floyd wanted to reach over the table and beat his one-time friend and savior unconscious. "You should have let them kill me in that alley. We'd both be better off."

"Maybe, maybe not." Paul shrugged and sighed. He thought of his football days and a time when his knee didn't constantly ache. "We'll never know. It doesn't matter now. I chose not to be a casualty of that circumstance. Just keep supporting the kid and strengthening his bonds to the family. Don't get caught up in the ethics of the situation. You'll lose sleep, and it won't change a thing. I've got to get back to the office. Are we done?"

"Yeah, Paul, we're done."

They stood and shook hands as though they'd come to some great consensus. The only agreement they'd achieved was an unspoken one. Neither of them liked Paul Harper.

Floyd crossed the square and headed south on Houston Street towards the old church. He'd befriended one of the staff there through an AA meeting and hoped he would be available to pray with him. He felt the filth of his past all over him. It was clinging to him like old fry grease at a fast-food joint. There were only two places he knew to go to wash it away, and he'd sworn that he'd never set foot in a bar again. Under the weight of his culpability, off to church he went.

Paul met Elton in the usual place. "Status?"

"The kid is back on track. Becky's got him preoccupied, and Floyd's relieved the money stress. I don't think he's fixating on Stowe anymore. We do have a new problem. My source says that Derick is the lead person of interest in the FBI's investigation. No hard evidence, but they're watching him."

"Predictable. Where are we on the other matter?" Paul was looking for the way forward with his plan.

"I made contact with the subject. He has a strong motive. No means or opportunity."

"What about his will? If he is given the means and opportunity, will he do it?" For Paul, this was transactional. It mattered not that the details involved killing a human being.

"I think so. I found him at a bar in South Beach, drinking heavily. He's a train wreck. No job or prospects. Angry. He's totally bought the idea that Stowe or his people leaked the affair. Wishes he was dead."

"Who, himself or Stowe? We're looking for a murder before a suicide."

"I'm not convinced he can pull off either. He's in rough shape. We may have to construct both. I don't like it." The prospect of facilitating a plot using this guy was perilous. If something went wrong, it would land squarely in his lap.

Paul didn't like the idea any better than Elton. The opportunity to deflect the FBI away from Derick and eliminate Stowe didn't outweigh the risk. The guy was too unreliable.

"Share the information from Florida with our associates in Illinois. Let them figure out what to do with it."

CHAPTER 41

Mike Thach spent all week working with members of his caucus. He didn't find much support. Less than half the caucus would commit to him, and most of them owed him big favors. Zimmerman and Jenkins had been on the phones too. They had already convinced many that shared power was better than no power.

Junior knew his father was in a foul mood. He soaked in the hot water, waiting for him to ask a question.

"What is the status of Plan 'A?'" Senior had resigned himself that it was the only way to stop this madness and preserve his way of doing things.

"I got some information from down South. Gave me the location of a guy with a plausible motive in Florida. It will reek of conspiracy, and you'll be blamed because of the anti-gay rhetoric. It will martyr Stowe and blow back on you."

Senior closed his eyes. "There's another way. Derick Harris."

Junior knew Derick was the subject of an investigation but didn't see how to make it work. "I thought that wasn't going anywhere."

"It's not. The FBI is sure he's the guy but has no actionable evidence. The president and AG have cautioned the FBI to tread lightly because of the Rockport connection. My source says they won't touch him without hard evidence. They have electronic surveillance warrants but can't search his premises."

"I still don't see how catching Harris eliminates Stowe."

"It doesn't, and that works in our favor. The FBI will give up on him soon. In a few more days, it will have been two weeks of nothing. Thanksgiving is Thursday, and they'll end surveillance so everyone can enjoy their holiday. My source says the boy is a ticking time bomb. They think he's off Stowe because of a new girl and help from his father. I bet if we stress him, he will refocus on Stowe."

Junior saw the possibilities. No repercussions for his father. Paul would lose his job, but a dozen more just like him were in the network. The benefits of the plan outweighed the loss of a single, yet powerful resource.

———

The Wednesday afternoon briefing was uneventful. No other serious persons of interest had emerged from the ongoing research. Admittedly there were just under a dozen young men, including Derick Harris, on the shortlist. Most were there only because they had expressed an extremist political view. Some had a documented mental disorder. All had known access to a weapon and their whereabouts during the incident at the University Club could not be verified. All their motives were weak except for Derick Harris'. That kept him in pole position.

Interagency cooperation meant that the daily briefings would include members from the Capitol Police until the detail assigned to the senator-elect was no longer required. No threats had been detected by the detail, and by all accounts, the Stowe family was secure in their residence. Being the holiday week, the children were out of school, and the family planned to receive guests at the farm for Thanksgiving. With the passing of the press conference, the circus at the edge of the property had moved on to other stories. The Capitol Police detachment was confident the probability of action at the farm was low.

The FBI agents monitoring suspect Harris reported nothing out of the ordinary in either his routines or contacts. They made note of his relationship with Becky and checked her out. Nothing of concern there. It was easy to trace her situation back to her birth in Parker County. By all measures, except for her extraordinary good looks, she seemed benign.

Derick didn't socialize at work and used his phone to communicate primarily with Becky, his mother, and more recently his father. He had a Facebook page that he had not updated or visited since shortly after his stepfather's implosion. His email consisted mostly of junk and the occasional bill notification. He did, however, have quite a few nasty notes from various people who relished in his misfortune.

Though greatly diminished in volume the further from the scandal time passed, Derick was still being trolled, so he kept a low profile on social media for someone his age. It was ultimately agreed to cut close surveillance on him, as nothing had turned up to confirm their suspicions. Electronic monitoring would continue for a few more weeks. If nothing developed suggesting he has an undue interest in Stowe, they'd shut it down entirely.

———— ◆ ————

Miranda carefully selected her wardrobe for the trip. In addition to the several sweaters and jeans, she selected a long-sleeved, cream-colored, designer blouse. It was paired with a calf-length khaki skirt to wear to Thanksgiving dinner at the Stowe farm. She'd round the outfit out with a two-inch leather belt, a matching pair of boots, and some silver and turquoise jewelry.

She was a refined, educated, single woman with no dependents consuming her hard-earned resources. As such, she often surrounded herself with the luxuries of life. Her wardrobe came from premier stores, fashioned from the most recent designs and finest materials. Everything was chosen to accentuate her natural beauty and pamper her feminine nature.

She found herself struggling for the right sleepwear. She was staying with Jason at his home. Miranda was facing a conundrum: fashion, comfort, or modesty? She dated, but it had been an extremely long time since she had found a worthy suitor. She had chosen to go without rather than settle for something substandard. This afforded her the option of buying expensive night garments for the way she looked and felt in them and not necessarily for either seduction or modesty.

Now faced with the prospect of sharing a nightcap or eating breakfast across from Jason, she was torn between exuding enough of her womanly wares to be appropriately attractive and going too far, making him uncomfortable.

She had no desire to test his resolve at the risk of servicing her ego. The irony of the situation fell on her. She realized that the one man in years she'd consider giving her body was also the one least likely to pursue her for it. In the end, she chose a lavender set of silk pajamas and a matching full-length robe. Elegantly modest.

CHAPTER 42

Even in the early years, when it had just been Parker and Roni, Thanksgiving at the house of Stowe had always been a grand affair. When the table couldn't be filled with family, friends and neighbors were invited to share the feast. They tried to remain true to the communal celebration modeled by the Pilgrims and Native Americans in all the history books of their youth.

Out came the fine china, silver, and linens. Though dressing up was unnecessary, there was an unspoken understanding among family that the affair required more than just jeans and a tee-shirt. The children were bathed and shiny when they took their seats, and either dignified and respectful or sent to eat by themselves in the kitchen, far away from those who could behave.

Parker and Roni always worked together on the meal. As they got older, the children found their way into the preparations too. Parker oversaw the meats, usually a traditional turkey. But as the number of people increased through the years, a goose, a salmon, and a roast beef had been added to the table to accommodate the varied interests of their palates.

Roni prepared the sides. She created dishes ranging from the simplest of creamed corn to a more robust roasted garlic asparagus with a homemade hollandaise sauce. There were four potato dishes, two types of stuffing trays, and a myriad of vegetable offerings of all colors and types.

Though dinner would not officially begin until five-thirty with an opening dish of shrimp cocktail, guests were encouraged to arrive as early as two o'clock in the afternoon. This gave them time to enjoy various appetizers while watching some football, visiting on the porch, or walking the grounds of the farm. Enjoying an afternoon in the country was good living. Inclusive of family, the Stowes expected a few more than thirty souls to grace their table and bless their home.

Ever punctual, Jason's black Lincoln pulled into the drive at exactly two in the afternoon. The family was on the porch receiving their first guests. Roni had yet to meet Miranda and vacillated between excitement for Jason and grief for his departed wife. Parker assured her that her trepidations were unfounded. No doubt it would be different, but he had hopes that they would forge as strong a bond with Miranda as they had with Lilly.

When Jason and Miranda approached the stairs to the porch, Roni excused herself from a conversation with her sister-in-law to greet them. "Welcome! You must be Miranda. I'm Roni, Parker's wife. We're so glad you could join us."

"The pleasure is all mine," Miranda responded. She was looking forward to meeting Roni and the rest of the Stowe family. Her conversation with Jason from a few weeks past had had such an impact on her that she would never look at meeting people in the same way again.

Interactions happen with a purpose. They can sharpen both people like iron on iron. Her revelation about her motivations to know Jason had begun to transfer into other areas of her life. She was now looking to surround herself with as many people like Jason and Parker as she could.

She used to believe that being vulnerable with people was about sharing personal pain and sorrow with others. But now she had come to see vulnerability as being honest and principled in a world of denigrations and dishonorable ways. It was about being courteous and kind to others when they were being rude and devious. She came to see vulnerability as demonstrating a disposition of courage, not being a magnet for pity. That conversation with Jason had profoundly changed her perspective, and she understood it was for the better.

"Come, let me get you something to drink." Roni took Miranda by the arm as an old friend would do. They moved toward the house with Jason in tow. Climbing the stairs, they greeted Parker on the platform of the porch. The mood was familiar and comfortable, but for someone who was used to operating behind the scenes, Miranda felt palpably exposed.

"Welcome," said Parker. "We're so glad you were able to come."

"Thank you, Senator." Miranda sensed her formality. The salutation may have been overplayed, but she chose to err on the side of respect. It was an instinct that served her well, and she was grateful her parents had instilled it in her.

"Please, call me Parker. I suppose titles have their place, but not among friends." His smile was endearing. It dissipated the cautionary stiffness on which she relied when confronted with being in the spotlight. He smiled endearingly. "I hate to blindside you, but after you get a drink, I'd like for you to join me on a walk."

Miranda was instantly intrigued yet surprisingly uncertain. She caught herself looking at Jason, as if for approval. The stakes were higher because of her budding relationship with Jason. Parker and Roni were his closest friends. She was precipitously more aware of how emotionally invested she was in Jason. Her newfound self-awareness reset the calculus of the entire situation.

She looked Parker in the eye with all the self-assurance of a person who is confident in who they are and the value they represent. With a big smile, she said, "Give me just a few minutes to get settled, and I'll come find you. I look forward to it."

Proceeding into the house, Roni asked Miranda, "So what will it be? Wine? Beer? Cocktail?"

"I think something more benign for now. I'll have tea, or lemonade if you have it. Otherwise, just water will be fine. By the way, you have a lovely home."

"Oh, thank you. It's been years in the making, but it has become quite the perfect spot for us. I have apple cider and tea, but no lemonade."

"Tea will be great."

"Sweet or unsweet?"

"Sweet, of course. We are both proper Southern women, aren't we?" Miranda read the situation correctly, and the compliment landed perfectly on Roni.

"That's right, you're originally from Texas, aren't you? I think Parker told me. I'm sure you know we spent some time in Dallas. It's nice to see that Washington hasn't taken the South out of the lady." It was Roni's turn to compliment Miranda. The tribute was well placed and even better received. "I can already see why Jason has taken to you."

"Taken to me?" Miranda blushed. "He's a hard man to read, but I think he's more curious than taken."

"Come on, Miranda. You're smart, beautiful, and charming. And just so you know, he is very particular. He is always purposed in what he does and with whom he does it. Jason must see something special in you to have brought you here today."

If Parker's invitation for a walk had heightened her situational awareness, Roni's comment focused it. Getting Miranda Cortez to feel out of control was a hard thing to do. Somehow, it was happening. She took a deep breath, pausing to search for the right response. She thought about Jason and Parker and how they might respond.

"I know what you mean. He does have a different way of looking at things, doesn't he? Your husband does too. They are a unique pair." Miranda could tell her answer wasn't quite satisfying Roni. Playing to her ego, matching her kindness, or meeting her wit with her own would not thwart her. *Be transparent. Be empathetic. Be humble.* Miranda remembered a previous conversation with Jason and forged ahead.

"I guess I mean that I think he's special too." Roni smiled, and it encouraged her. "It must be strange to see him with another woman besides Lilly. Jason shared with me how much she meant to both you and Parker. I want you to know I understand how significant Jason is and Lilly was to both of you."

Roni brought her a glass of tea. "Thank you," she said to Miranda.

"I should be thanking you." Miranda furrowed her brow, somewhat confused.

"I mean thank you for understanding. Lilly was like a sister to me, and I promised her I'd look out for Jason. Without Lilly, I'm the only momma bear left to watch out for him. I've heard nothing but good things about you from Parker and Jason, but I had to know for myself." Ronni smiled sheepishly. "I should have trusted the boys' judgment."

Miranda felt the pressure dissipate. She was not only more aware of her feelings for Jason but also moved by the love Roni expressed for Lilly. It was something authentic. A love that transcended Lilly's death, and Miranda found it endearing. There was no one in her life like these people. Before she could think it through, she said, "I hope we can share a friendship like that one day."

Roni took her hand. "I already think we're off to a good start."

The gravel road descended from the back of the house and traversed a manicured lawn the length of a football field. At the end, it reached an old barn, where it intersected with another gravel road edging a field where crops had recently been harvested. All that remained were the stumps of whatever bounty the ground had yielded to its keeper.

"How much land do you own?" Miranda was making small talk.

"Almost four hundred acres. Most are sublet. We only retain from the main road down to the barn and from that tree line over to that stone wall." Parker pointed to the landmarks and gave her the general lay of the property. "I'm sorry to pull you away from the holiday, but I wanted some time to get to know you better."

The irony of the statement did not escape her. Miranda was hoping to get to know him better too. She was grateful he'd conjured the opportunity.

"I'm glad you did. I've come to admire you and your ways. Not too many can take on Mike Thach and walk away unscathed, let alone victorious."

Parker nodded as if in agreement. "Tell me, who did you want to be when you were a little girl?"

The question took Miranda off guard. She looked at her feet and the grayish-brown surface passing beneath them. Like sand through an hourglass, she thought. "I wanted to be a mother."

"Why?"

She didn't need to think about her response. "I wanted to be to a little girl what my mother was to me."

Parker probed a little more. "What about your mother so inspired you to want to be like her?"

"She has a strength about her. I don't mean physical. It is more of character and disposition. She left Korea and her family to be with my father. She worked in the family business and raised me and my brother. It was her idea to expand the business beyond lawns and pools. She is not loud or boastful. On the contrary, she is quite quiet. She simply does what needs to be done and always with a sense of decency and honor."

"Do you still want to be that person?" Parker realized he was treading into very personal space, but he needed her answer.

She looked at him as if to say, 'That question is a little intrusive,' but Miranda chose to answer anyway. "Unfortunately, that ship has sailed. I'm not likely to be a mother at this point in my life. I am an aunt, and I still aspire to be a role model. I still want to honor my mother's example."

Parker stopped and looked at her. "I think you do that well. This is going to be abrupt and will take you off guard. I wanted to ask if you would consider coming on staff as my director of communications. You are overqualified for the position, and I probably can't pay you what you're currently making. But given the circumstances, you're exactly what I need."

The question left her speechless. She again began to walk toward the barn, seemingly oblivious to Parker's presence and his proposition.

"I need some time to think about it. I'm honored you'd consider me for such an important role. I get the feeling it entails more than just being a press secretary."

"Without a doubt," Parker answered. "You will report directly to me. This is necessary not only because of your relationship with Jason but because I need your knowledge and experience navigating Washington. I have an obvious lack of both. You will be part of my inner circle and a trusted advisor. I will count on you to help me exemplify what good leadership looks like to my colleagues in Congress, the chief executive, and indeed the world."

"There are plenty of people with more knowledge and experience than I have. Why me?"

"Your sense of loyalty. It's in your blood. Even in the sharing of your divorce at the White House, it was apparent that loyalty is central to who you are. I trust Roni and Jason. I believe that if you decide to come on board, I can trust you too. Your knowledge and experience are important to me, but who you are is essential for this position. First and foremost, I want you on the team because I believe many of our core values align."

Miranda laughed. "I should have expected that answer." She wanted to say 'yes' right then and there but was not prone to making impulsive decisions. "When do you need an answer?"

"Soon. By the end of next week, if possible."

"Can I discuss this with Jason?"

"I encourage you to. He knows the details. If you come on board, there will not be professional secrets between the three of us."

"I'll get back to you before next weekend."

CHAPTER 43

Annmarie chose to stay at the apartment rather than go with Derick and Becky to the all-you-can-eat buffet. Thanksgiving turkey at the local cafeteria was more than she could endure. Being more accustomed to fine china, crystal, and candlelight at her holiday affairs, the thought of eating with the huddled masses off plastic plates under fluorescent lighting was intolerable.

The sadness of her life hung heavy on her. She was determined to hide it from Derick for fear of having the Falls Lake conversation again. There had not been a drink in days, and, without saying anything to Derick or her doctors, she had reduced her medication intake. It was important to prove to him that she could pull it together. Going to the cafeteria on such an occasion would make hiding her true feelings impossible. It would ruin their dinner.

When Derick first walked through the door, he thought he'd accidentally entered the wrong apartment. Everything was sparkling clean, no hint of stale smoke or a wayward dish on the coffee table. He was careful to be quiet in the event his mother was sleeping. His usual heightened sense of concern for her wellbeing did not compel him to check on her. His mom had been surprisingly functional the last few days. Maybe she was emerging from her state of despondency.

Derick's gait was less burdened and his steps jauntier; he was feeling rather hopeful in general. His mom was seemingly doing better. Floyd was easing the money concerns, and things with Becky were certainly moving in the right direction.

Becky had spent the afternoon connecting with Derick over dinner and canoodling while Thanksgiving window shopping. The mall stores opened for early Black Friday shopping, and Victoria's Secret was no exception. They didn't buy anything, but she kept asking what he'd like to remove from her body their first time together. He played along as if the wrapping mattered, but his focus was certainly not on the packaging. Saying goodnight was hard for them both. Now that he was home, he contemplated a cold shower.

The Thach family celebrated Thanksgiving in Illinois. The multi-million-dollar condominium overlooked a frigid Lake Michigan. Modern opulence best described the décor, and it felt cold and sterile. Everything was painted white. The floors were dark hardwood to add contrast. Color came from expensive contemporary art and designer furniture. Father and son stepped out to the balcony with cigars in one hand and an expensive single malt in the other. Mrs. Thach refused to have her museum smell like an ashtray.

Being at home and with the November wind blowing full force off the lake, the men felt reasonably sure their conversation would be private. For good measure, they left their phones in the living room.

"The FBI has pulled back. Just like you said," Junior prompted his father.

Senior responded, "Does he have the means to perform the task?"

"We assume he does. The FBI could not find a record of gun ownership, but that means nothing. It's not likely he would have followed Stowe if he didn't have a plan."

Senior didn't like the uncertainty even though his source at the FBI was sure the kid would do the deed under the right pressure. "The stress points are the mother and girlfriend."

"The wheels are already in motion on Mom. Searching for the angle on the girlfriend."

CHAPTER 44

"He's a one-term senator," Jason remarked. He and Miranda were sitting at the kitchen table enjoying the morning sun and coffee. Simon the cat had already determined Miranda was acceptable. He had perched himself on her lap so she could scratch behind his ears and under his chin with her perfectly manicured nails.

"Now why do you say that?" Miranda could speculate and probably be mostly right in her reasoning, but she wanted to hear it from Jason.

"There are a lot of reasons. The obvious is that he didn't want the job in the first place. He believes in term limits, for another. More personally, he's got young children and wants to be available to them as they grow up. As it is, his daughter will be off to college when his class is up for re-election. Strategically, he knows that he will become increasingly less significant after each subsequent election cycle. Neither party can break a filibuster or garner a supermajority, even with his vote. When his term is up, he's out."

Miranda frowned. "Then why should I get on this ship to nowhere? I have a lot to lose. It might be hard to get a good-paying gig when he closes shop. I like him and what he stands for… I want to follow him, but…"

Then Jason did something he rarely did. He interrupted someone while they were mid-thought. "Miranda, have you ever pondered holding office yourself?"

"I've played with the idea."

"This could be your opportunity to explore that interest further, prepare for it. By joining the team, you will be around people who are passionate about developing each other. Parker wants you on the team because he feels you can help make him better." Jason's statement added a twist to her perspective.

"That's kind of funny. I want to take the position thinking he can make me better." Miranda was almost convinced to join the team.

Jason smiled. "See, it's a win-win. You both feel like you're benefiting from the relationship. That's kind of the point, isn't it? Parker always starts with the relationship as his focus, not the circumstance by which it is forged."

Miranda decided she'd take the position Parker offered. The choice seemed to transcend pure logic. It almost seemed spiritual. There was something about joining this endeavor with these people that felt right with her soul. Now she was ready to steer the conversation in a more personal direction.

"Where does that leave us? I mean if I follow this path."

He didn't see that coming and was suddenly embarrassed. "What you do should not change who you are. I like who you are, so I'm not too concerned with what you might do."

It was Miranda's turn to be embarrassed. This time, she did not try to hide her blushing face. She reached across the small table and took his hand. "I hope you're falling for me, Jay, as hard as I'm falling for you."

"The subject has not presented any signs of suspicious activity." Neil was giving the last status update. He continued reciting the final mundane events of Derick's Wednesday just before Oscar French canceled the twenty-four-seven surveillance.

If Derick Harris was the guy, it appeared he had abandoned his plans after his misstep at the university. There was just no hard evidence of an interest in Stowe. The words 'career-ending situation' echoed in the SAC's ears as he remembered the director's admonition.

"The last thing we want to do is draw attention to this investigation. If he's not our guy and the Rockports get wind of it, they'll crucify us." French was careful not to make the team feel like they had failed. "There's two more weeks authorized by the warrant to electronically monitor him. In the meantime, I suggest we revisit other subjects of interest to ensure we didn't overlook someone. Cosby, do you have anything to add?"

Special Agent Cosby from the Secret Service and Detective Cobb from the Capitol Police had been receiving the reports and attending the briefings via conference call.

"We will still maintain a detail for a few more weeks," said Cobb. "We will reassess the need at that time."

———

Meghan found Chief Moffatt in his office. She was deflated. How could French give up so soon?

"I don't know, Meghan. The boy has re-enrolled in school for the spring semester. Someone who is planning that kind of future doesn't usually plot to commit premeditated murder. You have good instincts. They will continue to make you a good cop."

She sighed. "Maybe you're right." Letting go was not her style. She liked the senator-elect, and she truly felt his life was still in danger.

Derick awoke late Friday to the alarm on his phone. He lay in bed for a few minutes as his eyes adjusted. The mid-November afternoon sun was casting odd shadows about the room. Rays of amber light snuck past the various holes in the blinds and curtains.

It was a peaceful enough setting, but he found himself in a foul mood. He had to go to work. The week had gone by so quickly. Having seen Becky every night, he was annoyed by the prospect of a prolonged absence. His phone vibrated with a text. He grabbed it, hoping for something good.

Becky: Are u awake sweetie? Hope you slept well. Sorry I won't see you tonight. ☹ I have something to ask u. Come see me in the morn when you get home. Kisses

Parker hung up the phone. Miranda and Jason had decided to call and give him the news. She accepted the position, and he was feeling good about the team he was building. Things were coming together.

Throughout the week, he fielded no less than thirty calls from both sides of the aisle. Most of the callers were vying for the position of their choice in what they perceived would be the new power structure. He was saddened by the number of senators whose primary interest was in self-promotion.

Only two of the calls stood out for the right reasons. One was from an old-guard Republican and the other was from a freshman Democrat who was elected just two years earlier. The Republican from Idaho had four years remaining on his fifth term. He was the ranking member of the Senate Judiciary Committee.

After congratulating Parker, he told him in confidence that his current term would be his last. He did not run through his accomplishments or tout his importance. He simply said to Parker, "You have a daunting task ahead of you. There will be many who will stand in your way. This city doesn't like change, especially those chosen few with power who aren't elected. Tread lightly, but don't give up on your vision. Whatever I can offer in support of your efforts, know I'm here to help."

His call with the Democrat from Arizona was also remarkable. She candidly expressed her sincere disappointment in the Senate. Everything was about positioning and posturing. No less than ten, and closer to twenty-five, percent of the members had ambitions to be president. She watched her colleagues change long-held positions as soon as the current person promoting it was from the other side of the aisle.

"I didn't come here to be the chairwoman of this committee or that one. I'm not here to position myself for president, vice president, or governor. I just want the ability to do what is best for Arizona and the people of the United States. Your recent statements in the press have reminded me I'm not alone. I wanted to call and thank you for that. I don't have much to offer, but I do have a voice. If you can use it, call me."

They stood out for the right reasons. Now he hoped they would stand up when he called them out for those reasons.

CHAPTER 45

Derick was already in an excited state as he pulled into the parking lot of the apartment complex. He'd texted Becky several times, but she kept her surprise a secret. Normally as he entered the breezeway, he'd be steeling himself to deal with fallout created by his unpredictable mother. This morning, he had other, more pleasant thoughts on his mind.

Her last text told him to just let himself into her apartment. She had given him a spare key in case he locked himself out. Or so she said. Derick didn't question why she did it.

The message instructed him to bring two mugs of coffee to the bedroom. His mind dabbled in the possibilities. They had messed around, but he'd never been in her bedroom. She'd let him know that her interest in him was more than just a friend but was unsure how far she would let him go with her body. He knew by the way she flirted and dressed it wasn't modesty driving that behavior. It seemed to be compelled by a need to be in control and command respect. He was sure Becky carried insecurity behind her façade of invincibility. However, his illusion of her as a strong, powerful woman made her even more attractive.

A note by the coffee maker read: *Cream, two sugars. Come crawl into bed with me. Leave your underwear on, you're not getting lucky.*

His mind was swimming, and he was drowning in conflicting thoughts battling for supremacy. He was fully aroused at her instruction. It was his body's natural reaction to the prospect of being almost naked with the woman he desired. How could he conceal his enthusiasm? What if his state scared her, repulsed by his lack of control? If he'd been in this situation just three months earlier, he'd already have had his clothes off, lying next to her, proud his body was sending her a strong message about his intentions.

A lot had changed in the past few months. He was no longer as self-assured as he'd once been. Old friendships evaporated when the money dried up. This made whatever he was forging with Becky even more significant to him. He couldn't afford to be cavalier with the only personal relationship he had going outside his dysfunctional family. Somehow, he needed to pull himself together.

He entered her room and quietly placed her coffee on the nightstand closest to her side. She was truly beautiful lying in the morning sun that glistened off her rich, thick, still perfect hair. He went around to the other side of the bed, where he placed his coffee on the opposing stand. She was still asleep. He watched her back and bare shoulder rise with each slow breath she took. He removed his shirt but decided to remain in his pants for the moment.

Derick was suddenly aware of the November chill in the room. He was eager to get in the warm bed next to Becky. Careful not to disturb the tranquility of the pallet, Derick settled himself before she woke. He lay still on his back, feeling each breath she took as the covers softly rose and fell with them.

He closed his eyes and absorbed the heat radiating from her side of the bed, tempting him to draw closer. The scent of her hair and the aroma of her lingering perfume snaked through his head, inebriating him with her essence. He was losing himself in a cocktail of desire where the line between reality and fantasy met. The paralysis created at that moment was blissfully painful, and it seemed as if time could only be measured by the soft tempo of the breaths she drew.

He didn't know how long it had been since he first slipped under the covers. Maybe only minutes, but it felt like hours. If he waited too long, the coffee would chill. His mind returned to contemplating the request which she'd used to initiate this adventure in frustration. As he set his mind on other things, his body's eagerness waned. His confidence to proceed as instructed surged with his newfound control. He shifted towards her and began to kiss her softly where her neck fell into her back and shoulder.

Following the nape of her neck to her ear, he softly whispered, "It's the wake-up call you requested, Ms. Lang. Your coffee is getting cold."

She pinched his chin between her head and shoulder in a hug of sorts as she reached for his arm and wrapped it around her. The motion pulled him closer to her, causing his body to envelop her perfectly proportioned frame. She wanted to be cradled, to be held. She reentered the world of the conscious in the tenderness of a caress. It was a purely selfish moment as she had not a thought, a care, or consideration for the needs, wants, or desires of the person fulfilling hers. It was immature and reckless, but utterly satisfying in the here and now.

Derick fought hard for control as his body began to once again exhibit his craving to be with her. His mind was racing and settled on a congratulatory thought for having the foresight to remain in his pants.

He refocused. "Good morning, sleepyhead." He squeezed her with the arm she'd pulled over her. His attention was now split between thoughts of what to do with his other arm, now awkwardly tucked under the weight of his own body, and how to get further away from her before his anatomy betrayed him. "Your coffee is right there." He raised the arm she had previously wrapped around her and pointed to the mug on the nightstand.

She pulled his arm down and in a girlish tone said, "I'm not done cuddling with you yet."

He laughed. "Okay, but you have to let me readjust. My other arm is falling asleep."

She raised her head and let him slip his arm under her neck. She pressed her body into him, and he felt the satin of her top against his bare chest. Her legs rubbed up against his.

"What are you wearing? Do you still have your pants on?" she inquired, knowing the answer.

"Yes," was the best he could muster in response.

"Why? I'd have been okay with you in your undies. Didn't you see my note?"

"I went commando today. No underwear." He didn't know where it came from, but the lie seemed plausible. He just had to remember to conceal the elastic of his briefs when he got up.

"Is that a normal practice for you?" She chuckled but still expected an answer.

Crap. This is now a topic of conversation, he thought. "No, it is not. It's just been a long week, and I didn't have a chance to do the laundry."

They both laughed.

"Boxers or tighty-whities?" She was on a roll, awake and now obviously spirited.

Derick played along. It kept his mind occupied and his body in a semi-subdued state. "Neither. Well, both. Boxer-briefs. All the security and warmth of a brief combined with the freedom of a boxer. A most perfect combination." Time to take control of the situation. "Now what's this thing you wanted to ask me?"

She rolled over and faced him. "How would you like to play my husband for a few days?" She asked him the question with all the uncertainty of a prom proposal. "I have my first quality check scheduled for next week. It's here in Raleigh. I can do it alone, but then you won't see me all week. But if we check in as a couple, we can both enjoy a luxury suite together on the company's dime. Pretty awesome, huh?"

"Sounds great to me. What are the exact dates? I'll have to go to work Friday night."

"We check in on Tuesday. I have a bunch of special requests I'm supposed to make, one of which is an early arrival. We check out Friday morning. I get to try as many amenities and services as possible, including the restaurants, room service, and spa. My boss told me that I was to put the staff and services of the Grand Banks to the test." Becky's excitement was uncontainable.

"What's our story?" Derick was hot to the idea of revisiting a lifestyle he sorely missed.

"We're a couple from Texas celebrating our first anniversary. This trip is my gift to you." She punctuated the statement by gently running her index finger down the bridge of his nose. She smiled her big, white, Texan smile and met his gaze with her inimitably blue eyes.

"I'm all in." He didn't know what he was feeling, but it was the most intense, positive emotion he'd ever felt toward another human being. He wanted to get lost in her, ingest her so that no one and nothing could distinguish one from the other. It had to be love. He rolled her on her back and kissed her with all the tenderness of possession and passion of desire.

She felt the urgency in his body. "Wait a few more days. I promise you won't be disappointed."

Trey Perkins opened the manila envelope that had been delivered to his home with nothing that betrayed its origin. Inside was a single sheet of typed paper providing the address and schedule of Annmarie Crockett. A single date and time-stamped photo showed her exiting a mental health and mental rehabilitation center a few days earlier. Several dozen more of these packages had been distributed to select individuals, news outlets, and tabloids.

Annmarie slammed the door shut and ran to close the blinds. The flashes from the cameras created spots in her vision that were still affecting her orientation. She was visibly shaking. The reporters were right outside.

They were yelling questions like, "Have you spoken with your husband? Do you know where your husband is? Did you know he liked men when you married him?"

The apartment felt small and cramped. The pictures on the bookshelf reminded her of her previous life. It was happiness that now seemed trivial and false. Her son should be excited about building a future. Instead, he was caretaker to his forty-year-old catastrophe of a mother. Her life was a tale of steady and measurable decline.

Sure, others had it worse. She saw them at her meetings and therapy. There was a bed in which to sleep and a roof overhead. She didn't have to sell herself to eat or get a fix. But rather than taking comfort from those blessings, all Annmarie could do was see how much farther she had left to fall. For over twenty years, there has been one major setback after another. Each one more brutal than its predecessor.

The story Annmarie was telling herself concluded with the same undeniable fact as everyone else's story. She would eventually die. While most people fretted over the how and when of the inevitable end to their journey, Annmarie's focus was on the in between. She presumed that the rest of her existence would be filled with more of the same dramatic loss. The prospect of living to endure a worse pain than she was experiencing scared her more than anything, even death. She could only see a bleak and tortured picture of the future. It was a story she had no desire to play out to its natural end.

Derick was in the middle of texting goodnight to Becky. It was part of their routine when he went on break at the warehouse. When the man unexpectedly sat down on the bench next to him, his annoyance at the interruption was obvious.

"Becky Lang is not who she appears to be. Ask your father about her." With that said, he left as quickly as he had arrived.

CHAPTER 46

Derick was looking forward to the suite life. Twenty-four-hour room service and someone to clean up after him for a change. The spa was full service, and he would be treated to the works. There'd be a massage and skin treatment. He'd get a manicure and pedicure. His hair would be styled and fashionable for the first time in months.

There would be a round of golf and a game of tennis. Then time in the hot tub with Becky. Ahh, there was Becky. The jewel in the crown. She was so incredibly sexy with those eyes. He couldn't wait to lose himself in her.

Sure, the mystery guy at work had rattled his cage. He'd texted Floyd and asked him to call him when he got up. In the meantime, he wasn't going to let the cryptic admonition interrupt his fantasy. Unfortunately, something else did.

Driving up to the complex, he saw the lights of the police cruiser and the news trucks at the edge of the property. With his sense of concern heightened, he thought, *They found us.*

The apartment still being clean and in order provided some relief. He went down the hall into his mother's bedroom. She wasn't there. He called her name but got no response.

When he tried the bathroom door, it was locked. Fear gripped his stomach. He stepped back and kicked it, cracking the Masonite just enough for the latch to give way. The broken shards from the wine glass crunched under his feet.

He rushed to the side of the tub and pulled her face from the water. She was cold, her body pale and limp. He lifted her out of the tub and carried Annmarie to the living room, all the while shouting for help. She had a pulse. It was shallow and hard to detect, but he was sure he felt one.

Becky tried to open the door from the outside, but Derick had locked it behind him. "Are you okay?"

"It's my mom. She's not breathing. Call 911."

***

"What happened?" Thach Senior inquired of his son as they exited church Sunday morning.

"Too many Valiums mixed with too much alcohol. She passed out in the tub and almost drowned. The kid found her just in time."

"Stressor number one. What about two?" Senior felt it coming together.

Junior said, "It's in motion. Father's on his way to him now. Hopefully, with everything that's going on with his mom, he'll remember to ask about Becky."

***

Floyd had hung up with Derick and booked the first available flight to North Carolina. He was angry. All of this was a game, and he found it grotesque. Paul and Lawrence were not just playing with money and careers. They were playing with sanity, the very lives of people he loved. The ends couldn't justify the means if the collateral damage was this great.

He called the number and left a message. He hoped that Steve would get back to him. Maybe the two of them could devise a sensible way out of this mess.

CHAPTER 47

"Why did you agree to a meeting with this guy?" Parker was preparing for his sit-down with Lionel Rockport. Jason and Miranda were both in the room, but it was Jason who responded.

"Because he asked. He said he read some of your material and was intrigued. We will need support from people like him if you hope to move these ideas into law."

"Buddy, I haven't even been sworn into office. We have so many things to do before we ever get to legislating. I'm less concerned about getting bills passed than I am with putting the right people in the right positions."

"You can walk and chew gum at the same time. We have to hit the ground running."

"I don't like this. Money and politics don't mix. They are opposing sides vying for power. It's the people in the middle who always end up losing."

———

Elton had gone dark. Paul knew something must be terribly wrong. It was now past the forty-eight-hour mark since his last report. They had a longstanding communication protocol in place, and Paul was watching the clock. As each milestone in the timeline came and went, he moved to isolate more of the organization from Elton.

At the seventy-two-hour mark, Paul was to assume Elton was either involuntarily confined or dead. This was an occupational hazard that Elton accepted but worked extremely hard to avoid. If someone got him, they were well organized and well-funded.

There were contingency plans for the programs and projects Elton oversaw. Paul could transition all of them to other staff, except for the most sensitive ones. He had to assume direct control of those for the time being. With Derick part of the Rockport family and Becky being his ex-lover, they were vaulted to the heights of the most sensitive list.

Becky was getting nervous. Elton had called every day for an update, but she had not heard from him in two. She tried calling the number he programmed on the cell phone. It would just ring until she got the standard message that the voicemail box had not been set up by the customer. She wanted to let him know about Annmarie.

The phone finally rang. She looked at the caller ID and it simply said "Cell Phone" with an 817 area code. She knew it was a call from Fort Worth but remembered Elton's rules for the phone. She did not answer it.

The same number called back immediately. She began to wonder if she should take the call. When the caller made a third attempt, she answered. "Hello."

"Becky, do not use my name, but do you recognize my voice?" It was Paul.

"Yes. I thought we weren't to speak again?" Becky was confused.

"Things have changed. When was the last time you spoke to Elton?"

"Saturday afternoon. What's wrong?"

Paul ignored the question. He was now convinced Elton was out of the game. "Don't worry about Elton. Give me a status on Derick."

"Annmarie is in the hospital. She overdosed. Derick found her Sunday morning. He's upset, but his dad arrived last night and has been a huge source of support. He seems to have calmed down a bit. We are checking into the Grand Banks tomorrow for my first quality review and…"

Paul interrupted. "What? The Grand Banks, when is this again? How long are you there?"

"Tomorrow afternoon until Friday afternoon. We're a couple from Texas celebrating…"

Paul interrupted her again. "You need to cancel. Derick cannot be there this week. I don't care what excuse you give him, but he cannot be at that hotel. Do you understand me?"

"But…"

"Becky, remember our arrangement? Well, it's evolving. I have a high-level meeting with my boss and the new senator-elect on Thursday at the Grand Banks. Under no circumstances can Derick be near that meeting. This is not negotiable. I will meet you at the bar Tuesday night at eight. I will approach you. Are we clear?"

"Crystal." She hoped he would give her a hint as to what was happening, but all she heard was the phone disconnect. She was totally confused and quite annoyed. What had happened to Elton? Why couldn't Derick be at the Grand Banks? How was she going to cancel on him?

Meghan watched as father and son exited the hospital. She was off duty, and with nothing else to do, she had decided to spend a few hours surveilling her prime suspect.

She was getting ready to start her car when she watched another vehicle turn on its lights and follow them. Odd. She noted the vehicle and its tags.

Falling in line behind the new players, Meghan was careful to avoid detection. As Floyd and Derick pulled into the apartment complex, the other vehicle circled and found a spot nearby. Meghan parked even farther away, pulled her camera from the back seat, and began to document as much as she could.

———

Derick lay in bed, wide awake and sure he was being hollowed out bit by bit. When he'd told Floyd about the strange warning he received regarding Becky, he was confident his father had not divulged all of what he knew. His information was enough to make him doubt her intentions, but he still held hope that their relationship had grown into something real.

After Floyd had dropped him at the complex, he'd stopped at Becky's place to finalize their plans at the Grand Banks. He'd been looking forward to a few days with her in luxury. She canceled on him. Something about a big event and heightened security. Blah, blah, blah. It sounded like an excuse.

She was cold, distant, factual. It was an uncomfortable, even awkward exchange. Just like he was sure Floyd had been deficient in his answers, he was sure Becky was purposefully being evasive. He felt out of control again. He could feel the wheels of his life coming off one by one in slow motion. He was heading into the ditch. Why did this stuff keep happening to him?

CHAPTER 48

Parker vacillated between admiration and disdain for Lionel Rockport. He was genuinely impressed with the "Fortuneteller of Finance." His ability to foresee market needs and be at the forefront of solution offerings was truly legendary. By all accounts, he was a generous benefactor to many charities, and he did so with as little fanfare as possible. He was smart, generous, and humble. All qualities Parker admired.

On the other hand, he sorely lacked any semblance of transparency. He was so secretive most considered him on the Howard Hughes end of the eccentric paranoid scale. He seemed to be great at investing in ideas and companies, but not in people and relationships. No wife or children. High expectations of the people who surrounded him. Severe consequences for crossing him. He seemed to lack any modicum of empathy or grace. Both were concepts so central to who Parker was that he was having difficulty seeing a way for him to connect with Lionel.

His phone rang and vibrated. He looked at the caller ID and said, "Thank God. It's about time."

Meghan ran the plates of the mystery car from the night before. They belonged to a rental car company. No big surprise. The good news was that rental car companies required credit cards for deposits. They would also have the driver's information on file.

***

Derick woke and felt as though he did not sleep at all. Things just didn't make sense. Why would his grandfather and Paul send Becky to spy on him? If Becky was meant to look after him, why did she abruptly cancel their plans? Why would she become romantically involved with him if all she needed to do was keep an eye on his moves? She could have done that as just a friend. Never had he been so invested in a woman, so why her? His inability to reconcile his feelings with his experience and the few facts he'd been given were maddening. He couldn't focus on anything else.

***

After the men from the phone call left the house, Parker sat with Jason and Miranda. "That was quite an earful. What do you think?"

Miranda looked at Jason and then Parker. "They came to us. I still think we listen to Rockport. We now know as much, if not more, than he does. We have the best insurance policy against anything underhanded. We have the truth."

"Jason?" Parker didn't like games. It was one thing to be thrown into the lion's den on principle. It was another to voluntarily walk into it.

"Don't overthink the circumstances. You have always defined them by being the best that can be. The right path forward will appear, even if it isn't the easy one. Remember who and whose you are."

Miranda was used to strategizing with Wade. What she was experiencing with Parker and Jason was entirely different. Their strategy was not about building a narrative to fit the facts. It was about the truth being revealed by the facts. No agenda. Only good judgment.

———

Derick thought the Pearl's Oyster, an upscale seafood restaurant in the lobby of the Grand Banks, was an odd place to meet Floyd and Steve Crockett. They sat in a dimly lit corner booth, affording them much privacy. The place was sparsely filled. Not only was it a Tuesday night, but the other restaurant on the property was serving a filet special.

Derick thought the whole situation was surreal. He could hear them speaking, see their lips move, but he felt a million miles away.

"Son, are you okay?" Floyd brought him back from the edge of collapse.

"No." He reached for his glass of water and looked the other man in the eyes. "Was it all a lie?"

Steve Crockett had tears in his eyes. He shook his head. "My love for you and your mom was never a lie. I didn't intend to hurt either of you. I'm ashamed of the choices I've made and the damage resulting from them. I was selfish."

Floyd said, "You didn't deserve me and my failures, or Steve and his, or even your mom and hers. We are flawed people, but we all love and care deeply for you."

"And Parker Stowe had nothing to do with any of this?" Derick's anger was welling in him but no longer had a target.

"Nothing at all," Steve replied. "He is a good and honorable man."

"It was your grandfather and Paul." Floyd was having trouble finding forgiveness for them himself. He didn't even know how to begin to direct Derick in that capacity.

"What about Becky?" He was trying to find an anchor. Something on which to orient his emotions.

"I don't know, Son." Floyd didn't have the heart to tell him about her intimate history with Paul. "You need to speak with her directly. She's the only one who can tell you what she's feeling for you."

He wanted to be angry and lash out at the world, but his father left him with hope. "If you don't mind, I'd like to be alone for a while."

Floyd and Steve left him at the table with instructions to charge anything he wanted to Floyd's account. He gave Derick a keycard to his suite, hoping he would stay and enjoy the hotel. Derick took it and said he'd think about it.

After they left, he ordered a premium double vodka tonic. He sat behind the tinted glass of the restaurant and surveyed the hotel lobby on the other side. Maybe he'd see Becky. Maybe they could salvage some time together after all.

Paul entered the lobby at seven-fifty. He walked to the Starbucks kiosk and ordered a venti chai latte. He sat patiently during its preparation, all the while taking stock of the people about the area. He saw Becky sit at the bar across from the Pearl's Oyster at seven fifty-eight.

Though it had only been a few weeks, she seemed even more attractive than he remembered. He had never seen her all dolled up. With her hair freshly styled and in her professional attire, she looked so sophisticated and mature. He surveyed his surroundings one more time and approached her. "Your new life suits you."

"Well, howdy! I'd give you a hug, but I don't know how I'm supposed to act around you." She was genuinely glad to see him.

"Just pretend we are strangers having a chat at a hotel bar. Keep your volume low. Where's Derick?"

"Not here, you told me to ditch him. He wasn't at all happy. I think it broke his heart." She hoped whatever reason Paul had for making her break her plans with Derick was worth it.

"You have that effect on men." Paul didn't mean to be flirting with her but couldn't help himself. "Do you like him?"

"Yes, I do. Very much, I think." It was an honest answer. It also felt good to flaunt Paul's "gift" in his face.

"Do you know if he's made any new friends? Is he hanging out or talking with anybody different?"

"You mean besides his father? No. His time is split between work, taking care of his mom, and now me. Frankly, I don't know how he does it. Can you please tell me what in hell is going on?"

Her Texas accent was so cute. Those brilliantly white teeth behind her full, red lips, just adorable, he thought. "I don't know what it is, but something's wrong."

"I've been doing what you told me." Becky was suddenly afraid her new life was about to be yanked away from her.

"You're fine. Elton is missing. I think something bad has happened to him. I'm under a lot of stress and maybe even a little afraid." It was an unusual moment of complete honesty with himself. For so many months, Becky had been his escape, his release from the tensions of his responsibilities.

She felt bad for him. Paul was holding it together, but clearly he was troubled. In all the months she had known him, never had she witnessed any weakness or self-doubt. She reached across the bar and put her hand on top of his.

Derick watched with dread as she reached across the bar but became physically ill when he witnessed Paul draw her to him. She didn't immediately pull away or rebuke him. There was no slap to the face. He saw them kiss, and he knew it wasn't the first time.

There was no room in his stomach for its contents. His chest felt tight, and his breaths were quick and shallow. He hastily headed to the restroom, hoping to avoid a scene. When he returned to settle his bill, they were gone.

Becky lay alone in her room. Though Derick had already looked away, she had ended the kiss. She wasn't going backward. Even if Paul pulled his support, even if it meant having to tend bar again, so be it.

She knew she wanted something different, something better. That meant making different choices, better choices.

CHAPTER 49

The car was rented at the airport by Elton Walker of Fort Worth, Texas. The clerk at the rental car company had no problem showing Meghan the paperwork, even without a warrant. She Googled his name. There wasn't much online about him. One link pointed to a company profile at IFH. There was a picture of a man in his mid-fifties with the title of Director, Security Services.

The dossier on Derick Harris detailed his connections to the Rockport family. This car following him was rented by a guy connected to the Rockports through IFH. Her eyes wandered over to the picture in the directory. She compared it to the ones she took of the men in the car. Neither of them was Elton.

The picture next to Elton caught her eye. JoAnn Weldon, president of Rygart Properties, Inc.

Didn't Becky Lang work for Rygart? She was from Texas. Meghan had just linked her to the Rockports through IFH, too. Who were these people and what was their interest in Parker Stowe?

Her time with Oscar French had turned her off to the FBI. She liked him well enough, but she saw how political pressures influenced his decision making. She had no doubt about why she'd gotten Derick's file. He had also prematurely pulled the active surveillance of Harris. That wasn't good policing, and she knew it. Meghan searched her phone and found the name she wanted. She had to leave a message.

"Detective Cobb, this is Meghan Fowler from the Stowe investigation. Please call me back as soon as you can. I have some new information for you."

Lionel and Lawrence Rockport exited the limousine. The general manager and Paul were waiting in the lobby of the Grand Banks to meet them. There would be no wait at the registration desk. After brief introductions, they were escorted to a waiting elevator tasked with providing an uninterrupted trip to the top. The Grand Banks was a modern, rectangular structure built with a central hallway that bisected the length of each floor. Banks of rooms flanked each side of the hall and offered outside views of downtown Raleigh. At either end of the hall were stairwells. The fourteenth floor was the pinnacle of the building and contained only six suites, each at a cost of over a thousand dollars per night.

The elevator came to rest, and the doors slid open. Lionel stepped into the hall first, followed by Lawrence and then Paul. Lionel thanked the general manager but made it clear no further assistance was required. He then made for the nearest suite door.

"Excuse me, Lionel," Paul said. "Your suite is at the end of the hall."

"I know," was all he said, and he proceeded to knock on the door he first approached.

Floyd opened the door, and Paul shot Lawrence a perplexed look. Lawrence seemed just as confused by the situation.

Derick never went to sleep. He spent the night pacing, wondering what curse plagued his existence. There was no shortage of alcohol in the apartment, and he drank heavily to calm his anxiety. It only worsened his depression. Alone in the quiet of his room, he was in free fall. The Glock was out of hiding and resting on the table. It was fully loaded and ready to conduct business.

The two men outside Derick's apartment reported back to their boss in Chicago. The boy was stressed but had no movement on Stowe. He hadn't left the apartment since returning from the hotel.

Chicago responded, "The backup is now primary."

The men in the car didn't like this. It meant direct contact with an unreliable asset and possible exposure. They pulled out of Derick's complex and headed to the motel to deliver the weapon and instructions to the backup.

CHAPTER 50

"Senator Stowe, it's a pleasure to finally meet you." Lionel Rockport was gracious in his greeting. "Let me introduce you to a few people. This is my brother Lawrence, and this is Paul Harper, one of the executives at Indiana-Fellows Holdings."

Parker shook hands with each of them and made introductions himself. "This is my chief of staff, Jason Tuttle, and my director of communications, Miranda Cortez."

The small group of people made their way to an ornate glass table near a bank of windows in the center of the suite. There was an assortment of refreshments available. Though the setting was intended to be comfortable, there was an uneasiness in the room that made the gathering seem forced and tense.

The newly elected senator was well versed in the few details available surrounding Lionel Rockport and Indiana-Fellows Holdings. He was quite surprised at the staggering lack of information available in the public domain about the man and rather impressed at the low profile he was able to maintain.

"I've recently read your book, Senator. Some of your ideas are quite fascinating." Lionel began with a compliment. "I had hoped to spend most of our time together exploring some of the finer details in depth with you. Unfortunately, something recently came to my attention that has altered that plan. It appears I owe you an apology and an explanation. Afterward, it is my sincere desire you will still indulge me, but perhaps another time."

Everyone in the room seemed even more on edge than when they had first sat down. Lionel had the complete attention of his guests. Paul's burner phone began to buzz in his pocket, and he reached down to silence it as Lionel continued.

"It appears that resources at IFH were used to acquire information on one of your recent opponents. That information was subsequently leaked to the press, and you benefited from and were blamed for that revelation."

"Are you saying your organization is responsible for outing Steve Crockett?" Miranda was the first to speak. She'd lost a lot of sleep between the disclosure and election day. Of all the people in the room, she was the most emotionally invested in Crockett's campaign.

"I assure you, Ms. Cortez, I knew nothing of it. But as the head of IFH, I take full responsibility. I am starting with this apology and disclosure today."

"Why interfere with the campaign?" It wasn't meant as an accusation.

Lionel looked across the table at his younger brother. Their gazes met for a moment. "We're still investigating, but we believe it was a misguided attempt by a trusted member of the executive staff to gain favor with a major stakeholder in the company. Steve Crockett is the estranged stepfather of Lawrence's grandson and my grandnephew. Regrettably, I became aware of this information too late to stop the release of a press statement, a copy of which is in the folder on the table before each of you."

Miranda was the first to finish reading. "You are publicly endorsing the senator's income gap proposal?"

"Yes, but that seems trivial now in respect to what I've just disclosed. That leak is the reason the senator won the election," Lionel replied with the proper amount of gravity in his tone.

"You released this before the meeting, and you want nothing in return?" Miranda was confused. In all her years in politics, she had never seen a captain of industry capitulate to reform, let alone endorse it, without extracting something in return.

Parker was frowning. "He's already made the deal, Miranda. We're just being informed of what we're getting in return. By telling us about the source of the leak and providing his endorsement of my plan, Mr. Rockport has implicated me in the plot. There is now no way for us to expose what his people have done without casting doubt on the credibility of his endorsement.

"He's forcing us to keep his secret or risk creating the illusion of a scandal. The public will be left wondering what deal I cut with Rockport to win the election and gain his endorsement. I'll be buried in controversy before I take office. Disclosure will undoubtedly inhibit my ability to affect meaningful leadership reform."

Lionel did not smile or gloat. He was as even as he had been throughout the meeting. "I value my privacy and the public image of my holdings more than anything else. I have simply given you a reason to value them as well. My preference is that you use discretion with the information I just gave you. However, if I must suffer the indignity of a public scandal, then keeping you from changing a system that has benefited me for most of my life will be the price you pay."

"And don't forget, Lionel, you will effectively own a member of Congress if I agree to keep your secret. You will always have leverage over me with the threat of exposing this closed-door deal. Mr. Rockport, you have greatly underestimated the power of truth and my character. We'll be going now." Parker stood. On cue, Jason and Miranda followed his lead. There were no pleasantries exchanged with their host as they departed the suite.

———

"Are you here? Good. We're on our way down now." Jason hung up his phone as they reached the bank of elevators. "They're in the lobby waiting for you, Parker."

The Capitol Police officer interrupted. "Senator, there are several news crews which have assembled in the lobby, and they are drawing a bit of a crowd. We'd like to take you out via a more secured route."

"It's okay," replied Parker. "I want to talk to the press."

When Parker exited the elevator, someone shouted, "There he is," and a flock of reporters and cameras descended upon him. The security detail was well prepared and positioned themselves between Parker and the mass of media personalities vying to get the first question answered. The senator-elect stopped and held up his hand.

"There's no need to shout. I'll take some questions, but first I have a joint announcement."

The reporters fell into order and the shouting over one another ceased. "I'd like to invite my former opponent, Steve Crockett, to join me in front of you, and I'll let him begin."

In the clamoring to be the first to get to Parker, no one had noticed Steve enter the lobby. He stepped in front of the cameras next to Parker, much to the bewilderment of all. This was the first time he'd been seen in public since he announced his withdrawal from the race.

Steve began. "There's been much speculation about the demise of my campaign and who leaked the story that ultimately led to my withdrawal. I am standing before you today with our newly elected senator to unequivocally state that I know for certain neither he nor anyone associated or affiliated with his campaign had anything to do with the discovery or disclosure of that information. I know Senator Stowe to be a good and righteous man who will represent the people of North Carolina with integrity and a servant's heart.

"Though many have speculated about the source of the information, be assured that I not only know who is responsible, but I also know the reasons why they did what they did. However, the ultimate responsibility is my own. Had I been transparent with everyone, there would not have been a story to leak in the first place.

"My personal failure has hurt many people, foremost my wife. No words can express my deep regret for having done so. I hope that by breaking my silence today, I can end the speculation about Senator Stowe's involvement in this controversy. My mistake should not cast a dark shadow of suspicion on him and his campaign. Thank you."

A visibly emotional Steve Crockett turned to Parker to shake his hand. Parker took the extended hand and pulled Steve into him. They hugged. He whispered in his ear, "I'm so proud of you. Thank you."

The reporters started shouting questions, and once again they scattered into disorder. Parker stepped forward and held up his hand. "One at a time, please."

Rather quickly, the fray stilled itself, waiting for Parker to recognize one of them. He found his mark and called upon Trey Perkins.

"Senator Stowe, do you know who is responsible for giving me the information about Mr. Crockett's affair?" Trey could be counted on to promote his self-importance and grab credit whenever possible.

"I recently became privy to that information, but it's not mine to disclose. Perhaps if you were as good at tracking down leads and uncovering sources as you are at dishing insinuation, you would have already discovered the truth for yourself. After all, it was you who first broke the story, was it not? You are either an incompetent journalist or a political mouthpiece for my opposition. I will never again lend you credibility in your profession by fielding another question from you." Parker intended to be brash out of the gate. He wanted the press to know that they had gotten it wrong and were either complicit in the hoax or easily used by the perpetrators. It was a warning to all that they needed to step up their game and vet the integrity of the information they disseminated.

"Next question from over here." He pointed to a guy two deep to his right.

"Rick Franklin, Channel 6 News. Do you have any reaction to Lionel Rockport's endorsement of your income gap proposal?"

"I am pleased that such a successful icon of financial prowess sees merit in the idea. Since so many of his companies benefit from the current, and might I add excessively complicated tax and regulatory structures, his support is especially refreshing. I promise that any legislation that is brought before the members of Congress will be simple and easily understood. It will be fully debated so that all sides have a chance to be heard."

"Do you know why he chose to get behind the proposal? He is usually a very private, apolitical personality." The question was asked before Parker could call on the next reporter. He thought to himself that he needed to spend more time practicing press conference management. Miranda was thinking the same thing.

"That's a question better asked of Mr. Rockport. One more question." Parker was ready to head back to the farm and his family. A woman, obviously not from a television station, seemed innocuous enough, and he pointed to her.

"Are you aware that Steve Crockett's stepson is related to the Rockport family? Were the Rockports involved with the disclosure of Mr. Crockett's affair?"

Parker paused for a moment. "I recently became aware of the connection between the two families. As Steve mentioned in his statement, he knows the details of the disclosure and is confident I had nothing to do with it. If he wanted to reveal any other information, I'm sure he would have. Thank you."

And with that, Parker ended the conference.

CHAPTER 51

Derick entered the lobby just in time to catch the remnants of the press conference. He paid no attention to it as he walked to the bank of elevators. The key he got from his father gave him access to the top floor of suites. As an IFH executive, Paul would be staying on that floor. Derick was sure. He suspected Becky would be in a suite on this floor, too. That had been the plan before she'd ditched him, anyway. He exited the elevator, entered his father's suite, and sat by the door.

Meghan Fowler followed Derick into the hotel, horrified that the senator-elect was in the open at a press conference. She made eye contact with Cobb as she whispered something into a mouthpiece. The security detail was at its most heightened state of alert. Meghan was only feet from Derick if he decided to do anything. To her amazement and relief, he simply boarded an elevator. She watched as it climbed to the fourteenth floor. Cobb caught up to her and handed her a card key, earpiece, and microphone. "Keep your eyes on him until we're gone."

As the conference came to an end, a well-dressed and professional-looking Parsons Pettit stood up from his seat at the lobby bar. He had witnessed Parker Stowe and his former employer, Steve Crockett, speak to the press. Parsons had neither heard their comments nor cared about them. He was drunk. As drunk as he had been every day since the story of his relationship with Steve had become front-page news.

Being shaved and well-groomed was a far better look on him than that of the disheveled beach bum he donned in South Beach. As the senator finished speaking and headed for the exit, Parsons reached inside his coat pocket for the small revolver. A single round left the chamber before the Capitol Police took him down.

Cobb grabbed Stowe by the collar and rushed him out the door and into the waiting SUV. Steve Crockett lay on the cold lobby floor with an ever-growing red blot staining his white shirt.

———•———

As Meghan exited the elevator, her earpiece crackled to life with the word "Gun!" She drew her sidearm and proceeded to clear the floor. Could Derick have made it back to the lobby so quickly?

She made her way to the north stairwell when a door opened on the opposite end of the corridor. It wasn't Derick. She watched a middle-aged man walk toward her and stop midway down the hall, right in front of a suite door.

Derick watched from his room through the peephole. He saw Paul knock on the door across from his. The Glock was one with his hand, the safety off. The door opened, and Becky came into view. His heart swelled and shattered as the object of his hope and the object of his hate once again occupied the same frame. The pain was like nothing he'd ever felt. Even worse than when he'd witnessed their kiss. It had to end.

When the door opened behind him, Paul had just enough time to see Derick's face before two shots ripped through his chest. Becky screamed and tried to close her door, but the force of Paul falling against it made that impossible.

Officer Fowler's bullet caught Derick in the shoulder as he leaped across the hall and into Becky's suite. It knocked him off balance, and he tripped over Paul's body. Falling into the room, he could hear a woman's voice shouting in the hall, "Stop! Police officer! Put the gun down!" Paul groaned, and Derick put a bullet in his head.

When Meghan heard the last shot coming from the suite, she didn't know what to think. She was sure she'd hit him. Did he kill himself? Did he shoot someone else? Cautiously, she approached the open door. He wasn't in sight. The body in the doorway was undoubtedly dead. There was a smear of blood on the wall and droplets leading to a locked door further within the suite.

Behind the door, Derick had Becky at gunpoint. Shooting Paul had released some anger, but the pain of all his loss still lingered. It was an insatiable void consuming every thought, every feeling, every desire.

"Why?" was all she could muster the courage to say.

"Because he took everything. He destroyed Steve and my mom. He took our lives, and he stole our sanity. He manipulated me and used whomever he needed to do it. He brought you into my life and then ripped you out of it. He was a horrible person."

Becky wasn't afraid anymore. Her tears turned from fear to ones of compassion. "He used me too."

"Derick Harris. You have no way out." Meghan's voice was clear and firm. "Unlock the door and come out with your hands on your head."

"I have a hostage. Don't come in, or I'll kill her." Derick didn't know what he was going to do, but he wasn't ready for the police. With the gun pointed at the door, he looked at Becky. "Was any of it real?"

She looked him in the eyes. "Yes," she began to sob again. "Yes, it was real. It might not have started that way, but that's where it went." Becky's Texas drawl sounded so sweet to his ears. Though filled with tears, her blue eyes pleaded with him. "You don't have to do this. Put the gun down. Surrender. It'll be okay."

His eyes were glassy, but he was too angry to cry. "I can't undo what I've done." He thought of Paul's last moments without any remorse. "My family will try to buy your silence. Don't let them do it. Talk only with my dad. Tell him I'm sorry. Thank him for me. Tell him I forgive him."

"But... No... Wait..."

Derick put the Glock into his mouth and pulled the trigger.

CHAPTER 52

Parker decided to spend some quiet quality time with his family, especially as the Christmas holiday approached. He had asked Miranda to issue a statement assuring the public that he was uninjured and was praying for the loved ones of those killed. Upon viewing video coverage of the shooting, he ventured out to the hospital.

Though intended to be a private moment to personally thank Steve Crockett for taking the bullet intended for him, the visit turned into a news event. Parker was recognized entering the building, and as he exited the hospital, a throng of cameras and news people began shouting questions.

"Senator Stowe! Senator Stowe! In the wake of these shootings, will you finally join the Democrats calling for stricter gun laws?"

Parker was calm. He knew the question would eventually come up and had already worked with Miranda to frame his response. He stopped and addressed the crowd of reporters. "I am always ready to have an open, honest, and direct conversation about the sanctity of life. However, I'm not going to be pulled into endless fights over the tools of death. Guns account for roughly the same number of deaths each year as motor vehicle accidents, approximately thirty-five thousand. Roughly six hundred and twenty thousand abortions are performed in this country each year. Are we going to talk about regulating cars and scalpels as well as guns? The tool is not the problem."

Something in this moment made him swell with righteous indignation, and he felt compelled to don his professorial hat. Parker entered lecture mode and continued. "There is a verse in the Bible that says a person should deal with the log in their own eye before they point out the speck in someone else's. Perhaps instead of blaming the inanimate object, or even the shooters, in this case, you—the media—should first look at the role you played in this tragic set of circumstances.

"While it was your right to report on Steve's affair, why was it relevant to the election? What business is it of yours, or even the public's, with whom he has sex? Why publish the pictures of his stepson on that beach with that model, years back? Did any of you ask yourself if you should report it?

"You hide behind freedom of the press as though it is an immunization against the consequences of your choices. Does that make you any different than the politicians you accuse of hiding behind the Second Amendment?

"This country doesn't need to have a conversation about gun control, abortion, gay rights, or even freedom of the press. We need to have a conversation about common decency, personal responsibility, and basic respect. We need to assert our shared values and frame our discussions in the context of what they mean. Our first question might better be what happens if we do something and not can we do it."

"It's handled, Dad." The junior Thach was visibly annoyed. They were in conference at the club in the hot tub.

"The FBI has pictures of two men who are persons of interest. It doesn't seem handled."

Junior huffed. "When they find the car and the bodies, it won't come back to us. The 'accident' happened in a friendly jurisdiction. Our people have already manufactured a narrative to fit the scene. Besides, the car and one of the bodies are connected to the Rockports. Be assured old Lionel will put his organization in motion to quash any serious investigation. The last thing he is going to want is more publicity."

Thach Senior didn't care about the loose ends. The details were just a focal point on which his thoughts could settle. After a long silence, he finally said, "I'm not worried about Stowe's politics. Policy ideas come and go with elections.

"The real problem with Stowe is the threat he represents to the structure of power. He is destabilizing the country. The world wants predictability, and especially from the government of the United States. We all talk about change in elections, but everyone falls into line once the ballots are cast." He snorted derisively. "He's introducing an alternative way. A single senator is going to turn Washington on its ear." Thach shook his head with mock sympathy for the soon-to-be majority leader. "By the time the bureaucrats have their way with him, he's going to wish he took that bullet the other day."

EPILOGUE

Marco ordered another beer as he waited to board his flight to Las Vegas. The television above the shelf housing the premium liquor was announcing that the Senate had finally organized itself after the uncontested appointment of the independent, Parker Stowe, as its leader. True to his promise, the committee structure had been turned on its head, and it had taken over two weeks for the parties to figure out how to share power under the guidelines Leader Stowe put in place.

"Thanks," he said as he placed a hundred-dollar bill on the counter to settle his tab. He watched as the bartender took it and proceeded to the cash register. As he took a sip, he contemplated his next assignment. His team screwed up the Stowe hit and now he had a debt to pay, hence the trip to Vegas.

Unfortunately, not only did his team fail, but his connections reminded him that his obligations would double unless he could successfully secure what they sought. Marco knew he would have a role in this dangerous game for some time to come, and he gulped the last of his beer.

In truth, there was a part of him that felt somewhat excited for the changes that were about to hit Washington, even if it meant more trouble for him in the short term. He hoped that eventually, it might release him from some of his problems.

As he placed the glass back on the bar and stood to leave, he smiled. However the next six years played out, Marco knew that Parker Stowe could not imagine what would be coming.

ACKNOWLEDGEMENTS

I first conceived of *The Independent* in 2007 but didn't write it until 2015. The first draft had a major problem of which I was aware. Unfortunately, I had to walk away from the story to find the solution and it wasn't until 2018 that I was able to resolve it.

Throughout this adventure, my biggest fan and greatest critic has been my wife, Susan. An avid reader of fiction, her feedback, sometimes chapter by chapter as I finished them, was invaluable. Blessed by God for bringing her into my life, I could not have asked for a better partner and helpmate in life.

My niece, Julia Billeci, and my Pastor, the Reverend Joseph Colman, were the first to read the story in its initial draft. They confirmed the initial problem but were quick to let me know I had a great story. They wouldn't let me give up on fixing it and periodically inquired about its "status." Thank you both for all your efforts, but most importantly, for gently encouraging me to keep at it.

For a few years in my life, Allen Forte invested in me, helping me to refine my development as a mature leader. An author, leadership coach, and consultant, Allen reminded me of the instinctual nature of leadership.

I also want to acknowledge Kellee Casebeer, David Fiedler, Shannon Garcia, and Angelique Schlosser for taking the time to read and provide their feedback. Their unique backgrounds and perspectives were instrumental in making sure the story would resonate with a diverse set of readers.

And finally, I want to thank David Blankley. David is a childhood friend without whom I would never have found Martina Faulkner at IOM, Peter Wacks at 25&Y, and the amazing teams they lead.

ABOUT THE AUTHOR

 Justin is a husband and father of three with a degree in Philosophy from Vanderbilt University. He has professionally built and led organizations ranging from just a few employees, to over four hundred. Born and raised in the New York Metropolitan area, Justin has also called Tennessee, Kentucky, and Texas home. In his spare time, he enjoys theology, history, traveling, and politics... and of course a good read!

Made in United States
North Haven, CT
17 September 2023

41678785R00221